Book # 2 Alarion and the Secrets of Tiderune

The Chronicles of Alarion, Volume 2

ANANT RAM BOSS

Published by ANANT RAM, 2024.

This is a work of fiction. Similarities to real people, places, or events are entirely coincidental.

BOOK # 2 ALARION AND THE SECRETS OF TIDERUNE

First edition. October 24, 2024.

Copyright © 2024 ANANT RAM BOSS.

ISBN: 979-8227831057

Written by ANANT RAM BOSS.

Also by ANANT RAM BOSS

1
The Chronicles of Alarion -Part-6 "Alarion and the Nexus of Netheron"
"The Chronicles of Alarion -Part-7-"Alarion and the Legacy of Luminarya"

2
Mystic Alliances

Alarion Chronicles Series
The Dawn of Magic
Shadows Embrace
Book#3: "Phoenix's Flight"
Book 4: "Warriors of Light"
Echoes of Wisdom
Captivated Woodland
Kingdom of Crystals
Book 8: "Lost Legacies"
Book 9: "Siege of Hope"
Book 10: "Veil of Light"

The Astral Chronicles
Awakening Shadows
Awakening Shadows
Celestial Convergence
Whispers of the Himalayas
Riddles of Rishikesh
Portals of the Past
Echoes from Vijayanagara
Veil of Varanasi
The Astral Nexus
Eclipse of Eternity
Beyond the Veil

The Chronicles of Alarion
Book # 1: Alarion and the Cryptic Key
Book # 2 Alarion and the Secrets of Tiderune

Standalone
Love's Delectable Harmony
Adventures in Candy land
Adventures in Candy land
Canvas to Catalyst: Parenting Mastery
Guardians of Greatness: Our Children Are Our Property in Cultivating Tomorrow's Leaders
Guardians of Greatness: Cultivating Tomorrow's Leaders
Space Explorers Club
The Enchanted Forest Chronicles
Mystery at Monster Mansion

Robot Friends Forever
Underwater Kingdom
Underwater Kingdom
Time Travel Twins
Time Travel Twins
The Giggle Factory
Dreamland Chronicles
The Case of the Vanishing Cookies
Dragon Knight Chronicles
The Wishing Well
Trade Tactics Unveiled: Mastering Profit Secrets
Whispers in the Graveyard
Love after Dawn: A Second Chance Romance
Exodus: A Hopeful Dystopia
Death at Blackwood Manor
Orient Express: Murder Redefined
Poirot & the Raven: Digital Legacy
The Brave Little Elephant
The Little Robot That Could
The Adventures of Little Star
Dream World
Unique Friendship
The Courage of the Lion
The Art of Building Wealth: A Strategic Guide

Table of Contents

.... 1
"The Chronicles of Alarion" 2
Book # 2 Alarion and the Secrets of Tiderune 10
Overview 11
Introduction 13
Description 15
Chapter 1: The Wobbly Boat 18
Chapter 2: The Mischievous Mermaid 22
Chapter 3: The Soggy Map 27
Chapter 4: The Wizard with Two Hats 31
Chapter 5: The Enchanted Forest Picnic 35
Chapter 6: The Riddling River 39
Chapter 7: The Fluffy Monster 43
Chapter 8: The Snoring Sorcerer 47
Chapter 9: The Juggling Jellyfish 52
Chapter 10: The Bubblegum Bridge 56
Chapter 11: The Daring Duck 60
Chapter 12: The Potion Party 64
Chapter 13: The Overly Polite Goblin 68
Chapter 14: The Invisible Ink 73
Chapter 15: The Dancing Rocks 78
Chapter 16: The Magical Puddle 82
Chapter 17: The Snarky Squirrel 87
Chapter 18: The Spell Gone Wrong 92
Chapter 19: The Singing Stones 97
Chapter 20: The Cheese Wizard 101
Chapter 21: The Frightening Fog 106
Chapter 22: The Cloudy Conundrum 110
Chapter 23: The Ticklish Toad 114
Chapter 24: The Forgotten Spell 119
Chapter 26: The Sneezing Dragon 128

Chapter 27: The Ice Cream Spell 133
Chapter 28: The Time-Telling Turtle 137
Chapter 29: The Floating Festival 141
Chapter 30: The Sneaky Wind 146
Chapter 31: The Potion of Giggles 150
Chapter 32: The Singing Riverbank 154
Chapter 33: The Shy Fairy 159
Chapter 34: The Bubble Trouble 163
Chapter 35: The Grumpy Gnome 168
Chapter 36: The Fuzzy Phobia 172
Chapter 37: The Magical Maze 176
Chapter 38: The Wizard's Challenge 180
Chapter 39: The Rainbow Chaser 185
Chapter 40: The Sleepy Sandman 190
Chapter 41: The Jumpy Jelly 195
Chapter 42: The Talking Tree 200
Chapter 43: The Dragonfly Dilemma 205
Chapter 44: The Bubblegum Potion 211
Chapter 45: The Funny Shadows 216
Chapter 46: The Flying Fish 221
Chapter 47: The Dancing Shadows 226
Chapter 48: The Topsy-Turvy Treehouse 231
Chapter 49: The Great Giggle Hunt 236
Chapter 50: The Celebration of Secrets 241
A Note of Thanks to Our Wonderful Readers 246
Acknowledgment 248
Disclaimer 250
About the Author Anant Ram Boss 252

In "Alarion and the Secrets of Tiderune," the enchanting sequel to Alarion's first journey, prepare to embark on a spellbinding quest that promises laughter, intrigue, and unforgettable friendships. As our young mage ventures deeper into the magical realm of Tiderune, he unravels hidden truths and confronts a world where magic and mischief intertwine!

Book # 2 : Alarion and the Secrets of Tiderune

"Unraveling Mysteries, Forging Alliances, and Confronting New Dangers in the Magical Realm of Tiderune"

"The Chronicles of Alarion"

A Magical Adventure Awaits
Overview

STEP INTO *"The Chronicles of Alarion,"* a captivating series filled with humor, adventure, and magical wonder! This enchanting journey follows the life of Alarion, an ordinary boy who stumbles upon an

BOOK # 2 ALARION AND THE SECRETS OF TIDERUNE

extraordinary artifact. This ancient key unlocks doors and a portal to an entirely new world. Each book in the series offers readers a fresh and exciting tale of magic, mystery, and hilarious mishaps as Alarion faces ever-evolving challenges in a realm where nothing is as it seems.

In the first book, *"Alarion and the Cryptic Key,"* readers are introduced to Alarion's quirky, fun-loving personality as he quests to discover the secrets of the magical world he accidentally stumbles into. Alongside his loyal but forgetful giant friend Grog, Alarion encounters talking keys, mischievous goblins, and sassy sorcerers—all while trying to figure out the deeper purpose of the mysterious key that appears to have its own psyche. This book sets the tone for a laugh-out-loud yet heartwarming journey from goblin negotiations to enchanted forest adventures.

Key Points of the Series:

- **Humor and Heart:** The series is packed with light hearted humor, fun twists, and relatable moments that make readers laugh aloud. Yet, beneath the jokes, there's a story about friendship, bravery, and self-discovery.
- **An Unforgettable Cast of Characters:** Alarion is joined by a colorful array of characters—like the lovable Grog, the giant with a knack for snacks, and a sarcastic, talking key who loves riddles. Each character adds charm and excitement to the series.
- **Unique Magical World:** The books immerse readers in a magical universe where logic bends, trees talk, and even mountains have personalities. The world-building is vivid and imaginative, ensuring every page is a new discovery.
- **Action-Packed Adventure:** From escaping goblin traps to bargaining with dragons, the series always has action. Alarion's journey is full of suspenseful moments, clever puzzles, and epic showdowns.

- **Themes of Growth and Courage:** Despite its fun tone, the series subtly explores important themes like finding courage, embracing one's uniqueness, and the power of friendship. Alarion's growth throughout the series is one that readers will relate to and cheer for.
- **Engaging for All Ages:** While designed with young readers in mind, *The Chronicles of Alarion* appeals to anyone who enjoys a well-crafted adventure story with heart, humor, and a touch of magic.

As the series progresses, each book unravels new layers of Alarion's quest, with more surprises and magical mysteries waiting around every corner. From deciphering cryptic clues to facing shadowy forces, Alarion's journey is a delightful blend of laughter, danger, and unexpected twists. Readers will be hooked as they root for Alarion to unlock the ultimate secrets of the key and fulfill his destiny.

If you're a fan of humorous, action-packed fantasy adventures, *"The Chronicles of Alarion"* will take you on a journey you won't want to end. Whether you're 12 or 112, Alarion's world has something magical waiting for you!

Book 1: "Alarion and the Cryptic Key"

Alarion's adventure begins when he stumbles upon a mysterious artifact—an ancient key that opens the gateway to a forgotten world. The discovery marks the start of his quest into the unknown.

Book 2: "Alarion and the Secrets of Tiderune"

As Alarion delves deeper into the magical realm, he uncovers the hidden truths of Tiderune. With new alliances and enemies at every turn, he must navigate treacherous waters to unlock the ancient knowledge within.

Book 3: "Alarion and the Oracle of Atheron"

An ancient oracle foretells Alarion's destiny, setting him on a path toward a dangerous prophecy. His quest for answers will lead him to Atheron, where fate and fortune are forever entwined.

Book 4: "Alarion and the Shattered Sigils"

In a race against time, Alarion must gather the broken Sigils of Thalos to restore harmony to the realm. Every step of the way, he encounters threats that challenge his resolve and test his growing powers.

Book 5: "Alarion and the Veil of Duskspire"

Dark forces emerge from the shadows as Alarion journeys to Duskspire. With the veil of secrecy unravelling, he faces unseen dangers that threaten to tip the balance of magic into chaos.

Book 6: "Alarion and the Arcane Crossroads"

Alarion finds himself at the crossroads of ancient and forbidden magic. At the heart of the mystical nexus, he must decide whether to embrace or resist the volatile powers of the Arcane, risking everything he holds dear.

Book 7: "Alarion and the Eternal Flame"

In the final chapter of his quest, Alarion seeks the legendary Eternal Flame, a source of unmatched power. The secrets of the past are revealed, and Alarion must confront his destiny as the future of his world hangs in the balance.

These new titles reflect the evolving depth of Alarion's journey while maintaining the original essence of each book's plot.

"The Chronicles of Alarion" – "A Magical Adventure Awaits"
Book # 1: Alarion and the Cryptic Key

Alarion and the Cryptic Key is the captivating first instalment in a thrilling fantasy series *"The Chronicles of Alarion* "A Magical Adventure Awaits** follows the journey of a young hero, Alarion, who stumbles upon a mysterious artifact—an ancient key with untold powers. This discovery marks the beginning of an extraordinary quest that takes him into a forgotten world filled with magic, danger, and untold secrets.

Key Points of the Book Series:

1. **A Mysterious Artifact**

The heart of the story revolves around Alarion's discovery of the Cryptic Key, an ancient, magical object that unlocks gateways to hidden realms. This artifact plays a pivotal role, in guiding Alarion's journey and unveiling long-lost secrets about the world and his own destiny.

1. **An Unlikely Hero**

Alarion is not your typical hero—he's a curious, brave, and occasionally clumsy young man who gets thrust into a world he didn't even know existed. Readers will relate to his everyman qualities while cheering for his growth as he learns to embrace his fate.

1. **A Forgotten World**

Through the key, Alarion is introduced to a world that's been hidden for centuries. This forgotten realm is filled with magical creatures, ancient wisdom, and dark forces that have been waiting to be unleashed. The world-building is rich, immersive, and full of surprises, offering readers a fantastical escape.

1. **Action-Packed Adventure**

From treacherous landscapes to intense battles, *Alarion and the Cryptic Key* is packed with action, ensuring readers are engaged from the very first page. Alarion encounters enemies, puzzles, and dangerous challenges that test both his courage and wits.

BOOK # 2 ALARION AND THE SECRETS OF TIDERUNE

1. **Intriguing Allies and Foes**

Along the way, Alarion encounters a range of unique characters, from loyal friends who help him on his journey to cunning enemies who seek to control the power of the Cryptic Key. Each character is thoughtfully developed, adding depth to the narrative and creating emotional stakes for readers.

1. **A Quest for Truth and Power**

At its core, the series is about the quest for knowledge, power, and identity. Alarion is not only discovering the world around him but also uncovering who he is and what role he's destined to play in the grander scheme of things. His journey is both external and internal, making this series a compelling read for anyone who loves character-driven stories.

1. **A Series with Layers**

While *Alarion and the Cryptic Key* is the first book, it hints at a much larger story that will unfold in subsequent volumes. Readers will be eager to follow Alarion's journey in future instalments, with deeper mysteries, powerful new enemies, and evolving friendships.

Features:

- **Epic Fantasy for All Ages**: This book series appeals to both young adults and older readers who enjoy immersive fantasy worlds, magical adventures, and relatable heroes.
- **Engaging World-Building**: The forgotten realms, magical artifacts, and mystical creatures in this series provide a rich and engaging backdrop that fans of fantasy will love.
- **Character-Driven Narrative**: Readers will quickly become invested in Alarion's journey, his struggles, and his triumphs as he grows from an ordinary young man into a hero.

- **Exciting and Accessible**: The fast-paced storytelling and mix of humor, suspense, and heart make this book an easy yet thrilling read for a wide audience.
- **Series Continuity**: With the promise of more books to come, readers will be eager to continue the adventure in future instalments, such as *Alarion and the Secrets of Tiderune*.

Perfect for Fans Like:

- *Harry Potter* by J.K. Rowling
- *Percy Jackson and the Olympians* by Rick Riordan
- *The Chronicles of Narnia* by C.S. Lewis
- *The Inheritance Cycle* by Christopher Paolini
- *The Hobbit* by J.R.R. Tolkien

Alarion and the Cryptic Key is perfect for fans of classic fantasy adventures, filled with magic, mystery, and a hero who must unlock his true potential to save the world. This series promises to take readers on a thrilling, magical ride they won't soon forget.

Don't miss the start of Alarion's epic adventure. Unlock the mystery of *Alarion and the Cryptic Key* today!

If you're a fan of humorous, action-packed fantasy adventures, "The Chronicles of Alarion" will take you on a journey you won't want to end. Whether you're 12 or 112, Alarion's world has something magical waiting just for you!

BOOK # 2 ALARION AND THE SECRETS OF TIDERUNE

Book # 2 Alarion and the Secrets of Tiderune

Overview

In "Alarion and the Secrets of Tiderune," readers are invited to join Alarion, an adventurous young mage, as he embarks on an exhilarating quest through the enchanting realm of Tiderune. With its vibrant landscapes, whimsical creatures, and hidden mysteries, Tiderune is where magic dances in the air and anything is possible—provided you can outwit the challenges ahead.

Alarion's journey begins as he discovers an ancient map hidden within the pages of an old spell book. The map hints at the existence of powerful knowledge buried deep within Tiderune, the knowledge that could change the fate of the magical realm forever. But as Alarion soon learns, the path to unlocking these secrets is fraught with challenges and unexpected twists.

Throughout his adventure, Alarion encounters a colorful cast of characters, each adding their unique flair to his journey. From Lila, the mischievous mermaid who sings off-key but charms him with her wit, to a grumpy gnome whose grouchy demeanor hides a heart of gold, every ally and adversary he meets shapes his understanding of friendship, courage, and the true nature of magic. Alarion learns that allies can emerge from the most unlikely of places, while enemies may sometimes wear friendly faces.

As he navigates the vibrant tapestry of Tiderune, Alarion faces peculiar challenges that test not only his magical skills but also his sense of humor and creativity. Whether he's accidentally summoning a troupe of clumsy fairies or engaging in a bubble-blowing contest that spirals out of control, every experience brings new lessons wrapped in laughter. The realm's whimsical elements provide ample opportunities for comedic mishaps, reminding readers that even the most serious quests can be infused with joy and light heartedness.

Alarion's journey is not without its perils. He must outsmart cunning foes who covet the ancient knowledge he seeks, all while keeping a watchful eye on the secrets of Tiderune. As he encounters a variety of magical beings—each with their own agendas and quirks—he learns that trust is a fragile thread that can either bind allies together or lead to betrayal.

Through his trials and tribulations, Alarion discovers that true power lies not only in knowledge but also in understanding and compassion. As he forges new alliances and navigates the treacherous waters of friendship and rivalry, he realizes that the real magic of Tiderune is found in the connections he makes and the laughter they share.

As the pages of "Alarion and the Secrets of Tiderune" unfold, readers will be drawn into a world bursting with imagination and humor. With each chapter, Alarion's adventures offer both excitement and heartfelt moments, encouraging readers to embrace their quirks, find joy in unexpected places, and celebrate the beauty of friendship. In Tiderune, the only limits are those of your imagination, and with Alarion leading the way, every reader is invited to embark on their own journey of discovery, laughter, and magic.

Prepare to be enchanted, entertained, and utterly charmed by Alarion's whimsical escapades as he uncovers the secrets of a realm where laughter truly is the best spell!

Introduction

Welcome, dear readers, to the enchanting world of Tiderune, a realm where the ordinary meets the extraordinary and where the only limit is your imagination. In this captivating sequel, "Alarion and the Secrets of Tiderune," we dive deeper into the life of our beloved protagonist, Alarion, a young mage with an insatiable thirst for adventure and a heart full of curiosity.

Alarion's story begins in a quaint village where magic is woven into the fabric of everyday life. However, the call of adventure beckons him beyond the familiar sights of his home. Armed with his wit and an old spell book filled with secrets, he embarks on a journey to uncover ancient truths that could change the very fabric of Tiderune. With every step he takes, Alarion finds himself entangled in a tapestry of magical encounters and unexpected alliances.

As Alarion delves deeper into the realm, he uncovers a world brimming with whimsical creatures, vibrant landscapes, and hidden knowledge waiting to be discovered. Tiderune is not just a place; it's a living, breathing entity filled with stories that yearn to be told. From the shimmering rivers that sing ancient songs to the towering trees that share their wisdom in whispers, every corner of Tiderune has a secret to reveal.

But the path is not always smooth. With every new ally, there lurks the possibility of new adversaries. Alarion must navigate treacherous waters as he encounters rivals who seek the same knowledge he does. Yet, he learns that the greatest challenges often lead to the most rewarding discoveries. As he grapples with betrayal, confusion, and the occasional magical mishap, Alarion's character is put to the test, teaching him that true strength lies not only in magical prowess but also in the bonds he forges along the way.

This tale is filled with humor and heart, offering readers a delightful blend of adventure and laughter. Alarion's escapades will have you chuckling as he finds himself in uproarious situations—whether he's engaging in a duel with a wizard who takes fashion advice too seriously or attempting to communicate with a dragon who can't stop sneezing. Every twist and turn is a reminder that life is full of surprises, and sometimes, the best adventures arise from the most unexpected moments.

As you journey alongside Alarion through the colorful landscapes of Tiderune, you'll discover the importance of friendship, the power of laughter, and the magic that resides within us all. This book invites you to unleash your imagination and embark on an adventure that celebrates the beauty of curiosity and the joy of discovery.

So, dear reader, prepare to turn the pages and dive into a world where laughter reigns, friendships flourish, and secrets of the past await to be uncovered. Let Alarion's adventures inspire you to explore your realms of magic and wonder. Welcome to Tiderune—where every adventure is a story waiting to unfold!

Description

Dive into a Whimsical Adventure!
In "Alarion and the Secrets of Tiderune," the enchanting sequel to Alarion's first journey, prepare to embark on a spellbinding quest that promises laughter, intrigue, and unforgettable friendships. As our young mage ventures deeper into the magical realm of Tiderune, he unravels hidden truths and confronts a world where magic and mischief intertwine!

Key Points:

Uncover Ancient Secrets: Join Alarion as he follows a mysterious map leading to powerful knowledge that could change Tiderune forever. What secrets lie hidden in the depths of this whimsical realm?

Meet a Colorful Cast of Characters: From the witty Lila the mermaid to a grumpy yet lovable gnome, each character adds a unique charm to Alarion's adventure. Discover who becomes an ally and who turns out to be a surprising foe!

Humor and Heart: Experience laugh-out-loud moments as Alarion navigates comical mishaps, from magical duels gone awry to hilarious encounters with creatures of the realm. Each chapter brims with delightful humor and lessons on friendship and courage.

Navigating Treacherous Waters: As Alarion faces challenges and confronts rivals, he learns that the path to discovery is often fraught with danger. Will he be able to outsmart those who seek the same knowledge?

A Journey of Self-Discovery: Amidst the magic and laughter, Alarion embarks on a personal journey, learning that true strength comes from within and that the bonds of friendship can weather any storm.

Enchanting Imagery and Whimsical Settings: Immerse yourself in the vibrant landscapes of Tiderune, where every corner is alive with magic. Experience the joy of a realm where anything is possible and imagination knows no bounds.

This captivating tale invites readers of all ages to lose themselves in a world filled with adventure, laughter, and heartwarming moments. "Alarion and the Secrets of Tiderune" is not just a story; it's an invitation to explore your own magical possibilities and discover the wonders that await when you dare to dream.

Join Alarion on this unforgettable journey today, and unlock the secrets of Tiderune!

BOOK # 2 ALARION AND THE SECRETS OF TIDERUNE

Chapter 1: The Wobbly Boat

A larion sets sail on a boat that looks more like a giant pancake than a vessel. As it wobbles on the water, he learns that even magical boats have their quirks!

The sun had barely risen over the horizon, casting a golden glow on the tranquil waters of Tiderune. Alarion, our intrepid young mage, stood at the edge of the docks, staring wide-eyed at the boat before him. To put it mildly, it looked like a giant pancake with a penchant for wobbling.

"Is this really the boat I'm supposed to sail?" Alarion asked his voice a blend of skepticism and entertainment.

"Of course!" twittered a little, cheerful animal roosting on the edge of the vessel. It was Pippin, the boat's magically inclined if somewhat overenthusiastic, assistant. "Try not to pass judgment on a boat by its... uh, flapjacky appearance! This beauty can take you anywhere you want to go in Tiderune!"

Alarion squinted at the boat, which was painted in bright shades of blue and yellow, the colors clashing as wildly as the ingredients in a chaotic potion. The mast leaned precariously to one side, and the sails seemed to be waving in an invisible wind. If it can take me anyplace, for what reason does it seem as though sleeping is about?"

Pippin chuckled, his small wings fluttering in delight. "That's just the boat's charm! It's called the Wobbleberry. It's a classic in these waters. Trust me, once we get moving, you won't even notice!"

Alarion hesitated but couldn't resist the infectious excitement radiating from Pippin. With a deep breath, he climbed aboard. The moment he stepped onto the deck, the boat let out a comical groan, and Alarion felt a shiver run through his spine.

"Easy there, Wobbleberry!" he said, tapping the railing as though it were an obstinate donkey. "We're friends now, right?"

The boat seemed to respond with a gentle bounce, and Alarion exchanged a wary glance with Pippin. "Could it be said that you are certain this thing would, you know, toss us into the water?"

"Not unless you give it a reason to!" Pippin exclaimed, hopping energetically around the deck. "Just give it a fragile push to start us off!"

With Pippin's encouragement, Alarion took hold of the tiller. The boat quivered beneath him, resembling a child on a pogo stick, ready to leap into action. He pushed it forward, and with a surprising burst of energy, the Wobbleberry shot off, cutting through the water like a confused fish.

"Woohoo!" Pippin cheered, his minuscule arms thrashing in the breeze. "Now, let's see if you can steer!"

The boat began to wobble more dramatically, veering left and right, sending splashes of water flying. Alarion tried to maintain control, but it felt as if the Wobbleberry had developed a mind of its own. Every time he aimed it straight, it would swerve wildly to the side, as if mocking his attempts at navigation.

"Okay, maybe a little less enthusiasm, Wobbleberry!" he shouted, laughing despite himself.

Suddenly, the boat lurched forward, propelling them toward a small island that loomed ahead. Alarion's heart raced. "Pippin! We're headed straight for that rock!"

"Not to worry!" Pippin replied, his eyes gleaming with mischief. "Just give it a little wiggle!"

"A wiggle?" Alarion repeated, befuddled yet able to have a go at anything. He wiggled the tiller frantically, and to his astonishment, the boat responded with a series of comical hops, twisting away from the rocky shore at the last second.

"See? You're getting the hang of it!" Pippin snickered, gripping onto a rope to consistent himself as the boat proceeded with its eccentric dance on the water. "Just think of it as a wobbly dance party!"

"More like a wobbly disaster!" Alarion shot back, chuckling as the boat dipped and swayed. He couldn't help but feel a strange sense of joy in the chaos, the unpredictable nature of their journey bringing a spark of adventure he hadn't expected.

As they ventured further, the landscape of Tiderune unfolded around them, vibrant colors and fantastical creatures popping into view. Alarion spotted a family of mermaids giggling as they splashed one another, and a group of grumpy-looking turtles, wearing tiny hats, glared at the Wobbleberry as it passed.

"Look! They like us!" Pippin said, beaming at the turtles. "Or maybe they're just impressed by our skills!"

"Right," "I'm certain they're just surprised by our... lopsided execution."

But even amidst the chaos, Alarion began to appreciate the boat's quirks. With every twist and turn, he discovered something new about the magical realm—an unexpected beauty in the unpredictability of the Wobbleberry. It wasn't just a vessel; it was a companion on this journey, one that would teach him to embrace the unexpected.

"Hey, Wobbleberry!" Alarion called out, smiling as the boat sunk into a steadier beat. "You're not so bad after all!"

Just then, the boat gave a little shake as if in response, and Alarion laughed again, realizing that perhaps even a wobbly boat could lead to the most wonderful adventures.

As they continued to sail, Alarion felt a sense of exhilaration welling up within him. The winds of Tiderune were calling, and he was ready to answer. With Pippin by his side and the Wobbleberry wobbling happily beneath him, he knew that whatever lay ahead would be filled with laughter, magic, and the thrilling promise of the unknown.

BOOK # 2 ALARION AND THE SECRETS OF TIDERUNE 21

Chapter 2: The Mischievous Mermaid

A mermaid named Lila appears, claiming to be the best singer in Tiderune. When Alarion challenges her to a duet, things get hilariously out of tune.

As the Wobbleberry wobbled its way across the shimmering waters of Tiderune, Alarion leaned back, enjoying the sun warming his face. He had almost forgotten about the chaotic antics of the boat, revelling instead in the breathtaking scenery. But just as he started to relax, a bright flash of color caught his eye.

Out of the waves leaped a vibrant figure, splashing water in every direction. With flowing hair like spun gold and a shimmering tail that sparkled in the sunlight, a mermaid emerged from the depths of the sea. Her laughter rang through the air like a tinkling bell, and Alarion found himself staring, awestruck.

"Greetings, sailor!" she called, her voice smooth as silk. "I am Lila, the best singer in all of Tiderune! Care for a song?"

"Wow! The best singer?" Alarion said, trying to keep his excitement in check. "I've heard some pretty great voices, but I've never met a mermaid before!"

Lila flipped her hair over her shoulder, striking a pose that would make any sea creature swoon. "Of course! I'm the best! Everyone says so! But I can't just sing solo. How about a duet? I'll show you how it's done!"

Alarion, ever the adventurer, felt a spark of challenge. "A duet sounds fun! But I hope you're ready for a little competition. Let's see if I can keep up!"

Lila's eyes twinkled mischievously. "Oh, you won't be able to keep up with me, land-dweller!

But let's have a go, shall we?"

As the two prepared to sing, Pippin, perched on the edge of the boat, looked back and forth between them, his little wings twitching with excitement. "This is going to be hilarious!" he squeaked. "You'll need all your magical skills to keep up with her!"

"Just watch me!" Alarion said confidently. "I've got a few tricks of my own!"

Lila took a deep breath and launched into a melody so sweet that even the birds seemed to stop and listen. Her voice soared, echoing over the water, filled with harmonies that made the waves dance in delight. Alarion couldn't help but be swept away by the enchantment of it all.

"Now it's my turn!" Alarion shouted over the sound of her singing. He cleared his throat dramatically and began to sing, trying to match her enchanting tone.

But instead of a sweet melody, what came out was a rather strange cacophony, reminiscent of a cat trying to play a violin. His voice wobbled and wavered, sending ripples of laughter through the water. Lila paused mid-note, her eyes wide with surprise before bursting into fits of giggles.

"Is that a song or a frog having a tantrum?" she teased, her laughter echoing like music through the air.

Alarion tried to regain his composure, determined not to back down. "Just wait! I'll show you a real performance!" He took another breath, channelling all his magical energy, and tried again, this time mixing in some dramatic hand gestures.

With a flourish, he belted out a line that he was sure would impress her. But instead, he accidentally summoned a gust of wind that sent Pippin tumbling off the boat and into the water.

"Pippin!" Alarion hollered, attempting to keep down his chuckling. The tiny creature emerged, spluttering and soaked, but grinning from ear to ear. "I'm okay! Just part of the show!"

Lila couldn't contain her giggles, the melodious sound ringing like chimes on a windy day. "If you had any desire to stir things up, you surely did!"

Alarion, now in on the joke, struck a pose, raising one hand dramatically. "Oh, but this is just the beginning! Let's turn this into a full-fledged concert!"

They took turns singing, Alarion adding ridiculous sound effects and silly dance moves while Lila tried to keep her composure. Her beautiful voice contrasted sharply with Alarion's playful antics, creating a delightful chaos that filled the air.

"Dancing and singing? What a combo!" Alarion snickered as he spun around, almost losing his equilibrium on the flimsy deck.

Just as he thought they were hitting their stride, Alarion attempted to leap into an impressive dance move, only to miscalculate and end up falling right into Lila's arms as she laughed uncontrollably.

"You really are a funny one!" she exclaimed, helping him back to his feet. "Maybe we should consider a comedy career instead of singing!"

"Comedy? With my voice?" Alarion laughed, scouring the rear of his neck timidly. "Maybe I'll just stick to being a mage."

As the laughter echoed over the water, they finally settled into a rhythm, their voices harmonizing in an oddly amusing way. Even though Alarion's singing was far from perfect, the joy of the moment turned out to be the true melody of their performance.

"Okay, one more song! Let's make this one our best yet!" Lila called, her eyes sparkling with excitement.

With renewed energy, they launched into a final duet. The Wobbleberry wobbled with delight as the two sang, a delightful blend of Lila's enchanting voice and Alarion's enthusiastic if slightly off-key, melody. The waves danced along, carrying their laughter and song across the waters of Tiderune.

As they finished their performance, Alarion fell back against the deck, panting with laughter. "That was one of the most amazing minutes of all time!"

Lila smiled, her tail flicking playfully in the water. ""You probably won't be the best vocalist, yet you sure skill to have some good times! Thank you for the most entertaining duet in Tiderune history!"

"Furthermore, thank you for being a decent game!"Alarion replied, feeling a warm glow of friendship blossoming between them.

As the sun began to set, painting the sky in hues of orange and pink, Alarion knew this was just the beginning of many more adventures. With Lila's laughter still ringing in his ears and the wobbly boat beneath him, he felt ready to face whatever mischief Tiderune had in store. Little did he know, this was only a prelude to the countless encounters and curious creatures waiting just beyond the horizon.

Chapter 3: The Soggy Map

While trying to read a magical map, Alarion accidentally spills his drink on it. Now, instead of landmarks, he sees pictures of his lunch! Can he still find his way?

After the delightful chaos of the duet with Lila, Alarion felt invigorated. The Wobbleberry, still wobbling merrily, glided across the water as the sun began to dip below the horizon, painting the sky with shades of lavender and peach. He sat at the boat's helm, gazing at the magical map he had acquired from an eccentric wizard the previous week. It promised to reveal all the secrets of Tiderune, leading him to hidden treasures and mystical creatures.

"Alright, let's see what this baby can do!" Alarion said to himself, unfurling the map on the deck.

The map shimmered with an array of colors, the landmarks glowing as if they were alive. There were mountains shaped like giant pancakes, forests that looked like candy canes, and rivers swirling like ribbons in a dance. Alarion's eyes sparkled with excitement as he traced his finger along the winding paths.

Just as he was about to decipher the route to the nearest enchanted waterfall, Pippin flitted over, holding a goblet filled with a mysterious glowing drink. "Care for a sip of my famous sparkling fizz? It's a new recipe!"

Alarion grinned, eager to try it. "Absolutely! Pour me a glass!"

With a twist, Pippin tipped the challis, yet similarly as Alarion went after it, he lost his equilibrium, sending the beverage sprinkling onto the mystical guide. "No!" he exclaimed, watching in horror as the bright fizz soaked into the parchment, swirling together in a fizzy mess.

As the bubbles popped and fizzed, the map's magical glow flickered. Alarion leaned in closer, desperately hoping the map wouldn't be ruined. "Come on, don't do this to me now!"

But instead of the shimmering landmarks he expected, the map transformed before his eyes. Where once there had been mountains and rivers, he now saw—his lunch! There was a cartoonish illustration of a sandwich, complete with googly eyes, next to a giant piece of chocolate cake waving cheerfully.

"Uh, what just happened?" Pippin asked, his head tilting to the side like a curious puppy.

"It's a soggy map!" Alarion cried, flipping the parchment over in disbelief. "Instead of guiding me through Tiderune, it's showing me what I had for lunch!"

"Maybe it's a special feature? Like a treasure map to your next meal?" Pippin suggested, giggling uncontrollably.

Alarion's brows furrowed in frustration. "This isn't funny! I need to find the enchanted waterfall, not a cartoon sandwich!"

As he scowled at the silly illustrations, a sudden thought struck him. "Wait a minute... maybe this isn't as useless as I think!" With reestablished assurance, he zeroed in on the food pictures.

"If I can just retrace my steps from lunch, perhaps I can figure out where to go next!" He pointed at the sandwich, which now had arms and legs, appearing to dance. "This sandwich was made before our journey! If I follow its path..."

With that, Alarion quickly began to analyze the map. "The sandwich!" he exclaimed. ""It's driving me to the recreation area where I had my lunch! That's near the enchanted waterfall!"

Pippin clapped his tiny hands, excitement bubbling over. "Brilliant! You're a genius, Alarion!"

With the soggy map still in hand, Alarion adjusted his course on the Wobbleberry. "Let's set sail for the park! Who knew my lunch would guide me on this adventure?"

As they approached the park, Alarion could see the towering trees and colorful flowers blossoming in all directions. Following the sandwich's instructions, they sailed closer to the shore, where Alarion hopped off the boat with the soggy map in hand.

"Okay, where to next?" he mused, squinting at the animated illustrations. The sandwich seemed to point toward a nearby grove of trees where a chocolate cake had taken up residence, wearing a crown made of whipped cream.

"Here we go!" Alarion exclaimed, dashing toward the grove with Pippin flying close behind. As they neared the trees, the cake illustration danced and wiggled, encouraging them onward.

Alarion laughed, his earlier frustration forgotten. "Who knew a soggy map would lead us to a cake? This is the most ideal sort of expedition!"

They finally reached the grove, and to Alarion's astonishment, there was indeed an enchanted waterfall, sparkling with colors that seemed to pulse with magic. The water cascaded down like liquid diamonds, sending rainbows shimmering into the air.

"This is amazing!" Alarion shouted, feeling the cool mist on his face. "And to think, it was all thanks to a sandwich!"

Suddenly, the chocolate cake illustration on the map began to giggle, and with a flicker of magic, the cake leaped off the map, forming into a real cake right in front of Alarion and Pippin. It was as if the map was celebrating their success!

"Now, that's what I call a sweet reward!" Alarion laughed, eyeing the cake hungrily.

As he and Pippin dug into their unexpected treat, Alarion couldn't help but feel grateful for the mishap with the soggy map. What had started as a disaster had turned into a delightful adventure, full of laughter and joy. He realized that sometimes, the most unexpected things can lead to the best experiences.

"Alright, let's find out what else this magical world has to offer!" Alarion declared, his heart swelling with excitement as they prepared to explore the wonders of Tiderune further. The soggy map might have been a bit silly, but it had led him to the waterfall—and that was just the beginning!

Chapter 4: The Wizard with Two Hats

Alarion meets a wizard who can't decide which of his two hats is more magical. A friendly debate leads to a fashion show that ends in a magical mess!

The sun shone brightly over the magical realm of Tiderune, casting glimmers of light on Alarion's path as he wandered through the vibrant forest. The sound of chirping birds and rustling leaves filled the air, creating a delightful symphony that made him feel adventurous. Today, he was determined to find new friends and learn more about the enchantments of this mystical land.

As he strolled deeper into the woods, he stumbled upon a clearing where a curious scene was unfolding. A wizard dressed in a shimmering cloak stood with his arms crossed, staring intently at two extravagant hats perched on a nearby stump.

"What's going on here?" Alarion called out, his curiosity piqued.

The wizard turned around, revealing a rather comical face, one half beaming with enthusiasm and the other half caught in a perplexed frown. "Ah, a traveller! Just in time! I am Wizard Whimble, and I have a most pressing dilemma!"

Alarion approached, trying to stifle a laugh at the sight of the wizard, who wore mismatched shoes—one was a sparkly red and the other a bright blue. "What seems to be the problem, Wizard Whimble?"

The wizard gestured dramatically to his two hats. "You see, I can't decide which of these hats is more magical! The pointy one with stars and moons gives me the ability to conjure fireworks, while the floppy one with sparkles makes delicious pastries appear at a mere thought!"

Alarion scratched his head. "That's quite a choice! But how can we decide which one is better?"

"Why not have a friendly debate?" Wizard Whimble suggested, his eyes twinkling with mischief. "We can put them through a fashion show, and the hat that dazzles the most will be the winner!"

Alarion chuckled, the idea sounding like great fun. "A hat fashion show? Count me in! But how do we even start?"

"Simple! Each hat will take turns showcasing its talents! And you, dear Alarion, will be the judge!" Wizard Whimble declared, adjusting his spectacles.

With a nod, Alarion agreed, ready to see what magical wonders awaited them. "Alright, let's get this fashion show started!"

First up was the pointy hat. Wizard Whimble wore it and paused dramatically, emphatically waving his wand. "See! Firecrackers of the best quality!" With a flick of his wrist, brilliant blasts filled the sky, blasting into states of mythical serpents and stars

"Wow! Impressive!" Alarion clapped, thoroughly entertained.

Next, Wizard Whimble switched to the floppy hat. He adjusted it and beamed, "Now, prepare for a feast!" He thought hard, and suddenly, a flurry of pastries appeared, floating in the air like fluffy clouds. Croissants, tarts, and cupcakes danced around them, showering Alarion with sprinkles.

"Yum! This hat is delightful!" Alarion giggled, getting a cupcake and taking a major chomp.

But as they continued, things took a turn for the chaotic. Whimble got carried away with his display of talents. "Let's combine their powers!" he shouted, wearing the two caps on the double.

"Are you sure that's a good idea?" Alarion asked, his eyebrows raised.

"Of course!" Wizard Whimble insisted, his excitement bubbling over. He waved his wand, trying to summon fireworks while imagining a pastry buffet.

In a split second, the combination unleashed a wild surge of magic! Fireworks erupted into a whirl of colors, and pastries flew into the air like they were caught in a tornado. Croissants tumbled through the explosions, and cupcakes landed in strange places—one even plopped right onto Wizard Whimble's head!

"Ah! My hats!" he shouted, attempting to get the airborne cakes while evading the brilliant explodes the scene was nothing short of a magical mess!

Alarion doubled over with laughter as the wizard spun around, desperately trying to juggle hats and pastries. "You've truly outdone yourself, Wizard Whimble!"

With a grand finale, a giant pastry exploded in a flurry of frosting, showering Alarion and the wizard in a sticky, sweet cloud. When the frosting settled, both of them stood covered in colorful sprinkles, laughter echoing through the forest.

"Indeed, it appears we've made another style: the pleasantly sprinkled look!" Alarion laughed, clearing icing off his cheek.

Wizard Whimble took a deep breath and surveyed the delightful chaos. "Perhaps I don't need to choose a hat after all! They both have their merits, don't you think?"

"Absolutely! Why not keep both?" Alarion suggested, grinning widely. "After all, who wouldn't want a wizard who can conjure pastries and fireworks?"

With a twinkle in his eye, Wizard Whimble adjusted both hats, one on top of the other, making quite a sight. "A fine compromise, my friend! Thank you for your help!"

As they cleaned up the sweet mess together, Alarion felt a sense of joy bubbling within him. He had made a new friend, and together they had created a memorable moment filled with laughter and magic.

"Well, Alarion, let's continue this adventure of ours! With both hats, the possibilities are endless!" Wizard Whimble exclaimed; his spirits high.

"Lead the way, Wizard Whimble!" Alarion replied, ready for whatever magical mishap awaited them next. With their spirits high and their hearts light, the duo set off into the wondrous world of Tiderune, both delighted by the enchanting possibilities ahead.

Chapter 5: The Enchanted Forest Picnic

In an enchanted forest, Alarion organizes a picnic, but the trees decide they want to join in. The food disappears, and the trees start a food fight!

The sun cast its warm, golden glow over the enchanting land of Tiderune, where magical creatures roamed freely, and the air was filled with the sweet scent of blooming flowers. Alarion, having enjoyed his adventures so far, decided it was time for a relaxing day—a picnic in the heart of the enchanted forest!

He packed a basket with an assortment of delicious treats: fresh fruits, crunchy nuts, delightful pastries, and a few sparkling juice bottles that promised a fizzy, refreshing drink. Alarion could hardly contain his excitement as he skipped along the winding path, humming a cheerful tune. The forest was alive with sounds; birds chirped sweetly, and the leaves rustled playfully in the gentle breeze.

After arriving at a sun-dappled clearing, Alarion spread out a beautiful cover and organized the food with care. "Awesome! he exclaimed, eyeing his spread with satisfaction. "A delightful picnic awaits!"

As he settled down to enjoy his feast, a peculiar rustling interrupted his blissful moment. Alarion turned, curious, and his eyes widened in amazement. Tall trees with twisting trunks and broad canopies seemed to lean closer, peering curiously at the colorful spread of food.

"Um, hello there?" Alarion waved awkwardly at the trees, wondering if they were truly enchanted.

"Did someone say picnic?" a deep voice echoed from the bark of the nearest tree, its branches waving animatedly. "We trees can't resist a good feast!"

"Yeah, yeah! Let's join in!" another tree chimed in, its leaves shimmering with excitement.

Alarion chuckled nervously, "I didn't plan for anyone else to join. But I suppose—"

Before he could finish, the trees shifted with enthusiasm, their roots rustling like children eager to dive into a pool. Suddenly, one tree extended a branch and plucked a juicy apple right off the basket!

"Hey! That was mine!" Alarion exclaimed, laughing in disbelief as the trees began to pass the apple around among themselves, their laughter echoing in the forest.

"Don't worry! We'll share!" another tree promised, its bark creaking with laughter as it tried to juggle an apple and a muffin.

"Okay, okay! Just leave some for me!" Alarion said, joining in the laughter, unable to resist the trees' infectious joy. But as he turned his back for just a moment to pour himself a sparkling juice, he heard the sound of rustling leaves turning into wild giggles.

Alarion whipped around to find the trees participated in what must be depicted as a brilliant food heist. "Stand by! Where did every one of the cakes go?" he asked, his eyes wide as he watched branches waving in amuse, throwing treats starting with one tree then onto the next.

A giggling tree responded, "We wanted to play! Food should be fun!"

With a shake of his head and a grin spreading across his face, Alarion decided to join the fun. "Alright! If we're having a food party, let's have a food party!"

Suddenly, the picnic transformed into a whimsical food fight! Alarion grabbed a pastry and aimed it at the closest tree. The pastry soared through the air and landed squarely on a tree's leafy crown, exploding into crumbs!

"Hey! That's not how you play!" the tree laughed, shaking off the remnants and throwing a handful of nuts back at Alarion, who ducked just in time.

Laughter filled the clearing as muffins, fruits, and nuts flew through the air. Alarion and the trees danced around, giggling like children, their spirits soaring higher with each thrown treat. The once-quiet clearing was now alive with joyous chaos.

Amid their laughter, Alarion managed to gather a few remaining pastries and held them triumphantly. "Alright, truce! How about we sit and enjoy what's left together?"

The trees paused, their branches hanging low as they considered his offer. "Alright, but only if you promise to tell us a story!" one of the trees replied, its leaves shimmering in anticipation.

"Deal!" Alarion concurred, settling back onto the cover, and tidying off the morsels from his garments. He began to weave a tale about daring adventurers and magical quests, his voice animated and full of excitement. The trees listened intently, leaning in closer, their leaves quivering with anticipation.

As the sun dipped lower in the sky, painting the forest with hues of orange and pink, Alarion and the trees enjoyed the remnants of the feast, sharing stories and laughter. It became a picnic he would never forget, filled with joy, friendship, and the delight of unexpected companions.

Eventually, as the stars began to twinkle overhead, Alarion waved goodbye to his newfound friends, promising to return for more adventures and, of course, more picnics.

As he walked back home, a grin plastered across his face, Alarion couldn't help but think about the delightful chaos of the day. He knew that in the magical realm of Tiderune, anything could happen, and the more friends he made, the more adventures awaited him.

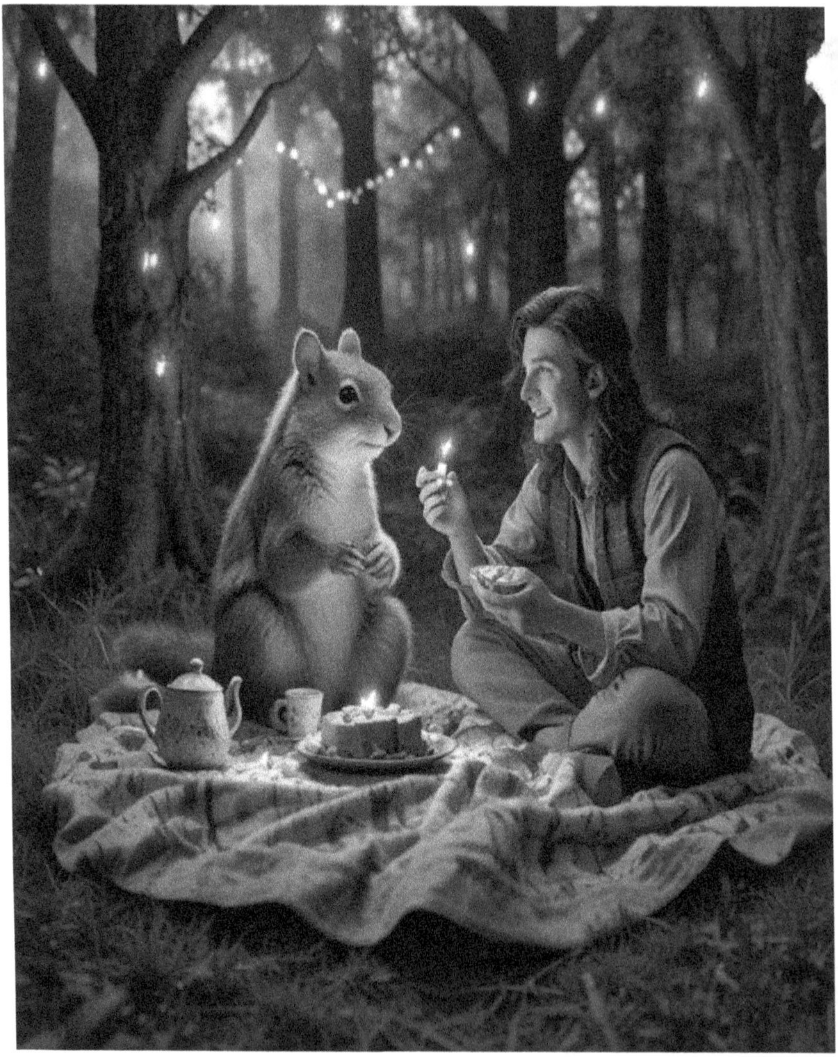

Chapter 6: The Riddling River

*A**larion encounters a talking river that loves riddles. Solving its puzzles is tricky, especially when the river starts tossing in random puns!*

As Alarion continued his adventure through the magical realm of Tiderune, he found himself wandering along a sparkling river that danced and shimmered under the sun. The gentle gurgling of water created a melody that seemed to beckon him closer. Curious, he stepped closer to the water's edge, peering into the clear depths.

"Ahoy there, traveller!" came a cheerful voice that echoed across the rippling surface. Startled, Alarion looked around, searching for the source of the voice. To his astonishment, the river itself was speaking to him, its waves bubbling with laughter.

"Who—who's talking?" Alarion stammered, half-expecting a fish to pop up and start chatting.

"It's me, the Riddling River!" the waiter replied, its surface swirling playfully. "I love riddles and puns! Care for a challenge?"

Alarion scratched his head, actually attempting to truly understand the possibility of a talking waterway. "Enigmas? Sure, I'm up for it! But what do I get if I win?"

The river rippled mischievously, "If you win, I'll grant you a delightful secret about the magical realm! If you lose, though, you must share a funny tale of your own!"

"Deal!" Alarion grinned, feeling a spark of excitement. "Let's hear your first riddle!"

"Alright, here we go!" the river bubbled. "What has keys but can't open locks?"

Alarion pondered for a moment, his brow furrowed in concentration. "A piano!" he exclaimed, his face lighting up with triumph.

"Ding Ding! Correct!" the river cheered, splashing playfully. ""Be that as it may, presently, here's a quip for you: For what reason did the stream part ways with the sea? Because it found someone deeper!"

Alarion chuckled at the river's whimsical nature. "Okay, that was pretty good! What's next?"

"Alright, here's another one!" The river swirled dramatically. "What can go all over the planet while remaining in a corner?"

"Hmm... a stamp?" Alarion speculated, feeling very satisfied with himself.

"Bravo!" the river cheered, sending a splash of water into the air. "But here's a riddle that's a little trickier: What has a heart that doesn't beat?"

Alarion scratched his head, trying to think outside the box. After a few moments of silence, he exclaimed, "An artichoke!"

"Spot on!" the waterway chuckled, making a rush of glad waves. "Now, for a pun: What do you call a fish with no eyes?"

Alarion couldn't help but burst into laughter. "I don't know! What?"

"Fsh!" the stream announced, its voice reverberating with entertainment.

"Alright, that one was a classic!" Alarion admitted, wiping a tear of laughter from his eye. "But I'm ready for another riddle!"

The river paused, its waters swirling thoughtfully. "OK, here's a difficult one: I'm tall when I'm youthful, and I'm short when I'm old. What am I?"

Alarion furrowed his brow again, pondering the riddle carefully. As he gazed at the river, an idea struck him. "A candle!"

"Brilliant!" the river cheered, splashing happily. "But, alas, you're too good at this! Let's mix things up a bit."

Suddenly, the river began tossing in random puns, and Alarion found himself in a delightful wordplay storm. "What do you get when you cross a river and a fish? A river fish that's too scaled for its own good!" the river shouted.

Alarion was caught off guard, laughing uncontrollably at the ridiculousness. "That's terrible!" he exclaimed, grinning from ear to ear.

"Terribly wonderful!" the waterway answered, shaking things up as it proceeded with its torrent of quips. "Why did the fish blush? Because it saw the ocean's bottom!"

Alarion shook his head, laughter bubbling up inside him. "You're quite the entertainer, River!"

As the river continued with its riddles and puns, Alarion realized that he was thoroughly enjoying himself. Each riddle was a test of his wit, while each pun brought a wave of laughter that resonated in the surrounding woods.

Eventually, the river paused, allowing Alarion a moment to catch his breath. "Alright, I must admit, you've outsmarted me today, traveller! But for your cleverness, here's your secret about Tiderune."

"Really? What is it?" Alarion leaned closer, anticipation tingling in the air.

"The trees of Tiderune whisper ancient tales when the moon is high. If you listen closely tonight, you might uncover secrets that even I don't know!" The river's voice danced with excitement.

"Thank you, Riddling River! I'll definitely listen tonight!" Alarion promised, feeling a newfound sense of wonder.

"Before you go, recollect: life is a puzzle, loaded with exciting bends in the road. Keep your sense of humor, and you'll navigate through it with joy!" the river called as Alarion waved goodbye.

With a heart full of laughter and a mind brimming with riddles, Alarion set off along the path. He couldn't wait for the night to fall, eager to listen to the secrets whispered by the trees. Little did he know, the journey through Tiderune was only just beginning, with each encounter more magical and whimsical than the last!

Chapter 7: The Fluffy Monster

Alarion faces a fluffy monster that looks more like a giant cotton candy. Instead of scaring him, it offers him candy, leading to a sticky situation.

Alarion was skipping along a winding path through the enchanting forest of Tiderune when a peculiar sight caught his eye. There, just off the trail, stood a creature unlike anything he had ever seen. It was enormous, fluffy, and looked remarkably like a giant ball of cotton candy—pink and blue swirled together in a dizzying array of colors.

"What in Tiderune is that?" Alarion whispered to himself, eyeing the creature with both curiosity and caution.

As he approached, the fluffy monster turned its head, revealing two enormous, round eyes that sparkled with friendliness rather than ferocity. "Hello there, little traveller!" it boomed in a cheerful voice that sent a few birds fluttering from nearby branches. "I'm Fuzzball, the Fluffy Monster! Would you like some candy?"

Alarion blinked in surprise. "Candy? You're offering me candy?"

"Of course!" Fuzzball said, puffing up a piece like a pleased peacock. "I have all kinds! Cotton candy, caramel apples, chocolate frogs—take your pick!" With a swish of its fluffy body, a rainbow of candies appeared around it, floating in the air like sweet little balloons.

Alarion's eyes widened. "Um, I think I'll go for the chocolate frogs!" he said, unable to resist the sugary allure.

"Excellent choice!" Fuzzball shouted, culling a chocolate frog from the air and throwing it toward Alarion, who got it in mid-air with a charmed smile.

But as he took a bite, things took an unexpected turn. The chocolate frog was not just sweet—it was sticky! Alarion felt the gooey chocolate begin to cling to his fingers, and before he knew it, he was stuck, waving his hands in the air like a flailing octopus.

"Ah! I can't move!" Alarion shouted, laughter bubbling up despite his predicament. "I'm turning into a chocolate statue!"

Fuzzball giggled, its fluffy body shaking. "Don't worry, my friend! It's just a bit of sticky candy! Here, let me help!" The cushioned beast inclined forward, and Alarion looked as its fluffy paws stretched out toward him.

In a flash, Fuzzball's fluffy paw wrapped around Alarion's hands, but rather than freeing him, it created an even stickier situation! The candy around him suddenly began to glow, and with a dramatic poof, Alarion found himself encased in a cocoon of candy floss.

"Now you really are a cotton candy creature!" Fuzzball roared with laughter, its eyes twinkling.

"Oh no! This is quite a sticky situation!" Alarion chuckled, realizing that he was more amused than alarmed. "What do I do now, gracious savvy, and cushy one?"

Fuzzball pondered, tilting its head adorably. "Well, there's only one way to get free! You must tickle yourself until the sticky candy melts away! It's a special Tiderune tradition!"

"Tickle me? That's absurd!" Alarion dissented, yet the prospect of being a treats sculpture forever appeared to be much more dreadful.

So, with a dramatic sigh, Alarion began to wiggle his fingers and tickle his sides. To his surprise, he burst into laughter! The more he tickled himself, the more he giggled, and soon the cocoon began to tremble and shake, bits of candy floss melting away with each peal of laughter.

Fuzzball clapped its fluffy paws in delight. "Yes! Keep going! You're almost there!"

With one final tickle, the last remnants of the sticky candy dissolved, and Alarion found himself free! He stood there, covered in fluffy bits, looking like he had just been through a sugar storm.

"Phew! That was... an experience!" Alarion said, shaking off the sugary remnants and grinning at Fuzzball. "You're not as scary as I thought you'd be!"

Fuzzball beamed, its fluff swaying. "Thank you! Most creatures run away from me because they think I'll eat them! But I'm just here to spread sweetness and laughter!"

"Sweetness and laughter? I can get behind that!" Alarion chuckled, tapping the goliath animal on its cushy side. "Would you like to go along with me on my excursion?"

"Absolutely! But only if we can have more candy along the way!" Fuzzball declared, bouncing excitedly.

"Deal!" Alarion said, and the two of them set off together, a strange pair wandering through the magical forest—one a curious adventurer and the other a fluffy monster with a heart as big as its size.

As they travelled, Fuzzball regaled Alarion with tales of sweet adventures and sticky mishaps, their laughter echoing through the trees. They shared candy and stories, making every step of their journey feel like a delightful escapade.

With each chuckle and sugary treat, Alarion realized that life in Tiderune was truly magical—and sometimes, a little bit sticky!

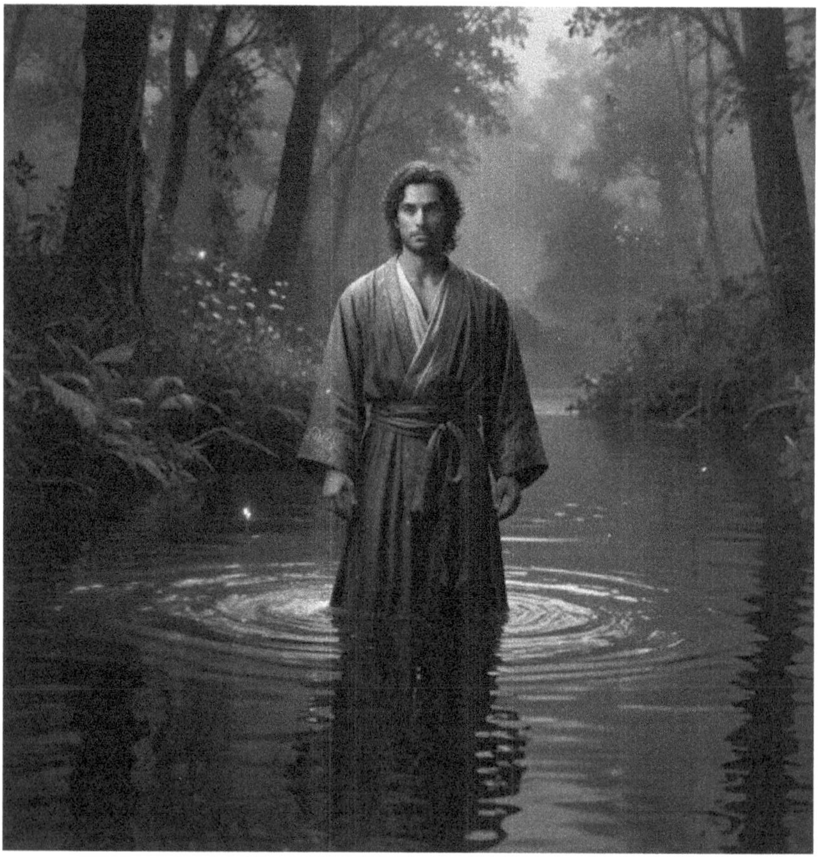

Chapter 8: The Snoring Sorcerer

While seeking knowledge, Alarion finds a sorcerer who snores louder than a thunderstorm. He must navigate through a snore-induced maze to find a hidden spellbook.

Alarion was on a mission—this time, he needed to find the ancient spellbook that held the secrets to unlocking the mystical powers of Tiderune. The map he had (the one that previously turned into a picture of his lunch) led him to the lair of a legendary sorcerer known as Snorri the Snoozing Sorcerer. Rumor had it that Snorri was a master of spells, but he also had one particularly notable characteristic: he snored louder than a thunderstorm.

As Alarion approached the sorcerer's lair, he could already hear the thunderous snores echoing through the trees. It sounded like a herd of elephants had taken up residence inside. "This is going to be interesting," Alarion muttered to himself, steeling his resolve.

He stepped through the entrance of the lair, which was surprisingly cozy, filled with colorful potions bubbling away and scrolls fluttering like birds. But the moment he stepped inside, the ground shook with a loud SNORRRRREEEEE. Alarion stumbled backward, his heart racing. "Goodness! Is that really a snore?" he exclaimed, trying not to laugh.

He tiptoed further in, trying to avoid making any noise. He peered around the room and spotted Snorri slumped in an enormous chair that looked like it was made of clouds. The sorcerer had a long, silver beard that seemed to float like a fluffy cloud, and a pointed hat that had a slight tilt to it, giving him a comically daft appearance. Each snore made his hat bob up and down as if it were dancing to a rhythm only it could hear.

"I need to find that spellbook," Alarion whispered to himself, glancing around for any signs of it. "Be that as it may, how could I should move beyond this wheezing behemoth?"

As if the universe were playing a prank, Snorri's snoring intensified. SNORRRRREEEEE! BOOM! The ground trembled again, and Alarion nearly lost his balance. "I guess I'll have to navigate a snore-induced maze," he said, half-laughing at his own predicament.

After a moment's contemplation, Alarion devised a plan. He would have to maneuver around Snorri's snores as if they were waves crashing in the ocean. He crouched low and began to creep toward a shelf overflowing with spellbooks, careful to time his movements with the rhythm of the snores.

As Snorri's snore reached a crescendo, Alarion darted forward, making a beeline for the nearest book. He reached for a bright blue tome with shimmering letters that read, "Spells for Everyday Occasions." Just as he was about to grab it, a massive SNORT! erupted from Snorri, causing Alarion to freeze in his tracks.

"Whoa! That was close!" he murmured, dots of sweat shaping on his temple. He waited, watching the sorcerer, who seemed blissfully unaware of the chaos his snores were causing. Finally, Snorri settled back into a deep snore, and Alarion took a deep breath.

"This is like a game of hopscotch!" he mumbled, attempting to keep the temperament light. He timed his next move perfectly and leaped over to another shelf filled with shimmering scrolls. But as he landed, a small vial fell from the shelf, shattering on the floor with a loud crash!

"Oops!" Alarion gasped, his heart racing as Snorri's snoring immediately ceased. The sorcerer's eyes fluttered open, and he sat up groggily, looking around with a befuddled expression. "Wha—who's there?"

BOOK # 2 ALARION AND THE SECRETS OF TIDERUNE   49

Panicking, Alarion ducked behind the shelf, hoping to remain hidden. He held his breath, his mind racing with thoughts. "I didn't mean to wake him up! How am I going to find the spellbook now?"

Snorri rubbed his eyes and peered around the room, squinting. "Hello? Is there someone here?" he called; his voice booming like thunder itself.

Summoning his courage, Alarion took a deep breath and stepped out from behind the shelf. "Uh, hello, great sorcerer! I'm Alarion, and I'm on a quest to find the ancient spellbook!"

Snorri flickered in shock, and afterward, a smile spread across his face. "Ok! A visitor! How wonderful! But why are you hiding? I promise I don't bite—unless it's during dinner, and then I prefer a nice roast!"

Alarion couldn't help but chuckle at the sorcerer's cheerful demeanor. "I was just trying to navigate through your impressive snoring, sir! It's a bit like a thunderstorm in here!"

Snorri laughed heartily, his beard shaking like jelly. "Ah, yes! I do tend to snore a bit, don't I? It's a curse of my magical abilities! Now, about that spellbook—what do you need it for?"

Alarion explained his quest and the knowledge he was seeking. Snorri listened intently, nodding with every word. "Well, you're in luck! The spellbook you seek is right behind my favorite napping chair! It's yours, my friend!"

Alarion couldn't believe his ears. "Really? That's amazing!"

"Of course! But you'll have to help me with something first," Snorri said, his eyes twinkling with mischief. "I'm facilitating a supernatural tea gathering this evening, and I want somebody to keep me conscious. How about you tell me your most hilarious jokes while I sip my tea?"

Alarion grinned, realizing he had struck a peculiar friendship. "Absolutely! I know a ton of jokes!"

As Snorri poured himself a cup of steaming tea, Alarion launched into a series of funny tales and jokes, his laughter mixing with Snorri's hearty chuckles. Each time the sorcerer laughed, his laughter was so powerful that it caused the shelves to rattle and the potion bottles to jiggle.

After a delightful tea party filled with laughter and light, Alarion retrieved the ancient spellbook, its pages glowing with magical energy. "Thank you, Snorri! You've been a fantastic help!"

"Just remember, Alarion," Snorri said, waving his fluffy hand. "Laughter is the best magic of all! Come back anytime, and I'll share more spells—and snore a few tunes too!"

With the spellbook safely tucked under his arm, Alarion stepped out of the lair, the echoes of Snorri's laughter still ringing in his ears. "What a day!" he thought. "A tempest of wheezing and a brilliant magician — who knew looking for information could be such a lot of tomfoolery?"

As Alarion ventured forth on his quest, he couldn't help but chuckle at the thought of the Snoring Sorcerer and the magical tea party that would always hold a special place in his heart.

BOOK # 2 ALARION AND THE SECRETS OF TIDERUNE 51

Chapter 9: The Juggling Jellyfish

In a vibrant underwater show, Alarion is enchanted by a jellyfish juggling glowing orbs. When it asks him to join, Alarion realizes he's better at making a splash!

Alarion had navigated many adventures in the magical realm of Tiderune, but nothing quite prepared him for what lay beneath the shimmering waves of the Emerald Sea. As he stood on the shore, the sun sparkling off the water like a thousand tiny diamonds, he couldn't shake the feeling that something extraordinary awaited him below.

He donned a magical diving suit—one that shimmered like a fish scale and allowed him to breathe underwater. With a deep breath, he dove in. The moment he entered the water, he was greeted by a dazzling display of color. Schools of fish darted past him like tiny, glittering arrows, and coral formations bloomed in every shade of the rainbow. Alarion couldn't help but giggle; it felt like he had swum into a living painting.

As he swam deeper, he began to hear the sounds of laughter echoing through the water, bouncing off the corals. Curious, he followed the joyous noise until he found himself in a grand underwater amphitheater, where an audience of fish, crabs, and even a few curious sea turtles had gathered. In the centre of the stage, a jellyfish was performing an astonishing act—juggling glowing orbs of light that floated gracefully in the water.

"Welcome, every last one, to the best show under the ocean!" the jellyfish announced, its tentacles moving rhythmically as it juggled the orbs. "I am Glimmer, the Juggling Jellyfish, and tonight, I shall mesmerize you with my skills!"

Alarion's eyes widened in amazement as he watched Glimmer toss the glowing orbs into the air, each one glimmering with colors that danced in the water. The crowd erupted in cheers, and Alarion found himself clapping along, unable to contain his excitement.

"Would you like to join me on stage?" Glimmer asked, noticing Alarion's enthusiasm. "I could use a charming assistant for my grand finale!"

"Me?" Alarion exclaimed, feeling a rush of exhilaration mixed with a tinge of nerves. "But I've never juggled before!"

"Oh, don't worry!" Glimmer replied with a twinkle in its gelatinous body. "Just follow my lead!"

Before Alarion could back out, he was swept onto the stage. The audience roared with laughter and applause as Glimmer handed him two small, glowing orbs. "Now, just toss them in the air like this!" the jellyfish expressed, showing with elegant style.

Alarion took a deep breath, feeling the weight of the orbs in his hands. He attempted to mimic Glimmer's movements. He tossed the first orb up with enthusiasm, but instead of catching it, he accidentally hit it, sending it spiralling off into the crowd. The fish squealed with delight, dodging the glowing orb like it was a game of underwater dodgeball.

"Oops! Not quite what I intended!" Alarion chuckled nervously, scratching his head. Undeterred, he tried again. This time, he tossed both orbs into the air, but instead of juggling, he ended up flailing his arms, splashing water everywhere, and sending one orb bouncing off the jellyfish's head.

"Nice shot!" Glimmer giggled, unfazed. The crowd erupted into fits of laughter, the kind that bubbled up from the depths of their watery homes.

With each failed attempt, Alarion's confidence began to wane. Just as he was about to give up, Glimmer floated closer. "How about we try something different?" the jellyfish recommended, its limbs twirling in a perky dance.

"What do you mean?" Alarion asked, intrigued.

"Let's make a splash!" Glimmer said with a grin, pointing its tentacle toward a pile of colorful seaweed and shimmering shells at the edge of the stage. "Rather than shuffling, for what reason don't we make a water show together? You splash, and I'll juggle!"

"Alright!" Alarion exclaimed, feeling a spark of excitement return. He dashed over to the pile of seaweed and began tossing it into the water, creating colorful fountains that spiralled and twirled. Glimmer started juggling again, this time with the glowing orbs, while Alarion splashed the crowd with bursts of sparkling water.

The audience was ecstatic, cheering and laughing as the two performers created a joyful chaos in the water. Glimmer would toss an orb high into the air, and Alarion would send waves crashing down to meet it, creating a symphony of color and light. The jellyfish's orbs glowed brighter with each splash, illuminating the underwater stage in a dazzling display.

"Now that's what I call teamwork!" Glimmer shouted over the cheers of the crowd. They were in sync, creating an unforgettable spectacle that left everyone in awe.

As the performance came to an end, Alarion and Glimmer took a bow, the audience erupting into thunderous applause. "You were fantastic!" Glimmer said, floating beside Alarion. "Who knew you had such talent for making a splash?"

Alarion beamed with pride, still catching his breath from the exhilarating performance. "That was way more fun than juggling! Thank you for letting me join you!"

"Anytime, my friend! You've got a natural talent for entertainment," Glimmer replied, its colors shimmering with joy. "Keep in mind, once in a while there's no need to focus on doing things impeccably — it's tied in with having a great time and gaining experiences!"

With that, Alarion said his goodbyes to the underwater audience and Glimmer, promising to return for another performance. As he swam back to the surface, he couldn't help but laugh at the day's adventures. He might not have mastered juggling, but he had certainly made a splash in Tiderune!

As he emerged from the water, the sun warmed his face, and Alarion felt grateful for yet another whimsical experience in this magical realm. With a heart brimming with giggling and bliss, he progressed forward with his excursion, eager to see what different undertakings looked for him.

Chapter 10: The Bubblegum Bridge

Alarion must cross a bridge made of Bubblegum to continue his journey. As he walks, he sticks and unsticks, making a giggly spectacle of himself!

Alarion had faced many peculiar challenges on his journey through Tiderune, but today was something entirely different. As he approached the next leg of his adventure, he stumbled upon the fabled Bubblegum Bridge. The bridge loomed ahead, a vibrant spectacle of pink and purple swirls that seemed to shimmer under the sun. It looked like a giant piece of candy, and Alarion couldn't help but wonder if it tasted as good as it looked.

"Just cross the bridge," he muttered to himself, trying to gather his courage. But as he took his first step onto the bridge, he realized this was not going to be an ordinary crossing. The moment his foot touched the surface, he felt a sticky sensation that made him giggle. "Oh, boy! What have I gotten myself into?"

The bridge was made of Bubblegum, and it squished under his feet, stretching and contracting with every step. Alarion took another tentative step, and the gum beneath him responded like a trampoline, bouncing him up and down. With each bounce, he felt more like a child on a sugar rush, and he couldn't help but burst into laughter.

As he made his way across, the sticky substance clung to his shoes, creating a hilarious sticking-and-unsticking spectacle. One moment he was bounding forward, and the next, he was stuck, wiggling his foot in a desperate attempt to free himself. "Come on, shoe! Let's not get stuck here forever!" he exclaimed, giggling at his predicament.

Just then, he heard a high-pitched giggle echoing from the other side of the bridge. Peeking over, he spotted a group of tiny creatures that looked like walking lollipops—colorful and full of energy. They were the Gumdrop Fairies, known for their playful mischief and love of Bubblegum.

"Hey there, traveller!" one of the pixies called out, her voice shimmering with charm. "Need a hand? Or should we say a wing?"

"Maybe a little help would be great!" Alarion answered, as yet battling to free his foot. The fairies flitted over, their wings sparkling like confetti in the sunlight.

With a flurry of tiny hands, they began to pull at Alarion's foot, but all it did was make the gum stretch even more, leading to an uproar of laughter from both Alarion and the fairies. "I think we're just making it worse!" Alarion chuckled.

The fairies, however, were undeterred. "Let's have some fun!" another fairy suggested. "On the count of three, we'll all pull together!"

"Okay!" Alarion agreed, excitement bubbling inside him. "One, two, three!"

With a united effort, they tugged, and for a brief moment, it seemed as though Alarion might just bounce right off the bridge. But instead, he popped free with a loud splat, sending the gum flying into the air like a gigantic, sticky water balloon!

As he landed back on his feet, he couldn't help but laugh, feeling a bit like a clumsy acrobat. "Well, that was unexpected!"

The Gumdrop Fairies erupted into fits of giggles, their eyes sparkling with joy. "You've got quite the flair for Bubblegum acrobatics!" one fairy chirped, doing a little twirl mid-air.

Feeling inspired by their laughter, Alarion decided to turn the whole experience into a game. "How about a race across the bridge?" he proposed. "How about we see who can come to the opposite side without stalling out!"

The fairies exchanged excited glances before nodding eagerly. "You're on!"

With a count of three, they all took off, racing across the bridge. Alarion bounded ahead, his long strides propelling him forward, but the gum beneath his feet had other plans. It stuck to him like a clingy friend, pulling him back with every step.

"Oh no, not again!" Alarion laughed as he felt himself slowing down. The fairies zipped past him, giggling and teasing, "Keep up, slowpoke!" But Alarion wasn't going to let sticky gum get the best of him.

Determined, he focused all his energy on each step, leaping and bounding, trying to overcome the gooey obstacle. "I'm not giving up!" he yelled, his voice filled with playful determination.

Just as he was about to lose hope, Alarion discovered a new technique. Instead of fighting against the gum, he started using it to his advantage. He would bounce, then land with a splat that sent him springing forward! With newfound enthusiasm, he laughed heartily, "This is way more fun than I thought!"

With one last mighty leap, he propelled himself across the final stretch of the bridge, landing perfectly on the other side. The fairies cheered, flapping their wings in excitement. "You did it! You crossed the Bubblegum Bridge!" they exclaimed, showering him with tiny gumdrop confetti.

Alarion, out of breath but exhilarated, joined in their celebration. "That was the most fun I've had all day! Thank you for the help, everyone!" he said, wiping a bit of Bubblegum from his forehead, a sticky reminder of their adventure.

One of the fairies floated close and whispered, "If you ever need a little magic in your life, just remember to embrace the stickiness!"

With laughter still ringing in the air, Alarion waved goodbye to his newfound friends. As he continued on his journey, he felt grateful for the joy and laughter that accompanied him through Tiderune, each adventure sweeter and stickier than the last. And with a smile on his face, he headed toward the next mysterious challenge that waited him.

Chapter 11: The Daring Duck

Alarion meets a duck with a penchant for adventure. Together, they embark on a quest to retrieve a lost treasure, only to discover the duck is the real treasure!

Alarion strolled along the shores of a shimmering lake, feeling the warm sun on his back and the gentle breeze rustling through the trees. The air was filled with the sweet scent of blooming flowers, and for a moment, he thought his day would be peaceful. Little did he know that adventure was just around the corner, quacking its way toward him.

As he leaned down to dip his toes in the water, a loud, raucous quack interrupted his moment of tranquillity. Alarion looked up to see a plump duck waddling toward him, wearing a tiny explorer's hat that looked suspiciously like it had once been part of a child's toy.

"Ahoy there, landlubber!" the duck shouted, puffing out its chest like a carefully prepared privateer. "I'm Commander Quackers, the boldest duck in all of Tiderune! And I could use a daring partner for an epic treasure hunt!"

Alarion raised an eyebrow, both amused and intrigued. "Treasure hunt? What treasure are we looking for?"

Captain Quackers flapped his wings dramatically, sending a few nearby butterflies fluttering away in surprise. "Legend has it that the Lost Ruby of Tiderune is hidden deep within the Great Marsh! They say it sparkles brighter than a thousand suns and grants wishes to anyone who possesses it!"

"That sounds incredible!" Alarion replied, his curiosity piqued. "But why do you need a partner?"

"Because," the duck said, lowering his voice to a conspiratorial whisper, "I'm terrified of getting my feathers wet. The marsh is soggy business, my friend! But with you on my side, I'll be as brave as a lion!"

"Then let's go find this ruby!" Alarion laughed, a grin spreading across his face. "Lead the way, Captain!"

With a confident quack, Captain Quackers waddled ahead, quacking out a marching song that seemed to echo through the trees. "We're off to find the treasure, yes indeed! With Alarion the brave, there's nothing we'll need!"

As they made their way to the Great Marsh, Alarion quickly realized that Captain Quackers had quite the adventurous spirit, but also a knack for the dramatic. The duck hopped and flapped with enthusiasm, often pausing to strike a pose as if he were on the cover of a treasure-hunting magazine.

"Look at me!" Captain Quackers exclaimed, standing atop a rock. "The fearless explorer, ready to conquer the wild!"

Alarion chuckled at the sight. "You're quite the character, Captain. I didn't expect to meet a duck with such flair!"

"Flair is my middle name!" Captain Quackers declared proudly. "Well, not literally, but it should be! Now, onward!"

As they entered the marsh, Alarion could see the lush greenery around them, interspersed with patches of glistening water. The air was thick with the sounds of chirping crickets and croaking frogs. But as soon as they stepped onto the muddy path, Alarion noticed Captain Quackers begin to wobble.

"Whoa, this mud is stickier than I thought!" Alarion said, trying to avoid the muck. But Captain Quackers, true to his adventurous nature, had already plunged in, getting his little feet stuck.

"Help! I'm sinking!" the duck cried, flailing his wings.

Alarion burst into laughter as he rushed to assist the flailing duck. "Hold still, Captain! Let me pull you out!"

With a swift tug, he managed to free Captain Quackers, but not without sending a spray of mud all over himself. Both the duck and Alarion burst into laughter, the sound echoing across the marsh.

"Looks like we're both treasure hunters now," Alarion joked, wiping mud from his face. "Mud-covered adventurers!"

As they continued deeper into the marsh, they encountered a series of comical obstacles: a group of frogs having a lively debate about the best method to catch flies, a family of otters sliding down a muddy slope, and a rather grumpy turtle who insisted on challenging them to a slow race.

"Come on, Captain, we can't let a turtle outpace us!" Alarion empowered as they ran past, their giggling ringing through the swamp.

Eventually, after navigating through the twists and turns of the marsh, they arrived at a small clearing. In the centre stood a rickety old chest, half-buried in mud and grass, just waiting to be opened.

"There it is!" Captain Quackers exclaimed; his eyes wide with excitement. "The Lost Ruby of Tiderune!"

With great anticipation, Alarion approached the chest and carefully lifted the lid. Inside, however, there was no sparkling ruby—only a pile of soggy, old bread!

Alarion blinked in disbelief. "Uh, Captain? I think we've found the treasure of the local ducks instead!"

The duck's expression shifted from excitement to confusion, and then to laughter. "Well, it seems I've found something just as valuable!" he said, pecking at the soggy bread. "It's the perfect picnic for a hungry duck!"

Alarion couldn't help but laugh at the absurdity of the situation. "So, you're saying the real treasure isn't the ruby, but the fun we had along the way?"

"Exactly!" Captain Quackers quacked joyfully, munching on the bread. "And I must say, Alarion, you've turned out to be quite the treasure yourself! Who knew a duck could have so much fun with a human?"

Alarion smiled, feeling a warmth in his heart. "I guess adventures aren't just about finding treasures; they're about the friends we make along the way."

With that, the two new friends sat down in the clearing, enjoying their makeshift picnic and sharing stories filled with laughter and joy. As the sun began to set, painting the sky in shades of orange and pink, Alarion realized that the real magic of Tiderune lay not in glittering gems but in the whimsical adventures and delightful friendships that unfolded in the most unexpected ways.

And so, with full bellies and happy hearts, Alarion and Captain Quackers vowed to embark on more adventures together, proving that sometimes, the best treasure is simply the laughter and camaraderie found along the journey.

Chapter 12: The Potion Party

At a potion party, Alarion accidentally mixes the wrong ingredients, creating potions that make everyone speak in rhymes! Chaos ensues with every silly verse.

In the heart of Tiderune, the air buzzed with excitement and the tantalizing scents of bubbling brews and fragrant herbs. Alarion was on his way to the most anticipated event of the season—a grand Potion Party hosted by the eccentric and brilliantly talented potion master, Elowen. This was no ordinary gathering; it promised a night filled with magical concoctions, laughter, and of course, the chance to dabble in a little potion-making fun.

As Alarion approached Elowen's workshop, he could hear the merry chatter of guests inside. He opened the door to find a colorful chaos of wizards, witches, and curious creatures, all crowded around tables overflowing with glass vials, strange ingredients, and whimsical decorations made of twinkling lights. The atmosphere was vibrant, with everyone wearing colorful robes and laughing as they experimented with various potions.

"Welcome, welcome!" Elowen greeted him with a beaming smile, her hair a wild tangle of curls decorated with tiny flowers. "Come join the fun! Tonight, we create potions that delight, inspire, and maybe cause a bit of mischief!"

Alarion's eyes sparkled with anticipation. He grabbed a pair of goggles from a nearby table, feeling like a true potion master. "What's first on the agenda?" he asked eagerly.

BOOK # 2 ALARION AND THE SECRETS OF TIDERUNE   65

"Let's start with something simple!" Elowen announced, clapping her hands together. "We'll make a Giggle Elixir! Just a few drops and it will make anyone who drinks it laugh uncontrollably!"

The guests cheered, and Alarion eagerly gathered his ingredients. There were vibrant petals, sparkling dust, and a hint of mint that smelled absolutely delightful. However, as Alarion mixed his potion, he noticed another table filled with intriguing bottles and jars. One in particular caught his eye—a shimmering, deep purple liquid labelled "Mystery Brew."

His curiosity piqued, Alarion wandered over to the mysterious concoction. "What's this?" he asked, unable to resist the temptation.

"That's the Mystery Brew!" said a nearby which, her eyes twinkling. "No one knows what it does. It's been banned from all potion parties for causing chaos!"

Alarion's heart raced with excitement. "Chaos? I love chaos!" he announced, looking back at Elowen, who was too in the middle of clarifying the Snicker Mixture to notice his devilish interest.

With a bold move, Alarion poured a splash of the Mystery Brew into his Giggle Elixir, not realizing the trouble he was stirring up. The potion bubbled wildly, sending off little puffs of sparkly smoke. A hint of worry flickered in Alarion's mind, but the excitement of the party drowned it out.

Once everyone had their cups filled with the Giggle Elixir, Elowen raised her glass for a toast. "To laughter and friendship!"

"To laughter and friendship!" the guests echoed, clinking their glasses together. They took hearty sips, and within moments, joyous giggles erupted around the room. Everyone laughed so hard that tears streamed down their cheeks.

But just as Alarion thought he'd blended the perfect potion, the room suddenly fell silent, as if a spell had been cast. He looked around, confused, until he realized that all the guests were staring at him, their expressions frozen in bewilderment.

"What's happening?" he wondered aloud.

To his horror, one of the guests suddenly broke the silence, but instead of speaking normally, she launched into a rhyme!

"Oh, dear Alarion, what have you done?
We're stuck in verses, oh, this is fun!
With every word, a rhyme shall appear,
We're all poets now, let's give a cheer!"

Chaos erupted as everyone began to speak in rhymes, each verse more nonsensical than the last.

"Pass the potion, make it quick,
Or I'll burst out laughing, and that's no trick!" yelled another, shuffling a carafe of brilliant fluid.

Alarion, now realizing the true nature of his potion mishap, burst out laughing. "Oh no! I didn't mean to create a rhyming spree!"

But his laughter only inspired more rhymes from the crowd.

"Don't worry, dear friend, it's a blast!
This is the best potion party we've ever had!"

As Alarion tried to explain, he found himself slipping into rhymes as well. "I figured it would be a straightforward beverage,
But now we're all poets—what do you think?"

Elowen, struggling to contain her laughter, clapped her hands. "This is the most amusing disaster I've ever witnessed! Let's make the most of it!"

So, the Potion Party transformed into a wild and whimsical rhyming fest. Guests danced and recited silly poems about potion ingredients, frogs in the bogs, and chasing after magic logs.

"Beware the toad, it hops with glee,
It's on a mission, can't you see?" one visitor yelled, jumping around the room.

Alarion joined in, waving his arms. "I've brewed a potion, oh what a mess,
But this laughter and rhymes? I must confess,

It's the best kind of chaos, don't you agree?
This magical night was meant to be!"

As the night wore on, the laughter became infectious, and the entire room was filled with joy. They created impromptu rhymes about everything and everyone, turning the Potion Party into a delightful spectacle of silliness.

Eventually, Elowen called for calm. "Alright, dear friends! Let's take a moment to regain our speech and fix this potion predicament!"

With great determination, they gathered around Alarion as he attempted to reverse the spell. With a few more carefully chosen ingredients (and a promise to avoid any more Mystery Brews), they mixed a new potion that, once sipped, would return everyone's speech to normal.

As the last drops of the potion were consumed, the room erupted into cheers and applause. The rhyming had brought them all closer together, and the shared laughter was something they would remember forever.

"I can't believe we rhymed all night!" Alarion said, shaking his head in disbelief. "What a wild ride!"

"You, my friend, are a true potion master!" Elowen said with a wink. "And remember, sometimes the best recipes are the ones that don't go according to plan!"

With hearts still light from laughter, the guests left the Potion Party, promising to meet again for another round of magic—maybe even a rhyme or two. Alarion walked home, a smile plastered on his face, grateful for the delightful chaos he had inadvertently brewed.

And who knew? Perhaps the next adventure would come with its own set of surprises, each more magical and ridiculous than the last!

Chapter 13: The Overly Polite Goblin

Alarion encounters a goblin who insists on saying "please" and "thank you" at every turn. Their interaction turns into a hilariously formal affair!

As Alarion ventured deeper into the magical realm of Tiderune, the sun began to dip below the horizon, painting the sky with hues of orange and purple. The air was crisp, filled with the scent of adventure, and Alarion felt a familiar thrill. With his trusty map (now mostly legible after the soggy fiasco), he continued his quest, looking for clues about the secrets hidden within Tiderune.

Out of nowhere, a stirring in the shrubs grabbed his eye. Curious, Alarion peered closer, only to be greeted by a small, green creature with oversized ears and a crooked nose. It was a goblin! But unlike any goblin Alarion had ever encountered, this one stood upright and wore a tiny waistcoat adorned with shiny buttons.

"Good day to you, fine traveller!" the goblin exclaimed, bowing deeply. "My name is Grumbleton, and may I please offer you my sincerest greetings?"

Alarion blinked in surprise. "Um, hello, Grumbleton! Nice to meet you. What are you doing here?"

"Thank you for asking, kind sir!" Grumbleton replied, straightening his waistcoat with a flourish. "I'm just watching out for my nursery, which, assuming you'll benevolently permit me to say, has been developing rather magnificently this season!"

Alarion chuckled, his confusion giving way to amusement. "A garden? I didn't expect goblins to be gardeners!"

"Oh, absolutely! Thank you for your interest!" Grumbleton beamed, clearly thrilled that Alarion was engaging in the conversation. "It's a marvellous hobby, filled with splendid herbs and delectable vegetables. Might I offer you some of my prized radishes? They are particularly crunchy this time of year!"

"Radishes? Uh, sure, why not?" Alarion replied, already intrigued by the goblin's charm.

As Grumbleton rummaged through his satchel, he continued, "Now, before I hand them to you, may I kindly ask if you have any allergies? I wouldn't want to cause you any distress, if I may be so bold as to inquire."

"None that I know of! Thank you for asking," Alarion said, stifling a laugh at how formal this little goblin was.

"Splendid! Here you go, one, two, three crunchy radishes, as fresh as the morning dew if I might say!" Grumbleton said, placing the vegetables in Alarion's hands with the utmost care. "I hope you find them delicious!"

Alarion took a bite and chewed thoughtfully. "These are actually really good! You've got a talent for gardening!"

"Oh, your praise warms my heart!" Grumbleton replied, puffing out his chest with pride. "Now, if I may be so bold, what brings you to this fine part of Tiderune? Is there something I could help you with?"

"I'm on a journey to reveal the mysteries of Tiderune!" Alarion pronounced, waving his guide emphatically. "I'm expecting to track down secret information about this enchanted spot."

"Ah, a quest! How thrilling! May I please wish you the very best of luck on your endeavour!"

Grumbleton said, bowing again. "And if I could possibly offer a suggestion, you might want to consult the Ancient Oak Tree at the centre of the Whispering Woods. It is known to have witnessed many secrets over the centuries!"

"Thanks for the tip, Grumbleton!" Alarion replied, feeling a wave of warmth wash over him from the goblin's earnestness. "I'll definitely check it out!"

"Wonderful! It would be my utmost pleasure to assist you further. If I may, can I ask if you need any provisions for your journey?" Grumbleton offered, motioning towards his garden. "Maybe a couple of additional radishes or a portion of my supernatural mint?"

Alarion couldn't help but smile. "I think I'm good for now, but I appreciate the offer!"

"Oh, but I insist! A traveller should never be without proper sustenance!" Grumbleton said, rummaging through his satchel once again. "Here are a portion of my best otherworldly mints. They're quite invigorating, and they may help you on your quest!"

"Thank you!" Alarion laughed, accepting the mints. "You're very generous!"

"Generosity is a virtue, and I'm ever so grateful to have the opportunity to share!" Grumbleton exclaimed, clapping his hands together.

As they chatted, Alarion began to realize that every interaction with Grumbleton was turning into a formal affair. "So, do all goblins speak like this?" he asked, incapable of containing his interest.

"For sure, assuming I might be so blunt, we don't need to! But I find that politeness brings about pleasant exchanges," Grumbleton said with a wink. "A 'please' here and a 'thank you' there can make all the difference!"

"Fair enough!" Alarion chuckled. "But isn't it a bit... excessive?"

"Overabundance is entirely subjective assuming that I could say! "Grumbleton replied, grinning widely. "Now, if I may inquire, would you like to join me for a spot of tea in my cozy little home? I assure you, it's very inviting and full of delightful knickknacks!"

Alarion hesitated. "I'm on a bit of a tight schedule, but tea does sound nice."

"Wonderful! Let us proceed posthaste!" Grumbleton exclaimed, leading Alarion down a winding path lined with flowers that danced in the breeze. As they walked, the goblin continued to pepper his sentences with polite expressions, causing Alarion to giggle at the absurdity of it all.

Upon reaching Grumbleton's home—a charming little cottage adorned with flowers and tiny lanterns—Alarion marvelled at how cozy it looked. "Wow, this is really nice!" he said as he stepped inside.

"Thank you, kind sir! It is my humble abode!" Grumbleton replied, moving about the kitchen with surprising grace. He began to brew a pot of tea, his tiny hands working with deft precision.

As they sipped their tea, the conversation flowed, with Alarion sharing tales of his adventures while Grumbleton interjected with polite remarks. The more they talked, the more Alarion found himself charmed by the goblin's quirky manners.

"May I please compliment you on your tales of bravery? They are quite inspiring!" Grumbleton said, his eyes sparkling. "And if I could be so bold as to ask, do you have any other quests planned after this one?"

"Actually, yes! There's a prophecy I need to investigate," Alarion replied, feeling encouraged by Grumbleton's enthusiasm.

"Oh, a prophecy! How thrilling!" Grumbleton exclaimed. "If I may offer my assistance, I can point you to the best sources of information! Please allow me to share my extensive knowledge of the local lore!"

Alarion couldn't help but laugh. "You really are the most helpful goblin I've ever met!"

"Thank you! That means a lot to me!" Grumbleton replied, beaming. "And if I may add, it's always a pleasure to make new friends!"

After a delightful afternoon filled with tea, laughter, and a few more crunchy radishes, Alarion knew it was time to continue on his journey. "Overabundance is entirely subjective assuming that I could say!" I will never forget this charming encounter."

"Nor shall I! It was an honor to meet you, dear Alarion!" Grumbleton bowed again, his petticoat fluttering somewhat. "Please do come back if you ever wish to share more stories or simply enjoy a cup of tea!"

With a wave and a smile, Alarion set off on his adventure, feeling lighter in spirit. He marvelled at the strange yet wonderful encounter with the overly polite goblin and thought about how a little kindness could make a world of difference.

As he walked away, he couldn't help but practice his own manners. "Thank you, Grumbleton!" he called back, laughing to himself. "Please let me know if you find any more magical radishes!"

And so, with a heart full of warmth and an eager spirit for adventure, Alarion continued his quest, ready to uncover the next secret of Tiderune, one politely spoken word at a time!

Chapter 14: The Invisible Ink

When Alarion receives a letter written in invisible ink, he enlists the help of a quirky ghost to decipher it, leading to more ghostly giggles than useful advice.

Alarion's journey through Tiderune had been nothing short of extraordinary. From wobbly boats to overly polite goblins, each day was filled with new adventures and quirky characters. One sunny afternoon, as Alarion strolled through a misty glade, he stumbled upon a small, shimmering envelope nestled among the wildflowers.

"What's this?" Alarion wondered aloud, picking it up with a curious grin. The envelope was perfectly ordinary, but as he opened it, he discovered that the letter inside was completely blank. Maybe somebody had composed it in undetectable ink!

He furrowed his brow and turned the letter this way and that, hoping to catch a glimpse of hidden words. "This is just great! I can't read anything!" he exclaimed, shaking the letter like it might magically reveal its secrets. But alas, it remained as blank as ever.

Just then, a soft chuckling echoed through the glade, making Alarion jump. "Oh dear, you look like you've just seen a ghost!" A transparent figure materialized before him, floating effortlessly with a wide grin and a playful twinkle in its ethereal eyes.

Alarion's eyes widened. "Uh, I mean, I'm pretty sure I did just see a ghost!"

"Guilty as charged!" the ghost said with a theatrical bow, causing its translucent form to swirl gracefully. "I'm Caspar, the quirkiest ghost in Tiderune. And you, my friend, appear to be in a bit of a pickle with that invisible letter!"

"Yes! Do you know how to read it?" Alarion asked, eager for help.

"Of course! But first, let me share a little ghostly wisdom!" Caspar floated closer; his expression mischievous. "You see, invisible ink is a specialty of the finest pranksters! I'm sure there's a trick to making it visible!"

"Great! But how do we find that trick?" Alarion replied, feeling a mix of hope and skepticism.

Caspar twirled in the air, a whirlwind of sparkles trailing behind him. "Leave it to me! The first thing we need is a dash of moonlight and a sprinkle of laughter! You see, laughter is the key to many secrets in Tiderune!"

Alarion raised an eyebrow. "Laughter? Really? That's the secret?"

"Absolutely! It works like magic, I assure you!" Caspar winked, floating back to Alarion. "Now, let's start with the laughter! How about you make me your best quip?"

Alarion scratched his head, trying to think of something funny. "Um... For what reason did the chicken go across the street?"

"To get to the other side?" Caspar replied, looking puzzled. "Oh, come on! That's an old one! You can do better!"

"Okay, how about this?" Alarion took a deep breath. "What do you call a phantom's genuine romance?"

Caspar tilted his head, intrigued. "I don't know, what?"

"A beautiful soul!" Alarion announced, unable to keep a straight face.

Caspar emitted an attack of chuckling, his spooky structure shaking as he moved in the air. "Ha! That's a good one! You've got the spirit of a true comedian!" he exclaimed between giggles.

Encouraged by the ghost's delight, Alarion continued. "Okay, okay! What do you call a beast with a funny bone?"

Caspar cleaned away a spooky tear of chuckling. "What?"

"A funny bone!" Alarion chuckled, his confidence growing.

Caspar clapped his hands with glee. "You're on a roll! Keep going!"

"Alright! Why don't skeletons fight each other?" Alarion said, feeling the excitement bubbling.

"Why?" Caspar asked, leaning in.

"They don't have the guts!" Alarion shouted, laughing at the pun.

Caspar's laughter filled the glade, echoing among the trees. Suddenly, a flicker of light burst forth from the envelope, illuminating the air. Alarion gasped in surprise as words began to materialize on the blank page, dancing in the glow.

"It worked! Look!" he shouted, pointing at the now-visible writing. "But it's all jumbled!"

"Ah, but you must decipher it, dear friend!" Caspar said, floating beside Alarion. "And perhaps it will lead you to even more giggles!"

As Alarion read the message, he realized it was a series of silly riddles mixed with random ghostly puns. "This is absurd!" he laughed, scratching his head. "I don't think this is helping!"

Caspar floated in front of him, a cheeky smile on his face. "Oh, but it is! The key is in the fun! You'll figure it out eventually! How about we add some more laughter to the mix?"

With renewed determination, Alarion sat down on a patch of grass, looking at the jumbled text. "Okay, let's turn this into a game. For every riddle I solve, you have to tell me a ghost story!"

Caspar's eyes gleamed with excitement. "Deal! Let the laughter lead the way!"

The two spent the afternoon engaged in a hilarious back-and-forth of riddles and ghostly tales. Alarion tackled the riddles one by one, and each answer met with a raucous story from Caspar's vast collection of ghostly mischief.

"What runs but never walks?" Alarion read aloud, grinning as he realized the answer. "A river!"

"Correct! Now, let me tell you about the time I haunted a riverbank and scared a fisherman so badly, he thought he caught a ghost fish!" Caspar exclaimed, his laughter echoing through the glade.

After a while, Alarion finally pieced together the strange message. It wasn't a treasure map or a warning; it was an invitation to a ghostly gathering taking place that very night!

"Caspar! This letter is an invitation!" Alarion said, beaming with excitement. "It says there's a party for all the spirits in Tiderune!"

"Ah, the annual Phantom Frolic!" Caspar clapped his hands in delight. "I'd almost forgotten! It's the one time of year when all ghosts come together for fun and games!"

"Can I come too?" Alarion asked eagerly. "I'd love to see what it's like!"

"Of course! Just bring your sense of humor!" Caspar floated around in circles. "What's more, I'll ensure you fit right in!"

As the sun began to set, Alarion and Caspar made their way to the party. With laughter and excitement in the air, Alarion felt grateful for the invisible ink that had led him to such an amusing companion and the promise of ghostly fun.

At the Phantom Frolic, Alarion found himself surrounded by friendly spirits, playing games, sharing stories, and indulging in sweet treats made from ectoplasm—though he wasn't quite sure how they could be sweet and gooey at the same time.

That night, under the shimmering stars, Alarion realized that sometimes the most important journeys are the ones filled with laughter and friendship, and he was glad to have a ghostly friend like Caspar to share it all with.

And so, with a heart full of joy and a belly aching from laughter, Alarion knew that the invisible ink had led him to something truly special—a whimsical adventure that would always stay with him, even long after the laughter faded into the night.

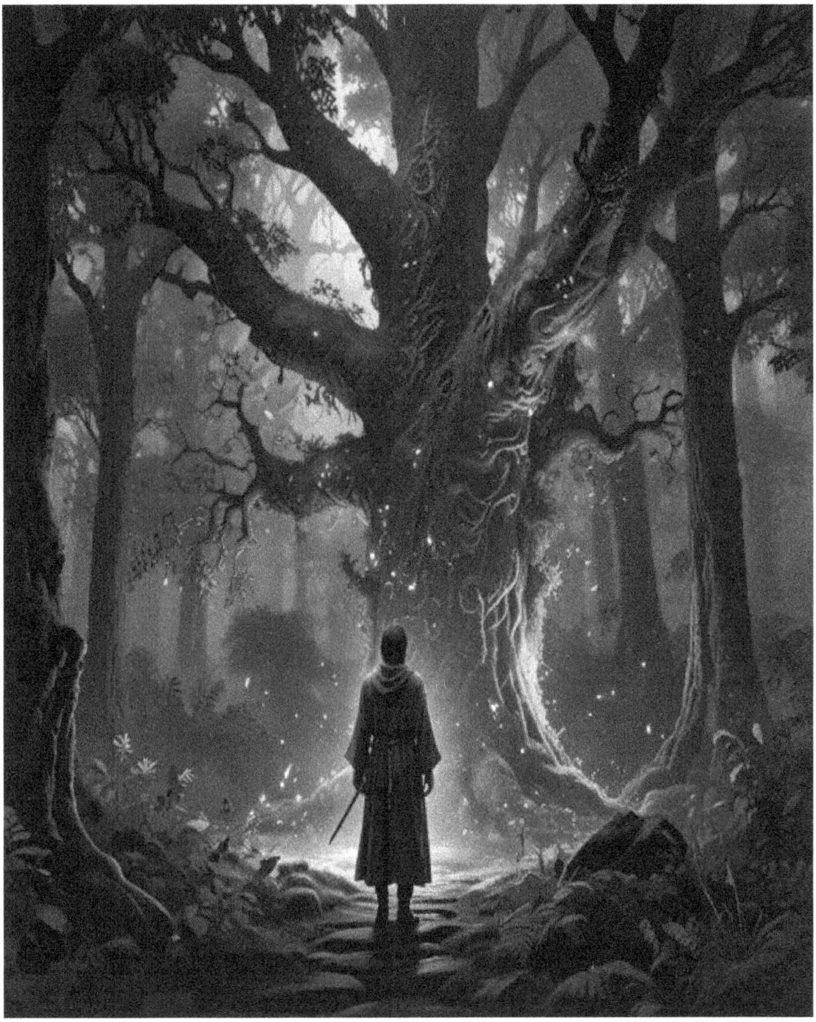

Chapter 15: The Dancing Rocks

In a rocky valley, Alarion stumbles upon dancing rocks that break into a lively jig. Trying to keep up, he discovers he has two left feet!

The sun shone brightly over the enchanting realm of Tiderune, casting playful shadows as Alarion wandered through a winding valley filled with peculiar rock formations. After his adventures with invisible ink and friendly ghosts, he was eager for more surprises. Nonetheless, nothing could set him up for what lay ahead.

As he strolled through the rocky landscape, Alarion heard a curious sound—a rhythmic thumping that echoed through the valley like the beat of a drum. Intrigued, he followed the sound, weaving around towering boulders that loomed like ancient guardians.

Suddenly, he stumbled into a clearing where the ground vibrated with energy. Before him, a group of rocks had come to life, bouncing and twirling in a merry dance! Their smooth surfaces glistened in the sunlight, reflecting the joy of their lively jig.

"What in the world?" Alarion gasped, unable to believe his eyes. The rocks spun and hopped, performing pirouettes and cartwheels with a grace that would put even the most skilled dancers to shame.

"Oh, come and join us!" called out one particularly bouncy rock, adorned with a bright blue hue. "We're having a dance party!"

"Dance party?" Alarion echoed, his heart racing with excitement. He loved dancing, though his skills were more akin to a wobbling chicken than a smooth-footed wizard. "But I've never danced with rocks before!"

"Don't worry! Just follow our lead!" ringed a more modest stone, doing a little shimmy that sent rocks flying every which way. "It's easy! Just let the music move you!"

Feeling emboldened by their infectious energy, Alarion stepped into the circle of dancing rocks, ready to join the fun. However, as he attempted to mimic their lively moves, he quickly realized he had two left feet—or perhaps even three! His legs flailed awkwardly as he tried to spin and twirl, each misstep leading to a cascade of giggles from his rocky companions.

"Oops! Not quite like that!" the blue stone prodded, jumping sideways to show a smooth mix. "Just relax and feel the rhythm!"

Alarion took a deep breath, determined to get it right. He tried again, this time focusing on the beat of the invisible drum that seemed to pulsate from the earth itself. He shifted his weight, took a step, and then—whoosh! His foot slipped on a stray pebble, sending him tumbling headfirst into a pile of very amused rocks.

"Ha! Look at him go!" one rock chortled, rolling back and forth in delight.

Alarion pushed himself up, dusting off the dirt with a sheepish grin. "Okay, I can do this! Just a little more practice!"

With a renewed spirit, he joined in once more, this time determined to find his groove. The rocks hopped around him, their laughter echoing like the sound of tinkling bells. Alarion tried to keep up, mimicking their bounces and shakes, though he felt as if he were doing a funny, wonky dance that might confuse even the most seasoned dancer.

"Just remember to have fun!" the smaller rock encouraged, doing a little jig that was so contagious Alarion couldn't help but laugh.

And then, unexpectedly, he found himself loosening up. He began to enjoy the silliness of the moment, letting the rhythm take over. He wobbled and jiggled, swaying from side to side like a leaf caught in the wind, and to his surprise, he was starting to keep up with the rocks!

With every bounce and spin, Alarion's laughter mixed with that of his rocky friends, and soon, the valley was alive with the sound of joyous dance. The rocks had no qualms about their imperfect partner, and Alarion felt the warmth of friendship wrap around him like a cozy blanket.

"Presently, we should check whether you can do the Stone Roll!" shouted the blue rock, launching itself into an intricate tumble that sent it rolling through the grass.

"Rock Roll?" Alarion echoed, eyes wide. "I'm not sure I can—"

"Just follow me!" the blue rock insisted, spinning and rolling as if it had no care in the world.

Taking a deep breath, Alarion watched closely, gathering his courage. The rocks cheered him on, their encouragement lifting his spirits higher than ever. "Here goes nothing!" he muttered to himself. He crouched down, trying to gather his momentum.

He launched himself forward, attempting the Rock Roll. But instead of a graceful tumble, he somersaulted awkwardly, landing in a heap next to a very amused blue rock. The entire dance party erupted in fits of laughter, their giggles bouncing off the valley walls.

"Bravo!" the smaller rock cheered. "That was a performance for the ages!"

Alarion couldn't help but chuckle at himself. "Maybe I need a little more practice!" he laughed, wiping away a tear from laughter.

"Don't you worry! You've got the spirit of a true dancer!" said the blue rock. "Now let's do a group dance!"

As the sun dipped lower in the sky, casting a golden hue over the valley, Alarion and the dancing rocks joined together for a final performance. With joyful abandon, they spun and twirled, a delightful mixture of clumsy moves and synchronized hops. The valley echoed with laughter and the rhythmic sound of their dance, an enchanting melody that seemed to awaken the very rocks around them.

When the dance finally came to a close, Alarion flopped down onto the soft grass, panting and breathless. "That was incredible!" he wheezed, gazing toward the perky rocks. "I've never had so much fun!"

The blue rock rolled over, settling beside him. "You did great! Remember, it's not about how well you dance, but how much joy you bring to the dance!"

Alarion smiled, his heart warm with happiness. "Thank you, friends! I may not have the best moves, but I had a blast dancing with you!"

As twilight fell over Tiderune, Alarion waved goodbye to the dancing rocks, promising to return for another jig. With laughter still ringing in his ears, he continued on his journey, filled with the memories of a wonderful day spent dancing among lively friends.

At that moment, Alarion knew that whether he had two left feet or a heart full of rhythm, the true magic of Tiderune lay in the laughter, friendships, and joy of embracing every quirky adventure along the way.

Chapter 16: The Magical Puddle

Alarion finds a puddle that shows his reflections in funny costumes. He starts an impromptu fashion show, showcasing the quirkiest outfits imaginable!

One sunny afternoon in Tiderune, Alarion was wandering through a lush meadow, the sweet scent of wildflowers tickling his nose. After a long day filled with dancing rocks and bubbly potions, he was hoping for a moment of peace and maybe a snack or two. As he meandered through the tall grass, something shiny caught his eye—a small puddle shimmering like a star had fallen right into the ground.

"Is that a puddle or a portal to another world?" Alarion pondered, tilting his head in curiosity. He stepped closer, and as he peered into the water, he realized it was no ordinary puddle at all! The surface reflected not just his image but a series of ridiculous, vibrant costumes that seemed to materialize from thin air.

"Whoa!" Alarion exclaimed, leaning closer to the puddle. One moment he was gazing at his usual attire—a simple tunic and trousers—and the next, he saw himself sporting a flamboyant feathered hat, oversized clown shoes, and a polka-dotted cape. He burst into laughter. "Is this what I look like in an alternate universe?"

Just then, the puddle rippled as if it were alive. The reflection shifted again, showcasing him in a sparkling disco outfit, complete with sequins that twinkled like the night sky. Alarion couldn't resist. "I have to try this out!"

Without a second thought, he stepped right into the puddle, feeling a tingling sensation as he was enveloped in a whirlwind of color.

When he emerged, he was decked out in the full disco ensemble, complete with a shiny mirror ball necklace that swung back and forth with every move.

"Look at me! I'm ready to dance the night away!" he declared, striking a pose that would have made any dance floor proud. The nearby flowers seemed to sway in approval, and Alarion couldn't help but do a little shimmy.

But the puddle had more surprises in store. As Alarion examined his reflection, it changed again, transforming him into a pirate with a parrot perched on his shoulder (which was really just a piece of fluffy moss). He let out a hearty "Arrr!" while brandishing an imaginary sword. "Avast, ye scallywags! Who's ready for treasure?"

Alarion burst into a fit of giggles as he played the part of the flamboyant pirate, pretending to sail the seven seas right there in the meadow. But the puddle wasn't finished yet. Next, it transformed him into a medieval knight, complete with a shiny helmet and an enormous sword that was almost too heavy for him to lift.

"Onward, noble steed!" he cried, claiming to rush into a fight while emphatically swinging his fanciful sword. However, rather than a wild call to war, what emerged from his mouth was a somewhat diverting "Huzzah!" as he lost his equilibrium and fell onto the grass, his protective cap rolling endlessly.

As Alarion lay there, laughter echoing around him, he realized he had to share this joy with someone. "This is too great to even consider minding my own business!" he said, his mind racing with ideas for a grand fashion show. With renewed energy, he called out to the surrounding forest, "Hey, everyone! Come see the magical puddle and its incredible costumes!"

To his surprise, a few curious critters began to gather. A rabbit with oversized glasses hopped over, followed by a couple of squirrels who chattered excitedly. Even a wise old owl perched on a nearby branch seemed intrigued, tilting its head to get a better look.

"Welcome to the first-ever Tiderune Fashion Show!" Alarion reported, pausing dramatically that would make any runway model desirous. "Prepare to be amazed!"

With a flourish, he leaped back into the puddle, and this time emerged wearing a flamboyant magician's outfit, complete with a top hat and a cape that sparkled like stars. "Ta-da!" he shouted, pulling a fluffy bunny from his hat (which was really just a small ball of moss). The audience erupted into cheers.

The rabbit adjusted its glasses and squeaked, "Bravo! I didn't know you were a magician too!"

Alarion, feeling inspired, decided to showcase every outfit the puddle had to offer. With each dive into the puddle, he transformed into silly characters: a superhero with a cape made of leaves, a chef with a giant spoon, and even a disco diva who danced with such flair that the flowers seemed to sway along with him.

Each transformation brought more laughter from the woodland critters. The squirrels began to imitate his dance moves, their tiny paws flailing as they attempted to keep up with his energetic routines. The rabbit joined in, twirling and hopping to the beat of an imaginary drum, while the owl hooted in approval, its head bobbing along to the rhythm.

"Next up is the royal jester!" Alarion proclaimed, hopping back into the puddle. This time, he emerged wearing a colorful jester's outfit, complete with bells that jingled with every step. He juggled invisible balls while prancing about, making silly faces that had the audience rolling with laughter.

"For what reason did the jokester carry a stepping stool to the party?" he quipped, pausing dramatically. "Since he needed to arrive at new levels of humor!" The critters laughed out loud, the owl, in any event, fluttering its wings in charm.

Just as he was about to present his final outfit, the puddle shimmered again, but this time, it didn't just show his reflection.

Instead, it began to project images of even sillier costumes—an octopus wearing sunglasses, a giant cupcake with sprinkles, and even a walrus with a top hat!

Alarion, inspired by the creativity of the puddle, exclaimed, "That's it! Let's make this the biggest fashion show Tiderune has ever seen!" He turned to his audience, his eyes sparkling with excitement. "Everyone can join in! Let's see what you've got!"

Encouraged by his enthusiasm, the critters began to participate. The rabbit hopped around with an imaginary crown, pretending to be the king of carrots, while the squirrels draped themselves in leaves, mimicking a fashion statement straight from the forest runway. Even the wise old owl decided to join in, fluttering down to sport a pair of comically large sunglasses.

Alarion clapped his hands, urging everyone to strut their stuff. "Let's have a parade of silliness!"

They paraded around the meadow, a delightful mix of costumes and laughter. Alarion led the charge, his jester's outfit jingling with every move, while the critters followed suit, each taking turns showcasing their quirky attire. The meadow transformed into a whimsical spectacle of color and joy, every participant shining brighter than the last.

After what felt like hours of laughter and fun, they all collapsed in a heap of giggles on the grass, panting but utterly happy. The magical puddle shimmered under the fading sunlight, its surface reflecting the joyful chaos of the impromptu fashion show.

"Thank you, magical puddle!" Alarion grinned, still catching his breath. "You've turned an ordinary day into an extraordinary adventure!"

As the sun dipped below the horizon, painting the sky in hues of orange and pink, Alarion knew he would always cherish the laughter and friendship that had blossomed in that magical moment. The puddle might have shown him silly costumes, but it had also revealed the beauty of spontaneity and joy.

With a final wave to his new friends, Alarion promised to return for more fashion fun. As he headed home, the sounds of laughter echoed in his ears, reminding him that in Tiderune, even the simplest things could lead to the most magical adventures.

Chapter 17: The Snarky Squirrel

A squirrel with a snarky attitude challenges Alarion to a game of acorn toss. Their banter and competitive spirit lead to some unexpected acorn shenanigans!

One bright and sunny morning in Tiderune, Alarion was exploring the edge of a glimmering forest. Birds chirped happily overhead, and the gentle rustle of leaves danced in the warm breeze. Alarion, always on the lookout for a new adventure, was feeling particularly cheerful as he skipped along the path, humming a little tune. Little did he know, he was about to encounter a creature whose sass could rival even the most spirited jesters in the land.

As he ventured deeper into the woods, he stumbled upon a clearing filled with acorn-laden oak trees. The ground was littered with acorns of all sizes, creating a perfect playground for any squirrel. Just as he was admiring the scenery, a small, bushy-tailed squirrel perched on a low branch caught his eye. This wasn't just any squirrel; this one had an air of confidence and mischief.

"Hey, you!" the squirrel called out, her voice dripping with a cheeky tone. "You seem as though you have probably as much point as a three-legged feline at a mouse show! Care to challenge me to a game of acorn toss?"

Alarion stopped in his tracks, slightly taken aback. "Acorn toss? Is that some sort of joke? I'm not afraid of a little competition!"

The squirrel chuckled, her eyes sparkling with mischief. "Oh, I'm not joking, fluffy! I'm Sassy, the best acorn tosser in all of Tiderune. You'd have to have the skills of a wizard to keep up with me!"

"Bring it on, Sassy!" Alarion replied, his competitive spirit igniting. "Let's see what you've got!"

They set up a makeshift tossing area on the grass, with Sassy's acorn stash glimmering in the sunlight. Alarion picked up a hefty acorn, eyeing it as if it were a magical artifact. "So, how do we play?"

"It's simple," Sassy explained, a smirk on her face. "We each take turns tossing our acorns into that mossy old bucket over there. The one who gets the most acorns in wins. And just to spice things up, I say the loser has to do a silly dance right here in front of the trees!"

"Deal!" Alarion giggled, changing his position like a carefully prepared competitor.

The first toss was Sassy's. She took careful aim, her little paws steady as she flung an acorn toward the bucket. It soared through the air with precision and landed perfectly inside with a triumphant thunk.

"Ha! One point for the squirrel!" she squeaked, doing a little celebratory jig. Alarion chuckled, shaking his head. "Alright, my turn!"

He took a deep breath and tossed his acorn, which veered off course and landed with a plop in a nearby bush. Sassy burst into laughter. "Nice throw! Maybe I should give you a lesson on aim!"

Alarion couldn't help but laugh at his blunder. "Okay, okay! That was just a warm-up!"

He retrieved another acorn and concentrated, channelling all his energy into this toss. With a determined flick of his wrist, the acorn soared into the air, spinning like a miniature comet. This time, it bounced off the edge of the bucket and rolled away.

"Still warming up, huh?" Sassy teased; her voice playful. "Going on like this, I should crown myself Sovereign of the Oak seeds!"

The playful banter continued as they tossed back and forth. Sassy nailed her next shot, landing two more acorns in the bucket, while Alarion, despite his best efforts, managed to send several acorns flying into the trees, where they got stuck in the branches. Each time an acorn got stuck, Sassy would mimic a dramatic gasp, and the laughter echoed throughout the clearing.

"Maybe you should switch careers!" Sassy joked, doing a mock imitation of a circus ringmaster. "Welcome to the Acorn Circus, where we have the world's first acorn-flinging magician who can make all his acorns disappear... into the trees!"

"Okay, okay! I get it!" Alarion replied, grinning. "You're good! But I'm just getting started!"

With newfound determination, Alarion decided to focus. He took a moment to meditate, channelling all his energy into the next toss. He felt a surge of confidence, picked up the largest acorn he could find, and aimed carefully at the bucket.

"Here goes nothing!" he announced, letting the acorn fly. It sailed through the air, spinning beautifully before landing perfectly in the bucket with a resounding thud.

"Woohoo!" Alarion cheered, dancing around the clearing. "Finally! That's what I'm talking about!"

Sassy, impressed despite herself, clapped her tiny paws together. "Alright, you're warming up! However, we should check whether you can keep up the force!"

The game continued, with both competitors tossing acorns and sharing witty banter. Alarion managed to land several more in the bucket, and to his surprise, Sassy began to struggle as she became increasingly distracted by their playful back-and-forth.

"Hey, Sassy, I think you might be losing your touch!" Alarion teased.

"Me? Never!" Sassy shot back, puffing out her little chest. "I just... wanted to try a different technique!"

However, as the game progressed, Alarion's growing confidence began to shine, and he pulled ahead, finally managing to land a string of acorns in the bucket.

In the end, it was a close match, but Alarion emerged victorious, with Sassy panting in mock defeat. "I can't believe it! I, the queen of acorns, have been defeated by a human! What will my squirrel subjects think?"

Alarion laughed heartily. "Indeed, I get it's the ideal opportunity for you to do the senseless dance!"

"Alright, alright! You win fair and square," Sassy said, rolling her eyes, but there was a playful glint in her eyes. "But only because I'm feeling generous today!"

With a dramatic flair, Sassy jumped onto a rock in the clearing and began a dance that was a wild combination of twirls, hops, and exaggerated gestures. Her little feet moved so fast it was as if she had sprung! Alarion couldn't help but join in, flailing his arms and attempting to mimic her squirrel-like moves.

"Look at me, everyone! I'm Sassy the squirrel!" he called out, trying his best to keep up.

The nearby trees rustled as if they were laughing along with them. Alarion's silly dance moves sent them both into fits of giggles, the joyful sounds echoing throughout the forest. They danced together, their laughter weaving through the branches above.

Eventually, after what felt like an eternity of giggles and ridiculousness, they collapsed onto the soft grass, panting and out of breath.

"Okay, that was actually really fun!" Sassy admitted, grinning as she nudged Alarion with her tiny paw. "Perhaps I'll allow you to win again sometime later!"

"Or maybe I'll just practice more!" Alarion replied, wiping tears of laughter from his eyes. "Thank you for the challenge, Sassy. You're a great opponent!"

"Just remember," she said with a wink, "next time, the acorn toss will be even more competitive!"

With that, Alarion waved goodbye to Sassy and made his way home, a big smile on his face. He couldn't wait to share the day's antics with his friends. Tiderune was a land full of surprises, and with every new adventure, he discovered that laughter truly was the best treasure of all.

Chapter 18: The Spell Gone Wrong

Alarion tries a new spell to make a friend but accidentally turns himself into a fluffy rabbit. Now, he must hop his way out of trouble!

Alarion was feeling particularly adventurous one sunny afternoon in Tiderune. The magical realm was bursting with vibrant colors, and the gentle breeze danced through the trees. He had just finished reading a new spellbook he found in the dusty corner of the Enchanted Library, its pages filled with curious spells for friendship, fun, and laughter. One spell, in particular, caught his eye: The Instant Friendship Spell. It promised to create a bond with anyone nearby, making it perfect for making new friends.

"Today's the day!" Alarion exclaimed to himself, determination shining in his eyes. "I will attempt this spell and make another companion!"

He decided to test it out at the edge of the Whispering Woods, a magical place known for its friendly creatures. After clearing a small patch of grass, Alarion pulled out his trusty wand, a beautiful piece of enchanted wood that had served him well on many adventures. He waved it in the air dramatically, feeling the excitement bubble inside him.

"Alright, let's see..." he muttered, glancing at the spell's instructions. "To make a friend near and dear, just whisper the words in their ear!"

With a flourish, he recited the spell, but as he reached the final line, a little hiccup escaped him. "Oh, and please, make it fluffy!"

A soft sparkle filled the air, swirling around him like fireflies. Just then, a gentle breeze swept through the clearing, and he suddenly felt an odd tickling sensation in his nose. "What's happening?" he thought, wide-eyed.

Before he could process what was going on, a bright flash of light enveloped him. When the light faded, Alarion looked down and gasped. Instead of his usual arms and legs, he now had fluffy white paws, twitching whiskers, and, worst of all, a fluffy tail! He had turned into a rabbit!

"What? No, no, no! This isn't what I wanted!" Alarion squeaked with dismay, his voice presently sharp and noisy. He patted his soft, furry body with his little paws, realizing that he had hopped straight into a furry fiasco.

Just then, he heard giggles from behind a nearby bush. Alarion turned his fluffy head and saw a group of playful forest critters peeking out: a chipmunk, a squirrel, and a curious bluebird. Their eyes were wide with amusement as they took in the sight of a bunny who looked remarkably like a flustered human.

"Oh my! Is that a rabbit trying to cast spells?" the chipmunk chuckled, clutching his tiny belly. "I've seen a few things; however, this takes the carrot cake!"

"Seriously! Who would try to make friends and end up as a snack?" the squirrel added, her eyes twinkling with mischief.

"Guys! This is a serious situation!" Alarion squeaked, hopping in circles, which only seemed to make the critters laugh harder. "I really want to turn around into a human before I become supper for an eager fox!"

The bluebird flapped its wings excitedly. "Well, why don't you hop your way to the Wise Old Owl? He might know how to reverse the spell!"

"Good idea! The Wise Old Owl is my only hope!" Alarion expressed, attempting to concentrate regardless of his fluffy quandary.

"But first, I need to figure out how to move like this!"

With a determined grunt, Alarion took his first clumsy hop. He wobbled on his tiny rabbit legs, tumbling into a patch of daisies, which erupted into a cloud of white petals. "Ahh! No! Not the flowers!" he squeaked, his fluffy ears flopping wildly. The critters roared with laughter, and Alarion couldn't help but chuckle himself, realizing how ridiculous he must look.

With newfound resolve, he practiced hopping again, this time attempting to gain some grace. He managed a few small hops toward the path leading deeper into the woods, where the Wise Old Owl resided. With each bounce, Alarion's confidence grew, though the critters continued to trail behind him, chortling and cheering him on.

"Look at him go! The Fluffy Wizard is on the move!" the squirrel shouted, tossing acorns in the air.

Despite the teasing, Alarion pushed forward, hopping along the path, determined to reach the Wise Old Owl. After a short while, he arrived at a grand old oak tree where the owl resided, perched majestically on a thick branch.

"Wise Old Owl!" Alarion squeaked, gazing up in awe. "I need your help! I accidentally turned myself into a rabbit while trying to cast a friendship spell!"

The owl tilted its head, eyes narrowing thoughtfully. "A rabbit, you say? An interesting predicament indeed!"

"Please, I want to turn around before I'm confused with supper!" Alarion pleaded, doing his best to look as adorable as a rabbit could manage.

The Wise Old Owl chuckled softly, his feathers ruffling. "Indeed, you'll have to track down the wellspring of your spell, dear Alarion. Friendship is important, but so is knowing how to cast spells correctly! Tell me, what exactly did you say?"

Alarion explained the spell and his final wish for it to be "fluffy." The owl's laughter echoed through the woods. "Ah, I see! The power of words can sometimes lead to unexpected results! To reverse the spell, simply say, 'Fluffy no more, I want to be me!' while hopping three times in the direction of the setting sun."

"Easy enough!" Alarion squeaked, feeling a surge of hope. He thanked the Wise Old Owl and hopped back toward the path, determined to follow the instructions.

With the critters cheering him on, Alarion began hopping—one, two, three times—toward the west. "Cushioned no more, I need to be me!" he called out, his voice ringing with determination.

Suddenly, a bright light enveloped him again, the forest fading into a blur. When the light receded, Alarion blinked, looking down at his hands—his human hands! He was back to being himself!

"Woohoo!" he cheered, siphoning his clench hands up high. "I'm human again!"

The critters erupted into cheers, clapping their paws and wings in delight. "You did it! The Fluffy Wizard is now a human again!" they exclaimed, bouncing around him with joy.

"Thank you, everyone!" Alarion laughed, feeling relieved. "And I think I'll stick to making friends the old-fashioned way—no more spells for a while!"

Just then, the squirrel poked her head up with a sly grin. "But Alarion, wouldn't it be fun to do an acorn toss competition now?"

Alarion laughed, shaking his head. "You know what? That sounds like a great idea!"

As they set off to gather acorns, Alarion felt grateful for the wild adventure he had just experienced. It turned out that sometimes, making friends—and a little mischief—was just as important as magic itself. With laughter ringing through the trees and a newfound appreciation for his furry friends, Alarion knew he had not only survived a fluffy mishap but also made memories that would last a lifetime.

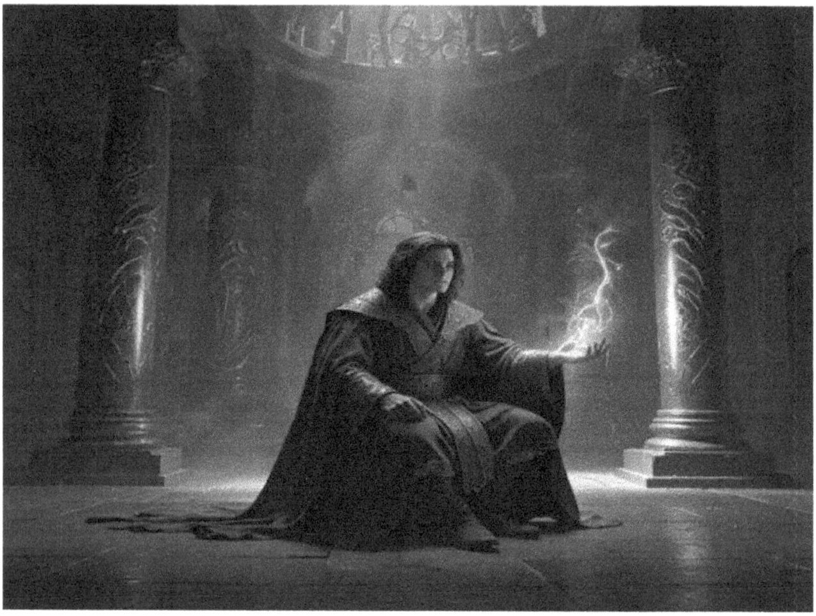

Chapter 19: The Singing Stones

*A*larion *discovers stones that sing when stepped on. Trying to dance along, he creates a cacophony that sends birds flying in all directions!*

The sun was shining bright over Tiderune, casting a golden glow across the vibrant landscape. Alarion was wandering through the Twinkling Glade, a magical place known for its unusual wonders and delightful surprises. With each step he took, the soft grass beneath his feet felt like a plush carpet, and the air was filled with the sweet scent of blooming flowers.

As he ambled along, Alarion spotted a peculiar sight up ahead—a patch of stones that glimmered in various hues of blue and green. Curious, he approached the stones, noticing that they seemed to hum softly as he got closer.

"What's this?" he mused, kneeling down to inspect the colorful stones. As he pressed his hand against one, it emitted a delightful chime, like a gentle bell ringing in the breeze. "Wow! These stones sing!"

Excitedly, Alarion jumped to his feet. "I wonder if they sing when you step on them!" With a decided smile, he arranged to evaluate this newly discovered disclosure.

He stepped cautiously onto the nearest stone, and to his delight, it let out a melodious ding that echoed in the glade. Encouraged, he hopped from one stone to another, creating a delightful melody. "This is amazing!" he exclaimed, his heart dancing along with the notes.

Feeling a rush of joy, Alarion began to dance. He twirled and spun, stepping on each stone as he went, the stones harmonizing in a cacophony of tunes. But as he picked up speed, the music transformed into a chaotic medley, the once-gentle notes spiralling into a wild symphony.

Ding! Dong! BONG! Ding-a-ling!

The sounds reverberated through the glade, and Alarion couldn't help but laugh at the sheer absurdity of it all. "I'm creating a masterpiece!" he declared, striking a pose mid-spin. But suddenly, the cacophony grew so loud that it startled a flock of nearby birds, sending them flapping into the air in a flurry of feathers.

"Oops!" Alarion exclaimed, watching as the birds squawked and scattered. He continued dancing, trying to regain control of his music. "Come back! I'm just trying to make art!"

With each tap of his foot, the stones reacted, creating an unpredictable tune that seemed to echo the frenzy in the sky. Alarion, still trying to dance gracefully, slipped on one of the stones and went tumbling forward, landing with a soft thud on the grass.

The stones, reacting to his fall, sang a sudden whoooop! that bounced off the trees. Alarion lay there for a moment, gazing up at the blue sky, slightly dazed but laughing at the ridiculousness of it all. "Maybe I should stick to less... adventurous music," he chuckled to himself.

Just then, a friendly voice interrupted his thoughts. "Well, aren't you a lively one!"

Alarion turned to see a wise old turtle slowly making its way toward him, its shell adorned with intricate patterns. "You're the first human I've seen dancing on the Singing Stones," the turtle said, its voice slow and soothing. "What brings you to this delightful chaos?"

"I didn't mean to create a ruckus! I just discovered these stones sing, and I thought I'd join in," Alarion replied, still chuckling as he brushed the grass from his clothes.

The turtle smiled knowingly. "Ah, the stones have their own rhythm. They appreciate a gentle touch, not a wild flurry. You must listen to their song."

Alarion nodded, realizing he had been so eager to create a masterpiece that he had forgotten to appreciate the beauty of the music itself. "You're right! I overdid it," he conceded, scouring the rear of his neck timidly.

The turtle took a seat beside Alarion, a soft smile still gracing its face. "Why don't we try it together? You step lightly, and I'll guide you through the dance. Let's see if we can make the stones sing a gentle tune."

Feeling excited, Alarion agreed. Together, they began to move, with the turtle leading the way. With each careful step, the stones chimed softly, creating a soothing melody that floated through the air like a gentle breeze. Alarion found himself swaying in time with the rhythm, laughing as the turtle showed him the slow, graceful movements.

As they danced, birds began to return, intrigued by the new tune that floated through the glade. They landed on nearby branches, their heads bobbing in time with the song. Alarion couldn't help but feel the magic of the moment—the glade was alive with music, laughter, and the flutter of wings.

"See? The Singing Stones just needed a little harmony," the turtle said with a twinkle in its eye.

"This is wonderful!" Alarion exclaimed, feeling the joy of the moment wash over him. "I could dance like this forever!"

And so, they danced, creating a beautiful symphony of sound that echoed through the Twinkling Glade. The sun began to set, casting a warm golden glow around them as Alarion and the turtle moved together, enjoying the simplicity of the moment.

As the last notes rang out, Alarion finally stopped, breathless but filled with happiness. "Thank you for showing me how to listen to the stones," he said gratefully, looking at the wise turtle. "You've made this adventure even better!"

"Remember, young one," the turtle replied, nodding sagely, "life is often about balance—between chaos and calm, laughter and music. Keep dancing through life, but never forget to listen."

With a heart full of gratitude, Alarion waved goodbye to his newfound friend and made his way back through the Twinkling Glade, the memory of the Singing Stones lingering like a sweet melody in his mind. He felt lighter and brighter, ready to embrace whatever adventure awaited him next in the magical realm of Tiderune.

Chapter 20: The Cheese Wizard

In search of knowledge, Alarion meets a wizard obsessed with cheese. Their discussion turns cheesy, literally, as Alarion gets trapped in a cheese fondue!

In the magical realm of Tiderune, where enchanting creatures roamed freely and the landscape changed with the flick of a wand, Alarion found himself on yet another whimsical adventure. This time, he was in pursuit of knowledge—not just any knowledge, but the kind that could help him unlock the secrets of a hidden treasure rumored to be buried deep within the enchanted land.

As he wandered through a charming village filled with colorful cottages and fragrant gardens, Alarion caught a whiff of something utterly delightful. It was a rich, Savory scent that made his mouth water. Following the aroma, he rounded a corner and was greeted by the sight of a whimsical little shop with a sign that read, "Cheeseria Magica: Home of the Cheesiest Wizard in Tiderune!"

Curiosity piqued, Alarion pushed open the door, and a little bell chimed overhead. The shop was a treasure trove of all things cheese—cheeses of every color and texture filled the shelves, from creamy brie to sharp cheddar, and even a glowing blue cheese that shimmered under the shop's magical lights.

Behind the counter stood an elderly wizard with a long, white beard that resembled a fluffy cloud. His robes were adorned with cheese motifs, and he was currently busy stirring a bubbling pot of cheese fondue. He looked up and grinned, revealing a toothy smile.

"Ah! A visitor! Welcome to my humble cheeseria! I'm Wizard Cheddar, the cheese connoisseur of Tiderune!"

"Hello! I'm Alarion," he replied, still mesmerized by the display of cheesy delights. "I'm on a quest for knowledge."

"Knowledge, you say?" Wizard Cheddar raised an eyebrow, his eyes twinkling with mischief. "Then you've come to the right place! But first, you must answer a riddle about cheese!"

"A riddle?" Alarion laughed, intrigued. "Alright, hit me with your best shot!"

"Very well! Here it is," Wizard Cheddar said, leaning closer as if sharing a great secret. "I am a type of cheese, but when I'm grated, I can become the life of the party. What am I?"

Alarion thought briefly, a smile spreading across his face. "Parmesan!"

"Correct!" the wizard exclaimed, clapping his hands together. "You've proven yourself worthy. Now, what knowledge do you seek?"

"I'm looking for information about the hidden treasure of Tiderune. Do you know anything about it?" Alarion asked, his excitement bubbling over.

Wizard Cheddar stroked his beard thoughtfully. "Ah, the treasure! Many have sought it, but few have succeeded. Legend says it lies beneath the Cheddar Mountains, protected by a powerful spell. To find it, one must first pass a series of cheesy challenges."

"Cheesy challenges?" Alarion echoed, trying to suppress a giggle. "What does that entail?"

The wizard chuckled, his eyes sparkling with amusement. "Oh, they are quite delightful! There's the Fondue Fiasco, the Cheesy Riddle Contest, and, my personal favorite, the Great Cheese Rolling Race. But first, let's see how you handle my fondue!"

With that, Wizard Cheddar brandished a ladle and beckoned Alarion over to the bubbling pot. "Care to try a dip? But be careful! It can get a bit messy!"

Alarion, feeling adventurous, dipped a piece of bread into the gooey cheese. As he brought it up to his mouth, the cheese stretched into an impressive string, and just as he was about to take a bite, a mischievous burst of energy crackled through the air. The cheese pot suddenly bubbled and flared, and before Alarion could react, he slipped and tumbled right into the pot!

"Whoa!" he hollered, thrashing his arms as the warm, messy goodness encompassed him. "I didn't intend to take a plunge like this!"

"Ah, it seems you've become part of the fondue!" Wizard Cheddar chuckled, unable to contain his laughter. "Now that's what I call a cheesy predicament!"

Alarion's laughter mixed with the cheese as he floated in the bubbling fondue. "I'm definitely in over my head—literally! How do I get out of this?"

"Simple!" the wizard replied, a twinkle of mischief in his eye. "Just say the magic word, and you'll be free!"

"What's the magic word?" Alarion asked, half-expecting something dramatic.

"Cheddarific!" the wizard exclaimed dramatically, his arms waving as if conducting an orchestra.

"Cheddarific!" Alarion shouted, and to his surprise, a golden light enveloped him, lifting him out of the pot and plopping him gently onto the floor. He landed with a soft splat, surrounded by a puddle of melted cheese.

"Now that was a bit cheesy!" Wizard Cheddar laughed heartily, his eyes sparkling with joy. "You handled that quite well!"

Alarion stood up, dripping in gooey cheese, and couldn't help but laugh at the absurdity of it all. "I guess I should have seen that coming! Do you have a towel?"

"Of course!" Wizard Cheddar waved his hand, and a fluffy towel appeared, floating through the air and landing in Alarion's hands. After wiping himself off, Alarion looked at the wizard with newfound determination. "Okay, what's next on this cheesy adventure?"

"Next is the Cheesy Riddle Contest!" Wizard Cheddar declared, excitement bubbling in his voice. "Are you ready to test your wits against my enchanted cheese wheels?"

"Bring it on!" Alarion said, ready to tackle whatever cheesy challenge lay ahead.

The wizard summoned two massive wheels of cheese; each one labelled with a different riddle. "To win, you must solve the riddle faster than the cheese can roll away!"

Alarion grinned, feeling confident. "Alright, let's do this!"

With that, the cheese wheels began to roll, and Wizard Cheddar shouted the riddles. "First riddle! What cheese is made backward?"

Alarion's mind raced. "Edam!" he yelled victoriously as he snatched a cheddar wheel, leaving it speechless.

"Very good!" the wizard exclaimed, and the next riddle was fired off. "What did the cheddar say when it thoroughly searched in the mirror?"

"Halloumi!" Alarion replied, laughing at the cleverness of the riddle.

The two continued to riddle and roll, laughter echoing throughout the shop as Alarion swiftly answered every question, his competitive spirit driving him forward.

Finally, after what felt like hours of fun, Alarion successfully answered the last riddle, leaving Wizard Cheddar thoroughly impressed. "You are truly a worthy challenger, Alarion! You've earned a special gift!"

With a wave of his wand, the wizard conjured a small, glowing cheese wheel. "This is the Cheesy Compass! It will guide you on your quest for the hidden treasure of Tiderune."

Alarion took the glowing cheese wheel, feeling a surge of excitement. "Thank you, Wizard Cheddar! I'll make sure to use it wisely."

As Alarion left the Cheeseria Magica, he felt giddy from laughter and cheese. With the compass in hand and memories of cheesy antics fresh in his mind, he set off on his next adventure, ready to uncover the secrets of Tiderune, one cheesy challenge at a time.

Chapter 21: The Frightening Fog

Alarion walks into a fog that whispers spooky tales. Instead of being scared, he starts adding funny endings, turning the eerie atmosphere into a comedy club!

The sun had just begun its descent over the magical realm of Tiderune, casting long shadows across the vibrant landscape. Alarion was meandering through the glimmering meadows, his trusty Cheesy Compass still glowing softly in his pocket. After his hilarious encounter with Wizard Cheddar, he was eager for his next adventure. Little did he know, an eerie experience awaited him just ahead.

As Alarion rounded a bend, he was met with a thick, swirling fog that rolled in like a carpet of white fluff. It was peculiar; instead of blocking his view, the fog seemed almost alive. Wisps of it curled around him, and as he stepped deeper into the mist, he began to hear whispers. At first, he thought it was just the wind, but the words became clearer: tales of ghostly figures and lost souls.

"Ah, welcome to the Frightening Fog," a voice seemed to drift from the haze. "Here, we share spooky tales that chill to the bone!"

Alarion paused, eyebrows raised. "Spooky tales, you say? I could use a laugh!" He stepped forward, crossing his arms with a mischievous grin. "Why not share one with me? I could use a good story to lighten the mood!"

The fog shivered, and suddenly, a disembodied voice echoed through the mist. "In a haunted castle, a ghost named Gerald lost his way. He wandered the halls for years, unable to find the door!"

Alarion couldn't help but chuckle. "Sounds like he needed a map! Or perhaps a ghostly GPS!"

The fog twirled, seeming to react to his laughter. "But then, one night, he met a friendly bat who offered to help him. They flew around, searching high and low, but they only found a stash of cobwebs!"

"Maybe they should have asked the spiders for directions!" Alarion added, laughing at the thought.

The fog, feeling encouraged, continued. "And so, Gerald and the bat decided to throw a party to attract other ghosts for help. They played music and danced all night!"

"Sounds like a real boo-ling good time!" Alarion exclaimed, striking a pose as if he were dancing himself.

Suddenly, the fog swirled faster, responding to Alarion's playful spirit. "But, alas! When the sun rose, all the ghosts vanished! Gerald was left with a mountain of snacks and no one to share them with."

"Classic ghost problem!" Alarion chimed in. "I guess it's hard to throw a good party when all your friends vanish at dawn! Maybe he should have served ghost pepper nachos instead!"

Laughter echoed through the fog, and it began to lighten, swirling around him in a playful dance.

Encouraged by the shift in atmosphere, Alarion decided to contribute his own tale.

"Alright, let me give it a try! Once upon a time in a spooky forest, a zombie named Zed tried to befriend a group of humans. But every time he approached them, they ran away screaming!"

The fog paused, intrigued. "Why did they run?"

"Because Zed was just so... dedicated to making friends!" Alarion replied, laughing at his own pun. "He didn't understand that his lack of a heart made him a poor candidate for romance!"

The fog giggled—yes, giggled! —and a whisper of warmth spread through the chilly air. "And what did Zed do then?"

"Zed decided to start a support group for misunderstood monsters. They all met under the moonlight, sharing their woes and figuring out ways to fit in! Even the werewolves showed up, but they kept howling every time someone told a joke!"

With each tale spun, the fog became less frightening and more whimsical, transforming into a place of laughter instead of fear. Alarion felt as if he had opened a comedy club in the middle of the mist!

"Tell us another one!" the fog encouraged, now fully engaged.

"Okay, how about this: in a dark, creepy mansion, a witch named Wanda had a pet cat named Whiskers. Every time Wanda tried to brew a potion, Whiskers would jump in and steal the ingredients!"

The fog let out a hissing laugh. "What happened next?"

"Wanda got tired of it and decided to make a potion that would turn Whiskers into a human!" Alarion continued, chuckling at the absurdity. "But instead of becoming a human, Whiskers turned into a pillow! Now he just lounges around, too lazy to do anything, while Wanda still yells at him to stop sleeping on her broomstick!"

More laughter erupted from the fog, and Alarion felt a warm glow surrounding him. "The tales are delightful!" the fog said, its voice now less spooky and more cheerful. "You've brought joy to the Frightening Fog, Alarion!"

Feeling a burst of confidence, Alarion leaned into the moment. "How about one last tale? Once, in a land far away, there was a dragon named Duke who was terrified of his own shadow. Every time he saw it, he would run away, flapping his wings and breathing fire!"

"What happened next?" the fog asked, clearly captivated.

"Well," Alarion said with a smirk, "one day he decided to face his fear. He invited all his dragon friends for a shadow party. But when they showed up, they all had massive shadows! Duke ended up fainting at the sight of his own shadow on a giant screen!"

The fog erupted in a fit of laughter, swirling into playful shapes and colors. "You've turned our spooky tales into something truly wonderful!"

Alarion felt a sense of accomplishment, proud of how he transformed the eerie atmosphere into a joyful gathering. "Thank you for the stories, dear fog! I had no idea whispers could be so much fun!"

The fog shimmered in gratitude. "And thank you for bringing laughter into our mist. May you always find joy, wherever your adventures take you!"

With a final swirl, the fog began to clear, revealing a stunning view of the Cheddar Mountains in the distance. Alarion waved goodbye to the whimsical mist and set off on his path, his heart light with laughter and his spirit uplifted.

As he continued his journey through Tiderune, he couldn't help but think of all the quirky characters he had met along the way. And if a little fog could turn from frightening to fun, he realized that every adventure held the potential for laughter, if only he looked at it from a different angle.

With that thought in mind, Alarion ventured forth, ready for whatever delightful mishap awaited him next!

Chapter 22: The Cloudy Conundrum

A larion meets a cloud that can't decide whether to rain or shine. They collaborate on a weather forecast that results in a hilarious downpour of giggles!

Alarion had seen many strange things on his journey through the magical realm of Tiderune, but today was shaping up to be particularly peculiar. After his comedic adventure in the Frightening Fog, he found himself walking through a meadow, gazing up at the sky. He had been enjoying the pleasant breeze and warm sunshine, when suddenly, the sky became... indecisive.

One moment, bright rays of sunlight bathed the meadow in warmth, and the next, a cloud drifted in, covering the sun and casting a chilly shadow. Then, just as quickly as it had arrived, the cloud moved away, letting the sun peek through once more. But before Alarion could get comfortable, the cloud came back. And forth. And back again.

"Well, this is annoying," Alarion muttered to himself, squinting at the sky. "Make up your mind already!"

As if it had heard him, the cloud stopped in its tracks and hovered directly above him. A deep, slightly embarrassed voice echoed from within it. "I... um... I'm trying to decide! It's just... really difficult!"

Alarion blinked, staring up at the hovering fluff. "Wait. Are you talking to me?"

"Yes!" the cloud said, its voice filled with indecision. "I'm sorry, but I just can't seem to make up my mind today. Should I rain? Should I shine? Should I just float around doing nothing? The choices are overwhelming!"

Alarion crossed his arms, a smirk tugging at his lips. "You know, most clouds seem to have this whole weather thing figured out. But you, my friend, seem to be in quite the conundrum."

The cloud let out a sigh—a gentle, misty breeze that ruffled Alarion's hair. "Tell me about it. Every other cloud I know is so confident. They either rain or they don't. But me? I always second-guess myself. What if I start raining, but people want sunshine? Or what if I decide to shine, but the farmers need rain for their crops? It's so stressful!"

Alarion chuckled and shook his head. "Well, when you put it like that, it does sound like a tough job. But, hey, you're talking to Alarion, master of magical mishaps! If there's anyone who knows about indecisiveness, it's me. How about we figure this out together?"

The cloud perked up a bit, its edges fluffing out in excitement. "Really? You'd help me decide?"

"Of course!" Alarion replied, his tone playful. "But first, I need to know—what's your name?"

"I'm Nimbus," the cloud said, sounding both proud and uncertain at the same time. "Named after the great storm clouds, but... I'm not really living up to that reputation."

Alarion gave Nimbus a reassuring smile. "Well, Nimbus, let's not worry about the storm cloud legacy right now. How about we focus on what you want to do?"

Nimbus floated in place, humming in thought. "Hmm... well, I kind of want to rain. But at the same time, the sun feels so nice today. I don't want to ruin anyone's picnic. Oh! And look at that rainbow over there! I don't want to block that either. Ugh, what a dilemma!"

Alarion tapped his chin, pondering the situation. "What if we came up with a plan? You know, like a weather forecast! We could schedule your rain and shine so that everyone gets what they want."

"A schedule?" Nimbus asked, intrigued. "That... that could work! But how would we do that?"

"Easy!" Alarion said with a grin. "First, let's assess the situation." He gestured grandly toward the meadow. "It's sunny and bright right now, perfect for picnics, daydreaming, and skipping through fields. So maybe, for the next hour, you let the sun shine."

Nimbus puffed out a small cloud of agreement. "I like that idea. But what happens after the hour is up?"

"After that," Alarion continued, "you can let loose with some gentle rain. You know, nothing too heavy—just enough to water the flowers and make that delightful pitter-patter sound that everyone loves. People who want sunshine can enjoy the first part of the day, and the gardeners will thank you for the afternoon rain."

Nimbus swirled in excitement. "Oh! That sounds perfect! But... what if I change my mind halfway through and start thundering? I'm terrible at sticking to plans."

Alarion stifled a laugh. "Well, if you start to thunder, we'll just add it to the forecast! Call it a 'surprise storm'—keeps things interesting."

Nimbus giggled, a soft rumbling sound that resembled distant thunder. "You're really good at this, Alarion! A surprise storm could be fun! But... what if it confuses people?"

Alarion waved a hand dismissively. "Confusion is part of life, Nimbus. And besides, who doesn't love a little excitement? Think of it this way: if they didn't get rained on every now and then, they wouldn't appreciate the sunshine as much. You're just helping them stay on their toes!"

Nimbus bobbed up and down in agreement, clearly warming to the idea. "You know, I never thought about it that way. Maybe being a cloud isn't so bad after all. I just need to embrace my indecisiveness!"

"Exactly!" Alarion said, smiling. "Being a cloud with options makes you special. You can bring sunshine and rain, laughter and surprise. And hey, if anyone complains, just send them my way. I'll explain it to them."

Nimbus let out a little burst of misty giggles. "Thank you, Alarion. You've really helped me see things in a new light—literally and figuratively!"

Alarion gave a dramatic bow. "It was my pleasure, Nimbus. Now, about that forecast... shall we make it official?"

The cloud hovered proudly above him, glowing slightly as the sunlight passed through its edges. "Yes! Let's do it!"

Together, they crafted the perfect weather schedule: one hour of glorious sunshine, followed by a gentle drizzle, and—just for fun—a surprise thunderclap at the end of the day. It was a forecast designed to keep everyone in Tiderune both happy and slightly amused.

As Nimbus floated higher into the sky, ready to deliver its carefully planned weather, Alarion waved goodbye. "Remember, Nimbus, it's okay to change your mind! That's what makes you unique!"

The cloud gave a final giggle before drifting away, leaving Alarion standing in the meadow with a grin on his face. As the sun continued to shine down, he couldn't help but marvel at the odd but delightful experience of helping a cloud find its purpose.

"Another day, another adventure," Alarion mused, starting back on the path. "Who knows? Maybe tomorrow I'll meet a talking tree or a bickering rainbow."

And with that, he continued his journey, knowing that even the most indecisive clouds could brighten someone's day—and, in Nimbus's case, add a little humor to the forecast too.

Chapter 23: The Ticklish Toad

While exploring a swamp, Alarion encounters a toad that laughs uncontrollably when tickled. Their playful antics turn into a hilarious chase!

Alarion had ventured through magical forests, sailed on mystical rivers, and even navigated a maze of snores, but nothing quite prepared him for the strange encounter he was about to have deep within the Swamps of Giggle fen.

The swamp was thick with mist, the kind that clung to his boots and made squelching noises with every step. Alarion wrinkled his nose at the smell of damp earth and something that vaguely reminded him of pickled frogs. The air was humid, the kind of heavy moisture that felt like it was hugging him too tightly. But being the curious adventurer he was, he pressed forward, always eager to uncover whatever mystery lay ahead.

As he made his way through the swampy muck, Alarion's ears caught an odd sound—a noise that didn't fit with the usual croaking of frogs or the chirping of crickets. It was... laughter?

Alarion stopped in his tracks, squinting into the fog ahead. He could hear it clearly now: a deep, booming laugh, followed by snorts and more giggles. It wasn't just any laugh—it was the kind of infectious laughter that made it impossible not to smile, no matter how strange the situation.

Cautiously, he followed the sound, stepping carefully around large mushrooms that seemed to blink at him and vines that wiggled like lazy snakes. The laughter grew louder until he found himself standing in front of a particularly large lily pad. And there, perched on top of it, was a massive, warty toad—green and brown, with bulging eyes that shimmered in the dim light of the swamp.

But what made the sight so peculiar was that the toad was rolling on its back, laughing uncontrollably.

"Well, this is new," Alarion said, crossing his arms as he watched the toad kick its legs in the air, gasping for breath between bouts of laughter.

Suddenly, the toad noticed him. With a dramatic flip, it rolled back onto its belly, wiping tears of laughter from its eyes with one pudgy webbed hand.

"Sorry, sorry," the toad croaked between snickers. "I didn't mean to startle you, lad. It's just—oh, I can't help it!" And with that, it burst into laughter again, shaking the entire lily pad.

Alarion raised an eyebrow, intrigued. "You seem to be in a good mood."

The toad nodded, still chuckling. "I'm Tickly. Tickly the Toad. And, well... it's kind of in my nature."

"Your nature? To laugh?" Alarion asked, stepping closer to the lily pad.

"To be ticklish!" Tickly exclaimed, hiccupping from another fit of giggles. "Everything tickles me—everything! A stray breeze, the touch of a leaf, even my own breath sometimes!" He slapped his knee, which only made him laugh harder. "It's both a gift and a curse, I tell you!"

Alarion couldn't help but laugh a little himself. "I see. So you just... spend your days laughing at everything?"

Tickly nodded, his massive belly jiggling with every laugh. "Pretty much! But you've got to admit, there are worse ways to live."

Alarion grinned, sitting down on a nearby rock. "I suppose that's true. Although, doesn't it get tiring after a while?"

"Sometimes," Tickly admitted, though his smile never faded. "But I've found it's best to just embrace it. After all, laughter's good for the soul, isn't it?"

Alarion chuckled. "You've got a point there."

Just as Alarion was about to ask more about Tickly's ticklish nature, a gust of wind blew through the swamp, carrying with it a flurry of tiny, glowing insects. One particularly brave bug landed right on Tickly's nose, its little legs brushing against his warty skin.

That was all it took.

Tickly exploded into laughter, his booming guffaws echoing through the swamp as he rolled off the lily pad and into the murky water below. Splashes flew everywhere, drenching Alarion from head to toe.

"Hey!" Alarion sputtered, wiping mud from his face. "Watch it!"

But Tickly was too far gone, laughing hysterically as he tried—and failed—to climb back onto the lily pad. His slippery webbed hands slipped again and again, sending him splashing back into the water each time.

Alarion couldn't help but laugh at the ridiculousness of it all. The scene was too absurd: a giant, ticklish toad having a full-on giggle fit in the middle of a swamp. "Here, let me help you," Alarion said, extending a hand.

But the moment his fingers brushed against Tickly's side, the toad shrieked with laughter and jerked away, splashing mud everywhere. "Oh no! Not the sides! Not the sides!" Tickly wailed through his laughter. "That's my most ticklish spot!"

Alarion raised an eyebrow, a mischievous grin creeping onto his face. "Oh really?"

Before Tickly could protest, Alarion reached out and tickled the toad's sides again. Tickly erupted in laughter, flailing wildly in the water, sending splashes in every direction. It wasn't long before the two of them were in the middle of an all-out tickle war—Tickly trying to swim away and Alarion chasing after him, laughing just as hard.

The swamp, which had been relatively quiet moments before, was now filled with the sound of laughter. The birds in the trees squawked in confusion, and even the swamp creatures poked their heads out to see what the commotion was about.

After what felt like ages, Alarion finally collapsed onto the lily pad, panting from laughter. Tickly floated beside him, still chuckling but clearly exhausted from the tickle battle.

"You... you're relentless!" Tickly gasped, trying to catch his breath.

Alarion wiped a tear from his eye, his sides aching from all the laughing. "You're not so bad yourself."

For a moment, the two of them lay there in the swamp, soaking wet and covered in mud, but content. It was one of the silliest—and most fun—adventures Alarion had ever had.

After a while, Tickly floated over to Alarion, his laughter finally subsiding. "You know, lad, it's not often someone joins me for a good laugh like that. Most folks run away when they see how ticklish I am."

"Well, they don't know what they're missing," Alarion replied, grinning. "This was... surprisingly fun."

Tickly smiled, though his cheeks were still a bit sore from all the laughing. "Aye, it was. You've got a good sense of humor, Alarion. You ever need a good laugh; you know where to find me."

Alarion nodded, standing up and wringing out his cloak. "I'll keep that in mind, Tickly. But for now, I think I need to find some dry clothes—and maybe a less ticklish traveling companion."

With that, Alarion waved goodbye to Tickly and set off back through the swamp, his footsteps squelching in the mud once more. But this time, there was a lightness in his step and a smile on his face that hadn't been there before.

Because if there was one thing Alarion had learned that day, it was that sometimes, the best adventures were the ones filled with laughter. And Tickly the Toad was certainly proof of that.

Chapter 24: The Forgotten Spell

Alarion tries to remember a spell from a dusty old book but ends up accidentally summoning a troupe of clumsy dancing fairies!

Alarion had spent a long, exhausting day in the depths of the ancient library of Thistle brook. The air was thick with the scent of old parchment and ink, and the only sound besides the occasional rustling of pages was the faint, echoing drip of water from somewhere deep within the forgotten catacombs below.

His eyes were drooping, but he couldn't leave just yet. There was one spell—just one—that he had been searching for. According to the rumors, it was hidden in an obscure, dusty old book, crammed into the back of one of the shelves no one dared approach due to a stubborn family of enchanted spiders that had taken up residence.

With a sigh, Alarion stretched his arms, feeling the weight of fatigue tugging at him. "How hard can it be to find one spell?" he muttered to himself. He glanced at the pile of ancient books around him, some so old they looked like they might crumble to dust if he turned the pages too quickly.

Finally, his gaze fell upon the thickest, most worn-out book in the pile. It was bound in faded brown leather, its cover creased and frayed at the edges, and the title was barely legible in gold-embossed script: "Arcane Oddities and Forgotten Magics."

"This has to be it," Alarion said, leaning forward and cracking the book open with a puff of dust. He squinted at the tiny, cramped handwriting on the first few pages. The text was barely readable, filled with convoluted sentences and unnecessary flourishes, but it had to contain what he was looking for.

Hours passed, and Alarion's patience was wearing thin. He flipped through page after page of odd spells and bizarre incantations: "The Shoes of Unstoppable Tap-Dancing," "The Spell to Grow Extra Elbows," and something about "Instant Goose Summoning." He groaned, resting his head in his hands.

"Who writes this stuff?" he grumbled. "All I need is a simple teleportation spell."

But the book had other plans. After a particularly frustrating page turn, Alarion's eyes lit up. There it was! A teleportation spell nestled between "Summon Suspicious Pudding" and "Temporary Baldness Charm." At least, he thought it was a teleportation spell. The faded words were hard to decipher, but it was the closest thing he had found all day.

"Finally!" Alarion exclaimed, sitting up straight. He cleared his throat and began to chant the words of the spell, his voice echoing slightly in the still air of the library.

"By the light of stars and moonlit breeze,
Let me move with the greatest ease,
From here to there and far away,
Take me now without delay!"

For a moment, nothing happened. Alarion furrowed his brow, confused. He had followed the instructions perfectly—hadn't he?

Suddenly, a loud POP echoed through the room, followed by a series of giggles. Alarion blinked in surprise as tiny, shimmering figures began to appear in front of him—one after another, until the air was filled with glowing, fluttering beings.

"Dancing fairies?" Alarion gasped.

But these weren't just any fairies. They were a troupe of the clumsiest, most disorganized dancers he had ever seen. The moment they appeared, they began to twirl and leap, but not gracefully. One fairy bumped into a bookshelf, knocking over a stack of books, while another spun too fast and tangled itself in Alarion's hair. A third tried to do a pirouette but stumbled mid-spin, crashing into the others.

"Ow! Watch it!" one fairy squeaked as she tripped over another's wings.

"Sorry, sorry!" the other fairy mumbled, trying to regain her balance but only managing to knock over a candlestick.

Alarion groaned, slapping his forehead. This was not the teleportation spell he'd hoped for. "What... is happening?"

The fairies, still in various states of awkward dancing, seemed utterly unfazed by Alarion's bewilderment. One fairy, who wore what looked like a tiny tutu made of cobwebs, gave him an apologetic smile as she tried to execute a clumsy curtsy.

"Sorry about the mess! We're the Dancing Fairies of Fluffing Hollow," she explained, wincing as one of her companions collided with a chair and sent it toppling over. "We, um, don't really get summoned much these days."

"Clearly," Alarion muttered under his breath, dodging another fairy who was attempting an aerial cartwheel but ended up plummeting into a pile of scrolls. "I was trying to cast a teleportation spell. Not... summon a circus!"

The lead fairy, still struggling to keep her balance, frowned. "Oh dear. You must have mixed up the words. Happens all the time with these old spells. They're tricky, you know. But don't worry—we can still be helpful!"

Alarion raised an eyebrow, dubious. "Helpful? How?"

The fairy brightened, twirling in place (this time without falling over). "We can dance, of course! Watch!" She clapped her hands, and the entire troupe gathered in a shaky formation. The musicless performance began, with fairies twirling, leaping, and flitting about like they were trying to imitate some kind of synchronized routine.

Except they weren't synchronized. At all.

One fairy kept bumping into others, sending them into a chain reaction of collisions. Another tried to lift a partner, but both ended up toppling over, knocking into Alarion's legs. A few fairies were so out of rhythm that they spun in the wrong direction entirely, bumping into bookshelves, sending scrolls flying, and creating a general whirlwind of chaos.

It was a disaster.

Alarion couldn't help but laugh. It was all so absurd—his grand quest to find a powerful spell had somehow devolved into watching the world's clumsiest fairy dance troupe wreak havoc in a library. "This... this is ridiculous!"

"Hey!" one of the fairies huffed, mid-tumble. "We're doing our best here!"

"You're doing something, all right," Alarion chuckled, dodging another fairy as she spiralled out of control. "But I'm not sure 'dancing' is the word I'd use."

The lead fairy sighed, finally collapsing onto a nearby stack of books. "Okay, okay, so we're not the best dancers. But we've got spirit!"

"I'll give you that," Alarion agreed, still grinning. "But I really need to figure out how to fix this spell."

The fairies stopped their awkward dancing, suddenly looking a bit sheepish. "Well, um," the lead fairy began, twiddling her tiny fingers, "you could always try undoing it?"

Alarion raised an eyebrow. "Undo it? How?"

"Just say the spell backward!" one of the fairies chirped, her voice high-pitched as she fluttered upside down.

"Backwards?" Alarion repeated, eyeing the fairies skeptically. "Are you sure that won't make things worse?"

The fairies exchanged glances. "Nope!" they chorused.

Alarion sighed, pinching the bridge of his nose. "Worth a shot, I guess."

With a deep breath, he stood up and recited the spell in reverse. It wasn't easy—halfway through, he got tangled up in the syllables and had to start over. But eventually, with some effort, he finished the incantation.

There was a moment of silence. Then, with a series of faint pops, the fairies disappeared, one by one, leaving the library in a mess of toppled books, scattered scrolls, and the lingering scent of fairy dust.

Alarion sighed in relief. "Finally."

But as he looked around at the chaos left behind, he couldn't help but laugh. The spell may have gone wrong, but it had certainly been one of the more entertaining mistakes he'd ever made.

And who knew? Maybe next time, he'd summon a troupe of dancing wizards. Now that would be something to see.

Chapter 25: The Gigglegrass

Alarion stumbles upon the grass which makes everyone who walks on it giggle. His friends can't stop laughing, leading to a fun-filled adventure through the giggle fields!

Alarion had been walking through the Meadow of Mirth for quite some time, his feet tired but his spirits high. The sun was warm on his back, the birds sang in the distance, and there was a gentle breeze that ruffled his cloak. The meadow was vast and seemed endless, stretching out like a sea of green under the blue sky. It was one of the most peaceful places he had come across in his travels. But, as he would soon learn, peace wasn't all that the Meadow of Mirth had to offer.

It started innocently enough.

Alarion noticed that with every step he took, his feet felt a bit... strange. It was as if the soles of his boots were tingling, a gentle tickling sensation crawling up his legs. At first, he thought it was just his imagination, or maybe some loose gravel stuck in his boots, but then, quite suddenly, he felt an overwhelming urge to laugh.

"Heh... ha-ha... what...?" Alarion tried to stifle a chuckle, but it was no use. The laughter bubbled up from deep inside him, and before he knew it, he was doubled over, laughing uncontrollably. "Hahaha! What in the world... is happening?!"

He looked down at his feet and noticed the strange grass swaying gently in the breeze. It wasn't like any grass he had ever seen before. The blades were a bright, almost neon green, and they shimmered with an odd glow. Every time the wind blew, the grass seemed to hum softly, and with every step Alarion took, the tickling sensation grew stronger.

"This must be... Gigglegrass!" Alarion exclaimed, laughing harder now. "Of course! I've heard of this stuff. They say anyone who steps on it can't stop laughing!"

As the giggles overtook him, Alarion tried to step back, but it was no use. The more he moved, the more he laughed. He fell to the ground, clutching his sides as peals of laughter escaped him. It was as though the meadow had cast a spell over him, and no matter what he did, he couldn't stop the infectious laughter.

"Hah... ha... ha-ha! Oh, I can't breathe!" he gasped between fits of giggles.

Just then, his companions appeared on the horizon, having been exploring the nearby hills. His best friend, Lydia, a skilled archer with a quick wit, was the first to spot him lying in the grass, laughing like a maniac.

"Alarion, what are you doing?" she called out, jogging over with a confused look on her face. "Did you trip over something?"

As soon as Lydia's boots touched the Gigglegrass, her eyes widened in surprise. She tried to take another step, but before she could say a word, a high-pitched giggle slipped from her lips. "What the... hee-hee! Oh no! What... ha ha ha... what's happening?!"

Alarion, still lying in the grass, laughed even harder at the sight of his friend trying to keep her composure. "It's... ha ha ha... the Gigglegrass! We're doomed! Hahaha!"

Lydia tried to move, but every time she did, the grass beneath her feet tickled her relentlessly. Soon, she was on the ground next to Alarion, laughing uncontrollably. "I... can't... stop... laughing!" she wheezed, clutching her stomach.

Moments later, the rest of their friends arrived, curious about the commotion. There was Tarin, the stoic dwarf with a penchant for grumbling, and Selwyn, the ever-optimistic wizard with an encyclopaedic knowledge of magical flora and fauna. Both of them approached cautiously, but as soon as their feet touched the Gigglegrass, they too were overwhelmed by the urge to laugh.

Tarin, usually gruff and serious, let out a deep, rumbling belly laugh that seemed to shake the ground beneath him. "Hahaha! What kind of cursed grass is this?! Hah... oh, by the beard of my ancestors, I can't take it!"

Selwyn, always the scholar, tried to speak through his fits of laughter. "It's... hah... a rare species of enchanted grass... known to... ha ha... induce laughter in anyone who... steps on it! Hahaha!"

Soon, the entire group was rolling around in the grass, tears streaming down their faces as they laughed uncontrollably. Even the usually grumpy Tarin was laughing so hard that his beard shook with every chuckle. The scene was nothing short of hilarious—a group of adventurers, usually so composed and serious, reduced to a giggling, helpless mess by a patch of enchanted grass.

"This... is... too much!" Alarion gasped, wiping away a tear. "How do we... get out of here?!"

Selwyn, still laughing, managed to pull himself up to a sitting position. "There's only... one way! You have to... stop walking! The more you move, the more it tickles!"

Lydia, who was clutching her sides in laughter, gave Selwyn a mock glare. "Oh, that's great advice, wizard! But how do we stop moving when the grass won't stop tickling us?!"

The group continued to laugh, trying to stand but failing miserably as the Gigglegrass worked its magic. It was as though the meadow had a mind of its own, and it wasn't going to let them go until it had its fill of laughter.

Finally, after what felt like an eternity of giggles, Alarion managed to calm down enough to think clearly. "Okay... okay... I think I have an idea. We need to... hop!"

"Hop?!" Tarin exclaimed, still laughing but trying to focus. "How is hopping going to help?!"

"Ha ha ha... because... if we don't let the grass touch our feet for too long... maybe it won't tickle us as much! Just... hop from spot to spot!" Alarion explained through his laughter.

It wasn't the most logical plan, but at this point, they were willing to try anything to escape the giggling madness. One by one, they all began hopping across the meadow, laughing less with each leap. The grass still tickled them, but it wasn't nearly as intense as before.

Lydia, ever the athletic one, was the first to reach the edge of the meadow, her giggles finally subsiding. "It's working! We're almost out!"

Alarion followed suit, hopping awkwardly but determinedly, with Tarin and Selwyn right behind him. As they leaped from patch to patch, their laughter grew softer until, at last, they reached the other side of the meadow and collapsed in a heap, exhausted but finally free of the Gigglegrass's grasp.

For a moment, none of them spoke, catching their breath after the giggle-filled ordeal. Then, Tarin let out a low chuckle. "Well, that was... unexpected."

Lydia, still wiping tears of laughter from her eyes, grinned. "I don't think I've ever laughed so hard in my life. That was ridiculous."

Selwyn, ever the scholar, adjusted his glasses and said, "I must say, that was quite the experience. I've read about Gigglegrass before, but experiencing it firsthand... it's something else."

Alarion, lying flat on his back and staring up at the sky, couldn't help but smile. "Well, at least we can say we survived the Meadow of Mirth. And who knows? Maybe next time we'll bring a picnic and make a day of it."

The group burst into laughter again, but this time it was from their own amusement, not the enchanted grass. As they lay there, surrounded by the gentle hum of the meadow, they knew this would be one adventure they'd never forget—an adventure filled with laughter, unexpected joy, and the magic of Gigglegrass.

As the sun set over the horizon, casting a golden glow over the meadow, Alarion couldn't help but think that sometimes, the best adventures are the ones that leave you laughing all the way through.

Chapter 26: The Sneezing Dragon

A *dragon sneezes fire whenever it laughs, and Alarion must keep it entertained without turning the forest into a barbeque!*

It was a crisp morning when Alarion ventured into the Thistlewood Forest. The trees towered high, their branches swaying gently in the breeze, casting long shadows over the forest floor. Alarion, ever curious and eager for adventure, was on a simple errand—a request from an old friend to retrieve a rare herb that grew only in the heart of the forest. He had expected nothing more than a peaceful stroll, a bit of foraging, and perhaps some quiet contemplation by the riverbank.

But, as it often happened in Alarion's life, things took a turn for the unexpected.

He had just bent down to inspect a patch of silver thistle, the very herb he was searching for, when the ground rumbled beneath his feet. The vibration was slight at first, but it grew stronger, shaking the earth in rhythmic bursts. Alarion stood up, his hand instinctively going to his wand as he scanned the treeline for the source of the disturbance.

Then, he heard it—a sound unlike anything he had encountered before. It was a deep, guttural laugh, followed by an enormous sneeze.

"ACHOO!" The sound echoed through the forest like thunder, and with it, a burst of flame shot into the sky, illuminating the canopy.

Alarion's eyes widened. "What in the world was that?"

He didn't have to wait long to find out. From behind a nearby thicket, there emerged a creature of myth and legend—a dragon. Its scales shimmered in shades of emerald and gold, catching the sunlight that filtered through the trees. Its eyes were a warm amber, but its expression was one of apology, as though it was embarrassed by the fiery sneeze it had just unleashed.

The dragon was massive, easily the size of a small cottage, but its demeanor was far from menacing. In fact, it looked quite friendly, if not a little sheepish. Alarion took a cautious step forward, his wand still in hand but lowered.

"Hello there," Alarion called out, trying to keep his voice calm despite the racing of his heart. "Are you alright?"

The dragon sniffled, its nostrils flaring slightly, but to Alarion's surprise, it didn't seem inclined to attack. Instead, it blinked at him with watery eyes and let out a soft, mournful sigh.

"I'm terribly sorry," the dragon rumbled, its voice deep but kind. "I seem to have caught a bit of a cold."

Alarion blinked in surprise. A cold? For a dragon?

"Wait," Alarion said, trying to process the situation. "You sneeze fire?"

The dragon nodded glumly, sitting back on its haunches and wrapping its tail around itself. "Whenever I laugh... or sneeze, which happens to be quite often when I'm under the weather." It looked around at the slightly charred trees nearby and winced. "As you can see, it's a bit of a problem."

Alarion couldn't help but chuckle. "That's... well, that's something you don't hear every day."

The dragon's face brightened slightly at Alarion's laughter, but then its expression grew serious. "I try to keep myself away from the village and the forest, but... sometimes, well... something funny happens, and I can't help it."

"Funny, you say?" Alarion raised an eyebrow. He was starting to understand the dragon's predicament. "So, what do you do when something makes you laugh?"

The dragon sighed again. "I try not to laugh, of course. But it's difficult, especially when you've been told to stay serious all the time." The dragon sniffed, its nostrils flaring again. "And now with this cold... well, you can imagine the chaos."

Alarion looked around at the singed foliage and nodded. "I can see how that might cause some trouble."

Just then, the dragon sneezed again, and a small burst of flame shot into the air. Alarion ducked instinctively, though the flames were nowhere near him.

"Bless you," he said with a grin.

"Thank you," the dragon mumbled, looking thoroughly embarrassed.

Alarion couldn't help but feel sorry for the creature. He had always imagined dragons as fearsome, fire-breathing beasts, but this one seemed more like a clumsy, overgrown puppy with an unfortunate habit of setting things on fire. And the more Alarion thought about it, the more ridiculous—and endearing—the situation became.

"I'm Alarion, by the way," he said, taking a step closer to the dragon, whose mood seemed to lift slightly at the introduction. "And you are?"

The dragon's amber eyes sparkled. "I'm Thistle... after the forest, you know. I've lived here for centuries."

"Well, Thistle," Alarion said, "I think we can work something out. But first, maybe we can do something about your cold?"

Thistle's snout twitched. "You know how to cure a dragon cold?"

"I know a few things about herbs," Alarion said, smiling. "And I happen to be gathering some silver thistle, which is great for colds, dragon or otherwise. I just need to mix it with some honey root, and you should feel better in no time."

Thistle's eyes lit up with hope. "That would be wonderful! But... what if I laugh in the meantime?"

Alarion thought for a moment, then grinned mischievously. "We'll have to make sure nothing too funny happens."

But as it turned out, keeping a dragon from laughing was no easy task. Alarion, with his quick wit and natural charm, had a habit of making even the grumpiest creatures laugh. And Thistle, with his warm personality, seemed particularly susceptible to Alarion's accidental humor.

As Alarion gathered the herbs, he recounted stories of his past adventures—tales of clumsy wizards and talking squirrels, of magical puddles and enchanted forests. Thistle tried to stay serious, but the more Alarion spoke, the harder it became for the dragon to contain his laughter.

At one point, Alarion slipped on a particularly slick patch of moss and fell flat on his back. Thistle let out a deep, rumbling laugh that shook the trees, and before Alarion could scramble to his feet, another fiery sneeze shot into the air.

"ACHOO!"

A small burst of fire singed a nearby bush, but neither Alarion nor Thistle could stop laughing.

"You... ha ha... really shouldn't laugh when I'm telling you to keep it in!" Alarion said between gasps of laughter.

"I'm sorry!" Thistle wheezed, trying to compose himself. "But you're so... clumsy!"

The two of them were soon laughing so hard that Alarion had tears in his eyes, and Thistle's fiery sneezes were lighting up the forest like a series of small fireworks. But despite the chaos, neither of them could stop.

Eventually, after several more sneezes and more than a few singed bushes, Alarion managed to brew a remedy using the silver thistle and honey root. He presented the potion to Thistle, who eagerly gulped it down.

"Ahh," Thistle sighed, his sneezes finally subsiding. "That feels much better. Thank you, Alarion. You've saved me—and the forest—from quite the fiery disaster."

Alarion smiled. "All in a day's work."

As the sun began to set, casting a golden glow over the forest, Thistle gave Alarion a grateful nod. "You're always welcome here, friend. And next time, I promise to keep the sneezes to a minimum."

Alarion chuckled. "I'll hold you to that."

And as he walked away, leaving the now-contented dragon behind, he couldn't help but think that sometimes, even the fiercest creatures just need a little laughter—and a lot of understanding.

As for Thistle, he would go on to be known as the Sneezing Dragon, but thanks to Alarion's cleverness and kindness, the forest would remain standing—and filled with laughter—for years to come.

Chapter 27: The Ice Cream Spell

After finding a spell for making the best ice cream, Alarion accidentally covers the entire village in delicious, sticky goodness. A sweet disaster ensues!

Alarion had been poring over ancient spell books in his cozy study for hours. The evening light filtered through the windows, casting a warm, golden glow across the room. The gentle crackling of the fireplace was the only sound that interrupted his intense concentration. His quest? To find a spell so special, so irresistible, that it would bring joy to the village after a long, hot summer.

And what better way to spread happiness than with ice cream?

While flipping through one of the dustiest, oldest tomes in his collection, Alarion stumbled upon a recipe for "The Perfect Ice Cream Spell". The instructions were simple, yet promising—an enchanted incantation that would conjure the most mouthwatering, irresistible ice cream ever tasted. It had the power to make anyone who took a bite smile, no matter how gloomy they felt.

Excited by the prospect, Alarion leaned back in his chair with a grin. He could already picture the delighted faces of the villagers as they tasted the frozen treat on this particularly hot day. He wasted no time, gathering his ingredients: a pinch of frost berry dust, a few sugar crystals from the enchanted sugar fields, and a dash of vanilla essence from the magical beans he kept in his pantry.

"This will be a sweet spell to remember," Alarion chuckled, rubbing his hands together in excitement. He stood in the middle of his kitchen, wand in hand, ready to cast the spell. "Let's make this the best ice cream the village has ever seen."

He spoke the ancient words of the spell, swirling his wand in the air, and a burst of light filled the room. At first, everything seemed perfect. A gentle frost spread across the kitchen counter, forming into a tub of creamy, smooth ice cream. The aroma of vanilla and sugar filled the air. Alarion dipped a spoon into the mixture, giving it a taste.

It was exquisite—smooth, rich, and utterly delightful.

But just as he was about to conjure up more servings for the village, something strange happened. The ice cream tub began to bubble. Slowly at first, but then it started expanding—growing larger and larger.

"Uh-oh..." Alarion muttered, his eyes widening as the tub began to overflow, spilling sticky sweetness onto the floor.

In seconds, the ice cream wasn't just expanding—it was multiplying. Buckets of it appeared from thin air, overflowing in every direction. Scoops of different Flavors—chocolate, strawberry, mango, and more—began rolling across the floor, each more delicious-looking than the last.

"I think I overdid it," Alarion groaned, scrambling to control the situation. But before he could cast a counter-spell, the ice cream spilled out of his house and began rolling down the hill into the village below. He could only watch in horror as his creation turned into an ice cream avalanche.

By the time he made it down to the village square, the damage had already been done. The entire town was covered in a thick, sticky layer of ice cream. Trees were draped in whipped cream, rooftops had scoops of strawberry and pistachio stuck to them, and the streets were flowing with rivers of melted chocolate.

The villagers stood in the midst of the chaos, staring in disbelief at the sweet disaster that had befallen them. But their shock didn't last long.

It started with a single laugh from a small boy, who was gleefully licking a chocolate-covered tree. Then, a group of children nearby began tossing scoops of vanilla ice cream at one another, giggling uncontrollably. Before long, the entire village was swept up in the hilarity of it all.

"This is the best accident ever!" one villager shouted as they waded through the streets, scooping up chunks of ice cream with their hands.

Alarion, now knee-deep in a sea of cookie dough ice cream, couldn't help but laugh. "I guess I gave them more ice cream than I planned," he said to himself.

As the villagers enjoyed the unexpected treat, Alarion noticed a figure approaching through the swirl of whipped cream and sprinkles. It was none other than Liora, the village baker and one of Alarion's dearest friends. Her apron was splattered with chocolate sauce, and she held a massive scoop of mint ice cream in her hand, but she didn't seem upset—in fact, she was smiling, her eyes twinkling with amusement.

"Alarion," she said, laughing as she wiped a bit of whipped cream from her cheek, "I should have known this was you're doing."

Alarion scratched his head sheepishly. "I was trying to make a small batch of ice cream, not... well, not this."

Liora's laughter was infectious. "Well, I'd say you've succeeded in making everyone's day much sweeter, even if it's a little... messy."

Just as Alarion was about to apologize, Liora took a spoonful of the mint ice cream she was holding and playfully flicked it at him, hitting him squarely on the nose. He blinked in surprise, then burst into laughter.

"Oh, so that's how it's going to be?" he grinned, grabbing a scoop of his own. "I hope you're ready for an ice cream battle!"

What followed was nothing short of a joyous, sticky war of sweetness. Liora and Alarion chased each other through the streets, tossing scoops of ice cream back and forth, laughing until their sides ached. The villagers, seeing the fun, joined in, turning the entire village square into an impromptu ice cream battleground.

By the time the sun began to set, the village was still a delicious mess, but the laughter and smiles were worth every bit of the sticky chaos. The air smelled of sugar and cream, and everyone had their fill of frozen treats. The village had never been so happy.

As the day wound down, Alarion and Liora sat together on a bench, both covered in a rainbow of melted ice cream. Liora leaned against him, a soft smile on her face. "You know, Alarion, you may have accidentally turned the village into a dessert, but you also brought a lot of joy."

Alarion, his heart warmed by her words and her closeness, smiled back. "I guess even magical mistakes can have sweet outcomes."

They sat in comfortable silence for a moment, watching the sunset over the village, the sky painted in shades of pink and orange that mirrored the strawberry and mango ice cream beneath their feet.

Liora turned to him with a teasing smile. "Just promise me that next time you try a new spell, you'll let me help."

Alarion chuckled, giving her a playful nudge. "Deal. But no promises that we won't end up covered in cake next time."

And with that, the day ended in laughter, sweetness, and a little more romance than Alarion had expected. Despite the ice cream catastrophe, he couldn't help but feel that things had turned out perfectly—messy, but perfect.

As the stars twinkled above and the village slowly returned to normal, Alarion couldn't wait for his next magical adventure, especially if it meant sharing it with Liora by his side.

Chapter 28: The Time-Telling Turtle

A larion meets a turtle that boasts about knowing the exact time. When asked, it answers with a riddle, leading to a race against time to figure it out!

Alarion had always been fascinated by strange creatures, but none intrigued him more than the rumor he heard from a group of traveling merchants. They spoke of an ancient turtle who not only could tell the time, but claimed to know time itself. Supposedly, it could tell the exact time of day, down to the last second, without ever needing to look at the sun, moon, or stars.

Intrigued and always eager for a mystery, Alarion set off on yet another adventure. Deep in the enchanted forest, beneath a canopy of towering trees and lush greenery, lay the turtle's abode, a small pond known to be untouched by time. The pond's surface was still, reflecting the sky like a perfect mirror. It was the kind of place that made time feel slow, yet oddly important—like every second was both precious and eternal.

As Alarion approached the pond, he noticed something peculiar: a trail of clocks, some broken and others ticking away, leading towards a large rock in the centre of the pond. And on that rock sat the most unusual creature he had ever seen—a massive turtle with a shell patterned like a clock face. Its wrinkled skin suggested centuries of wisdom, but its expression held a playful glimmer, as if it enjoyed being at the centre of such a grand mystery.

"Well, well, well," the turtle spoke, its voice slow and deep, yet filled with amusement. "What brings you here, young mage? Seeking the time, are we?"

Alarion grinned, already sensing this was going to be an interesting encounter. "You must be the famous time-telling turtle I've heard about. I have to admit, I'm curious. Do you really know the time—right now?"

The turtle chuckled, a sound that seemed to stretch out, much like its words. "Oh, I know more than just the time, my dear. I know time itself. But it's not so simple. To know time is to understand the riddle of life. And no answer comes without a question."

\Alarion raised an eyebrow, already sensing the twist. "So, you're saying that you'll tell me the time... if I can answer a riddle?"

"Indeed," the turtle replied, its wise eyes gleaming. "But beware. Time is slippery, and not all who chase it find what they're looking for."

Alarion nodded. "I accept your challenge, wise one. Let's hear this riddle of yours."

The turtle shifted slightly on the rock, its large, creaky body moving with the grace of something that knew the world better than most. "Here it is," it began, slowly and deliberately:

"I am in every moment, yet I'm never seen.

I'm always ahead but never have been.

I tick without a sound, I run without a race.

Though you chase me, I vanish without a trace.

What am I?"

Alarion stood there, pondering the words carefully. The riddle seemed simple enough at first glance, but like all good riddles, it twisted his thoughts the more he thought about it. It spoke of something that was both there and not there, something elusive and ever-present.

"Time," Alarion thought immediately. But knowing this was the turtle's specialty, he suspected the answer was not so direct.

While he considered his next move, a soft voice interrupted his thoughts. He turned to see Liora, the village baker, approaching from the forest path. She had been delivering pies to a neighbouring town when she saw Alarion disappear into the forest, curiosity driving her to follow.

"Alarion, what are you up to now?" she asked with a playful smile, her eyes gleaming with the kind of fondness that always made Alarion's heart flutter a little. She walked up beside him, her basket of pies swaying gently from her arm.

"Oh, just trying to figure out what time it is," Alarion said, grinning at her in return. "But apparently, I have to solve a riddle first."

Liora's curiosity was instantly piqued. "A riddle? Let me hear it. I've always loved a good puzzle."

Alarion repeated the turtle's riddle, and Liora listened carefully, her eyes narrowing in thought. As they stood there in silence, trying to work out the answer, the turtle chuckled again, clearly enjoying the spectacle of two minds at work.

"It's not just time, is it?" Liora said after a moment, her voice soft but thoughtful. "The riddle says 'I'm always ahead, but never have been.' That sounds like... the future, doesn't it?"

Alarion's eyes lit up. "Of course! The future! It's always ahead of us, but it's never something we've experienced. That must be it!"

He turned back to the turtle. "The answer is the future."

The turtle's eyes gleamed, its mouth curving into a slow, knowing smile. "Ah, you're sharp, young ones. The future indeed. Ever ahead, never grasped. Well, done."

Alarion grinned triumphantly, but the turtle wasn't done. "Now that you've answered my riddle, I shall tell you the time..." It paused for dramatic effect. "But there's one more catch."

Alarion's face fell slightly. "Another one?"

The turtle nodded, chuckling again. "Time isn't as easy to tell as you think. For you see, time changes depending on who asks."

Liora tilted her head, intrigued. "What do you mean?"

"I mean, dear Liora," the turtle said, "the time for Alarion is not the same as the time for you. Time is a personal thing—ever moving, ever flowing. For Alarion, the time is one of adventure, of seeking knowledge, and of discovery. But for you, Liora, the time is... sweeter. It's a time for connection, for laughter, and perhaps, for something more."

The turtle's eyes twinkled mischievously as Liora blushed, her gaze briefly meeting Alarion's.

Alarion, however, didn't quite catch the deeper meaning. "So, what you're saying is that time isn't just numbers on a clock?"

"Exactly," the turtle replied. "For you, young mage, the time is now to pay attention to more than just spells and adventures. There's something—someone—right in front of you who holds time just as dearly as you do."

This time, Alarion caught on, his heart skipping a beat. He glanced at Liora, who was still smiling shyly at the turtle's words. For a moment, the world seemed to slow, as if time itself had paused to let the two of them share that one fleeting look.

"Well," Alarion said, breaking the silence with a grin, "I suppose the time is also ripe for some pie. What do you say, Liora? Fancy sharing one of those pies by the pond?"

Liora laughed, her blush deepening but her smile bright and genuine. "I'd love that. But next time, I'll ask the turtle for the riddle."

As the two of them sat by the pond, sharing pie and laughter, the turtle watched with a contented smile. It had known the time all along—not just the hours or the minutes, but the perfect moment for something new to begin.

In the distance, the sun began to set, casting a golden glow over the pond. The future, ever ahead, was already looking bright.

Chapter 29: The Floating Festival

During a floating festival, Alarion accidentally ends up in a hot air balloon that floats a little too high. The view is amazing, but how will he get down?

It was a day of celebration in the magical village of Valtorin, and the air was buzzing with excitement. Alarion had arrived just in time for the Floating Festival, an annual event where villagers sent colorful lanterns into the sky and floated their wishes into the heavens. It was a day full of joy, laughter, and most exciting of all—hot air balloons. Every year, balloonists from all corners of the land gathered to show off their vibrant, whimsical airships, each one more elaborate than the next. The balloons weren't just transport; they were floating works of art, with massive balloons shaped like dragons, unicorns, and even a giant teapot bobbing up and down in the breeze.

Alarion, ever the adventurer, had heard about this festival and simply couldn't resist. As he wandered through the festival grounds, the smell of sweet cinnamon buns and roasting chestnuts filled the air. Children ran around with sparkling wands, and couples held hands as they gazed up at the balloons. The atmosphere was light, magical, and full of the kind of cheer that made Alarion feel like he had stumbled into a fairy tale.

"Care to take a ride?" a voice interrupted his thoughts.

Alarion turned to see a young woman with a mischievous grin standing beside a particularly large hot air balloon. The balloon was shaped like a giant fish, with shimmering scales that reflected the sunlight. Its basket was large enough to carry a small group, but at the moment, it was empty except for the woman and a few stray ropes dangling from the sides.

"I promise the view is worth it," she added, tilting her head and giving him a wink. She had deep auburn hair and eyes that sparkled with the same energy as the festival itself. Her name, as Alarion would soon learn, was Elira, and she was the pilot of this magnificent flying fish.

Alarion was sold. He had flown on many magical creatures, but never in something as whimsical as a flying fish hot air balloon. He hopped into the basket with enthusiasm. "Why not? I could use a little height to appreciate the whole festival from above."

Elira pulled a lever, releasing the ropes that held the balloon to the ground. Slowly, the basket began to rise. The village, with its busy stalls and cheerful faces, shrank beneath them as they ascended into the sky. The festival grounds turned into a patchwork quilt of color—reds, blues, and golds from the floating lanterns dotting the horizon.

"This is incredible!" Alarion shouted, the wind whipping through his hair. The view was, as promised, breathtaking. Below them, the river shimmered in the sunlight, the forests beyond the village swayed gently, and the entire world seemed to stretch out infinitely.

Elira laughed, clearly enjoying his excitement. "First time in a hot air balloon?"

"First time in a fish-shaped one, that's for sure!" Alarion joked, leaning over the edge to get a better look at the tiny festival-goers below.

However, as the balloon continued to rise, something unexpected happened. A sudden gust of wind hit them, and before Elira could react, the fish balloon drifted higher—much higher than intended. Alarion grabbed onto the edge of the basket, his eyes wide as they soared upward into the clouds.

"Elira, uh... I think we're going a bit higher than planned!" he called out, trying to keep his voice steady as the ground below became a distant blur.

Elira, for her part, didn't seem particularly worried, though a smirk played on her lips. "Relax, Alarion. What's life without a little adventure?"

The balloon swayed as they entered a fluffy cloud, turning the world around them into a hazy mist. Alarion could barely see anything but white. His heart raced, but part of him couldn't help but feel the thrill of it all. The rush of the wind, the unknown of how they were going to get down—it was the kind of unpredictable twist he thrived on. But this time, he wasn't alone.

"Tell me," Elira's voice cut through the mist, "are you always this serious, or is that just because we're dangling thousands of feet above the ground?"

Alarion blinked, caught off guard by her playful tone. He glanced over at her and noticed how at ease she seemed, her auburn hair floating slightly in the breeze, her grin as wide as ever. There was something infectious about her energy, something that made him want to laugh despite their predicament.

"Me? Serious?" Alarion chuckled. "I think you've got the wrong wizard. I just wasn't expecting to be sky-bound quite so... enthusiastically."

Elira laughed. "Well, welcome to the Floating Festival, Alarion! It's full of surprises—just like life, don't you think?"

There was a pause as Alarion considered her words. He had been on countless adventures, solved riddles, fought monsters, and faced dangers of all kinds, but this moment—this strange, light hearted ascent into the clouds with a stranger who seemed to find joy in everything—felt different. In the midst of his thoughts, the clouds began to part, revealing a sunset that painted the sky in hues of pink, orange, and purple.

"Wow," Alarion breathed, leaning on the basket's edge to take it all in. "That's... stunning."

"See? Sometimes, all it takes is a little height to get a new perspective," Elira said softly, standing beside him. Her arm brushed against his, and for a moment, the world seemed to slow down.

Alarion glanced at her, his heart beating a little faster, though he wasn't sure if it was from the height or the company. "You might be onto something," he admitted, feeling a strange warmth in his chest that had nothing to do with the sunset.

But just as the moment grew a little too quiet, a loud, rumbling sound echoed from above them. Alarion looked up, and his eyes widened in shock. "Uh, Elira... is that...?"

"Yep," Elira replied with a grin, not looking the least bit concerned. "That's a flock of sky eagles."

Before he could even think to ask what a sky eagle was, the giant birds swooped down, their powerful wings causing the balloon to rock violently. Alarion clutched the side of the basket as the balloon tipped, sending them spinning and swaying.

"Hold on!" Elira shouted, though she was laughing as she fought to regain control of the balloon.

The ride became a whirlwind of chaos and laughter. Alarion found himself clinging to the edge of the basket, laughing despite himself as the birds darted around them. Somehow, amidst the flurry of feathers and frantic flapping, they began to descend slowly, the wind now carrying them back toward the festival grounds.

Finally, after what felt like an eternity of laughing, shouting, and the occasional dive to avoid an eagle, the balloon touched down—albeit a bit roughly—just outside the village.

Alarion stumbled out of the basket, his legs shaky but his spirits high. Elira followed, landing gracefully on her feet, her eyes still sparkling with mischief.

"Well," she said, brushing off her dress, "that was a ride to remember, wouldn't you say?"

Alarion looked at her, then back at the sky, then back at her again. A grin spread across his face as he shook his head. "You certainly know how to keep things interesting."

Elira winked. "What's life without a little fun?"

As they walked back toward the festival together, Alarion couldn't help but feel that this was one adventure he'd never forget—especially since it wasn't the sky that had left him breathless.

Chapter 30: The Sneaky Wind

A *playful wind swirls around Alarion, stealing his hat and causing a ruckus. Their chase turns into a hilarious game of tag!*

The sun shone brightly over the village of Valtorin as Alarion set out for a leisurely stroll. After the adventures of the Floating Festival, he felt refreshed and invigorated, ready to enjoy a peaceful day. The flowers were in full bloom, their colors vibrant against the green of the grass, and the air was filled with the sweet fragrance of spring. But as Alarion took a deep breath, a mischievous breeze rustled through the trees, catching his attention.

"Hey there, little wind!" he called out, grinning as he tipped his hat toward the playful gust. It was one of those magical days when everything felt a little more alive. But the moment he settled his hat comfortably on his head, the wind seemed to take offense.

With a sudden swoosh, the breeze whipped around him, lifting his hat right off his head and sending it soaring into the air!

"Hey! Come back here!" Alarion shouted, watching his favorite hat float away like a feather. It was no ordinary hat; it was a whimsical creation he'd fashioned himself, decorated with tiny stars and moon charms that twinkled in the sunlight. The last thing he wanted was for the sneaky wind to carry it off to who-knows-where!

The wind swirled around him, taunting him with little gusts, as if daring him to chase it. Alarion felt a mix of frustration and amusement. "Is this some sort of game to you?" he yelled, starting to run after the retreating hat.

As he sprinted down the village path, the wind picked up speed, dancing just out of reach. Alarion chased after it, zigzagging through market stalls where vendors were setting up for the day, all while trying to avoid knocking over anything that might be in his path.

"Watch it!" an elderly lady shouted, clutching her basket of apples as Alarion narrowly avoided her.

"Sorry! It's the wind!" he called back, but the lady just shook her head, muttering about young people these days. The wind only seemed to get more playful, swirling around Alarion, blowing his hair into a wild mess.

It darted around a corner, and Alarion, determined not to lose sight of his beloved hat, followed with an eager grin. The chase led him to the village square, where a group of children were playing. The wind swooped low, teasing them, making their kites flap wildly as it danced in delight.

"Look out!" one of the children shouted, laughing as Alarion barrelled into the square, his arms flailing as he tried to catch up with the elusive breeze.

"Stop that wind!" another child yelled, joining in the chase. It seemed like Alarion wasn't the only one enchanted by the cheeky gust. The children chased after him, squealing with laughter as they joined forces against the wind that had stolen Alarion's hat.

Alarion could hardly contain his own laughter as they all ran around, the wind continuing to swirl and dart, now accompanied by a band of giggling children. It felt like a scene out of a storybook, one filled with laughter and joy. But as they ran, the wind took an unexpected turn and darted toward the fountain in the middle of the square.

"No, no, not the fountain!" Alarion shouted, but it was too late. The wind teased the water, swirling it into a mini whirlwind that shot droplets high into the air, glistening like diamonds in the sunlight. And right in the middle of that watery dance, Alarion's hat landed—plop!—right in the centre of the fountain.

"Great," he muttered, watching as the wind circled back around him, as if to say, "You're not getting your hat back that easily!"

The children burst into giggles at the sight of Alarion's predicament. "You'll have to jump in!" one of them teased.

With a dramatic sigh, Alarion approached the fountain, glancing at the cool water. "I suppose it's better than letting it get soaked," he reasoned, grinning at the thought of what a silly sight this was.

"On the count of three!" he called, and the children gathered around, excited to see what would happen next. "One… two… three!"

With that, Alarion leaped into the fountain, splashing water everywhere as he landed. The coolness enveloped him, and he let out a laugh that echoed in the square. The wind, now swirling playfully around him, seemed to encourage his antics.

"Gotcha!" he exclaimed, reaching for his hat, which was bobbing on the surface like a buoy. Just as he grabbed it, the wind blew in a gust, sending a wave of water cascading over him and the children.

"Alarion's making a splash!" one child shouted, doubling over in laughter.

"Watch out for the sneaky wind!" another chimed in, pointing at the way the breeze darted in and out, almost as if it was enjoying the chaos.

Soaked but triumphant, Alarion pulled his hat out of the water and placed it back on his head. The hat was a little soggy, but it still looked charming against the backdrop of his dishevelled hair.

"Thanks for the chase, my whimsical friend!" he called out to the wind, grinning as he turned to the children. "Who knew a hat could lead to such fun?"

The wind swirled around him one last time, lifting the hat slightly as if to say goodbye, before it dashed off toward the hills, leaving behind a trail of laughter.

As Alarion climbed out of the fountain, dripping wet and utterly carefree, he was met with a chorus of applause from the children. He took a theatrical bow, feeling lighter than air. This silly, spontaneous adventure had reminded him of the simple joys in life, the kind that were often overlooked in his quest for grand adventures.

"Want to play another round?" Alarion asked, winking at the children. "I'm sure the wind will be back for more fun!"

With that, the chase resumed, laughter ringing through the village square as they all took off again, ready to take on the next gust of mischief. The playful wind might have stolen Alarion's hat, but it had gifted him a day of joy and camaraderie—an adventure that would live on in the hearts of everyone involved. And as he chased after the children, Alarion couldn't help but think that sometimes, it was the smallest things—a mischievous wind and a hat— that created the biggest memories.

Chapter 31: The Potion of Giggles

Alarion accidentally drinks a potion that makes him laugh uncontrollably. His laughter becomes contagious, turning the whole village into a giggle fest!

In the heart of Valtorin, nestled between the bustling marketplace and the tranquil river, lay the curious little shop of Zilba the Potion Master. The shop was renowned for its colorful concoctions, each with a distinct charm—some to heal, others to enhance, and a few that promised the most delightful surprises. Today, Alarion felt particularly adventurous and decided to visit Zilba's shop, hoping to find something unique.

As he entered, the fragrant scent of herbs and spices enveloped him like a warm hug. Bottles of every size and color lined the shelves, each labelled with names that piqued his curiosity: "Elixir of Endless Energy," "Potion of Purring Kitties," and "Serum of Super Strength." But it was the brightly colored bottle labelled "Potion of Giggles" that caught his eye.

"What's this one do?" Alarion asked, picking it up and examining the contents—a swirling mixture of vibrant blues, pinks, and yellows.

Zilba, with her wild hair and twinkling eyes, emerged from behind a counter stacked high with potion ingredients. "Ah! The Potion of Giggles! It's a delightful concoction that induces laughter and joy! Just a sip will have you chuckling for hours!" She winked playfully.

Alarion's curiosity piqued even more. He loved a good laugh and could use a bit of fun, especially after the somewhat serious adventures he had recently endured. "How much?" he asked, eager to bring home a little joy.

"For you, dear Alarion, just one shiny gold coin!" Zilba replied, her eyes sparkling.

Without hesitation, Alarion handed over the coin and took the potion. "Cheers!" he said with a grin, raising the bottle to his lips. He took a hearty sip, savoring the sweet, fruity flavour. But almost immediately, a peculiar sensation washed over him.

"Uh-oh," he mumbled, feeling a tickle in his throat. Before he knew it, an uncontrollable laugh erupted from his mouth, a deep belly laugh that echoed through the tiny shop. Zilba burst into laughter alongside him, the joy infectious.

"Looks like it works!" she exclaimed between giggles.

Alarion stumbled out of the shop, still laughing, unable to contain the overwhelming mirth bubbling up inside him. The moment he stepped into the village square, his laughter rang out, and passersby turned to see what was happening.

"What's so funny?" a baker called out from his stall, flour dusting his apron.

"I don't know!" Alarion managed to gasp out between giggles. "But you should try it!"

And with that, the laughter spread like wildfire. The baker, intrigued, joined in Alarion's contagious giggles, clutching his belly as he doubled over. Soon, the giggles became a symphony of laughter, echoing through the square, drawing in more villagers.

"Why are we laughing?" one villager asked, bewildered but unable to resist the light hearted spirit.

"Who knows?" another replied, laughing even harder. "But it's the best feeling!"

The entire village seemed to come alive with laughter. Mothers pulled their children into the giggle fest, and even the grumpy old man who never smiled cracked a smile and joined in the ruckus. Children rolled on the ground, laughing until tears streamed down their cheeks, while couples shared gleeful glances, caught up in the joyous chaos.

But then, just as the laughter reached its peak, Alarion noticed a figure standing a little to the side, arms crossed and a bemused expression on her face. It was Lila, the girl he had been secretly smitten with for ages. She was watching the scene unfold, her lips pursed but her eyes sparkling with amusement.

"Lila!" Alarion called, trying to stifle his laughter enough to be coherent. "You have to join us!"

"Oh, really?" she teased, raising an eyebrow. "What's so funny?"

"Everything!" Alarion exclaimed, unable to hold back his chuckles. "Just take a sip! You'll see!"

With a playful glint in her eyes, Lila stepped closer, clearly intrigued despite her initial skepticism. "Alright, but if I end up laughing like a fool, it's your fault!"

"Deal!" Alarion replied, extending the potion bottle toward her. She took it, eyeing it as if it were a ticking bomb, before taking a cautious sip. Almost immediately, her expression shifted. A smile broke across her face, and then, in a heartbeat, she was engulfed in laughter.

"Alarion!" she gasped, her laughter infectious as she doubled over, clutching her stomach. "This is ridiculous!"

"Isn't it wonderful?" Alarion said, his heart racing. He couldn't remember the last time he had seen her laugh so freely.

As they laughed together, Alarion felt a warmth spread through him—something more than just joy. It was connection. It was camaraderie. And he realized, in that moment, that he was falling for her even more.

But the potion had more surprises in store. The laughter spread beyond them, attracting even more villagers, and soon, they were all dancing in the square, swept up in a wave of joy. Alarion twirled Lila around, both of them laughing uncontrollably, and in the chaos, he caught her gaze.

"Maybe this potion is a bit too effective?" he joked, his heart racing.

"Or maybe we just needed a reason to laugh!" Lila replied, leaning in closer, her eyes sparkling with mischief.

As they shared a moment, their laughter mingled with the symphony of joy around them, and Alarion realized how much he cherished this light-hearted connection with Lila. For a brief moment, everything felt perfect—like the universe had conspired to create this delightful day.

Finally, as the sun began to set, the laughter began to fade, and the villagers started to catch their breath. Alarion and Lila stood together, still giggling, the magic of the potion lingering in the air like a sweet perfume.

"Thank you for today, Alarion," Lila said, her cheeks still flushed with laughter. "This was the most fun I've had in ages!"

Alarion grinned back, feeling a flutter in his chest. "You know, I think I'll be visiting Zilba again. Who knew laughter could be so enchanting?"

As they walked back toward the river, side by side, Alarion felt a new excitement blooming. Perhaps the Potion of Giggles wasn't just about laughter. Maybe it was a catalyst for something deeper—something romantic blooming right before his eyes.

And as they chatted and chuckled together, Alarion knew that this was just the beginning of many more delightful adventures to come, filled with laughter, joy, and maybe—just maybe—a little love.

Chapter 32: The Singing Riverbank

Alarion visits a riverbank where the water sings. He attempts to harmonize but ends up splashing water everywhere, creating a comedic spectacle!

Alarion awoke one bright morning, the sun spilling golden rays across the land, warming his skin and invigorating his spirit. Today was the day he had long anticipated: a visit to the famous Singing Riverbank. Tales had spread throughout Valtorin about a magical river where the waters sang melodious tunes that could charm even the most hardened heart. Naturally, Alarion's heart—filled with curiosity and a bit of mischief—was drawn to it like a bee to blooming flowers.

He packed a small satchel with some essentials—a few snacks, his trusty lute, and a journal to capture the day's adventures. With a bounce in his step, he set off toward the riverbank, imagining the kind of melodies he might hear and the songs he could contribute. His heart raced at the thought of harmonizing with the river's song.

After a short hike through a vibrant forest teeming with flowers and chirping birds, Alarion finally reached the riverbank. He stood in awe. The water sparkled under the sunlight, and as he approached, the gentle flow of the river greeted him with soft, enchanting notes. It was as if the river was alive, its bubbling laughter resonating in the air, weaving in and out of a melody that was both calming and uplifting.

"Wow," he murmured, unable to take his eyes off the glimmering surface. "This is incredible!"

Not wanting to miss out on the opportunity, Alarion plopped himself down on the soft grass by the riverbank and took out his lute.

He tuned it carefully, then strummed a few gentle chords, trying to match the river's rhythm. But as he began to sing, the river's melody shifted, as if it were trying to respond.

"♦ Flowing water, dancing light,
Underneath the sun so bright.
Join me in this song so sweet,
Let's make magic, oh what a treat! ♦"

As he sang, he became more animated, completely lost in the moment. He swayed and strummed, trying to encourage the river to join in harmony with him. But just as he was getting into the groove, he leaned too far over the bank to catch a better note, and with a mighty sploosh, he fell right into the water!

"Whoa!" Alarion gasped as he splashed around, the cool water wrapping around him like an unexpected embrace. He couldn't help but laugh at himself, his voice mingling with the river's melody, creating a comical tune of its own.

"♦ Splashing Alarion, in the stream,
What a sight! What a dream!
With water everywhere, oh what a scene,
Dancing like a silly marine! ♦"

Just then, amidst the laughter and splashing, he noticed a figure standing on the opposite bank, doubled over with laughter. It was Lila! She had come to join him on his adventure, but it seemed she was getting an unexpected show instead.

"Alarion!" she called out between giggles. "You look like a fish out of water—literally!"

He wiped the water from his face, his cheeks reddening with a mix of embarrassment and delight. "I was just trying to harmonize! It seems I've made a splash instead!"

Lila stepped closer, her laughter echoing against the sweet melodies of the river. "I've never seen anyone perform a solo quite like that! You've turned this riverbank into a comedy show!"

Emboldened by her presence and laughter, Alarion decided to turn his misfortune into an opportunity for fun. "Join me! Let's create the silliest duet this river has ever heard!"

"Alright!" Lila said, crossing to his side, her eyes sparkling with mischief. She kicked off her sandals and waded into the water, her laughter blending with the river's song.

They began to sing together, Lila's voice rising melodiously with Alarion's. Their playful lyrics reflected the delightful chaos around them, and the river responded with bubbling enthusiasm, amplifying their joy.

"♦ Two friends in the river, oh what a sight,
Singing and splashing with all their might!
Water's a-waltzing, the sun shining bright,
In this happy moment, everything's right! ♦"

Alarion strummed his lute, trying to keep up with Lila's voice, but every time he leaned in to get closer to her harmonies, he'd splash water everywhere, drenching them both. Lila's laughter rang out as she playfully retaliated, splashing him back.

"Hey! No fair!" he laughed, trying to dodge the waves of water that she sent his way.

They continued their light hearted battle, laughter echoing across the riverbank. At one point, Lila splashed him so hard that he lost his balance and fell backward, sending a cascade of water splattering up into the air. The sun glinted off the droplets, creating a rainbow of colors that danced between them.

"Look! You've created a water rainbow!" Lila exclaimed, pointing at the shimmering spectacle above them. Alarion gazed in wonder, his heart swelling with happiness. In this magical moment, surrounded by laughter and beauty, everything felt perfect.

"Let's celebrate our artistic talents with a real performance!" Alarion suggested, regaining his footing. "How about we create a water dance?"

"A water dance?" Lila repeated, raising an eyebrow, clearly intrigued.

"Yes! We can jump and splash around while we sing. It'll be a grand spectacle!" he declared; his enthusiasm contagious.

And so, with the river as their stage and the sun casting a warm glow around them, Alarion and Lila began their grand water dance. They splashed and twirled, their voices blending into a melody that echoed through the trees, enchanting everyone who passed by.

"◇ Dancing, splashing, singing free,
Come and join this jubilee!
With laughter ringing through the air,
Let's dance and splash without care! ◇"

As they twirled and leaped, Alarion felt an undeniable connection to Lila. Her laughter filled his heart with warmth, and he found himself wishing the moment would never end.

After a while, they finally collapsed onto the grassy bank, panting and giggling. The river continued its song around them, a gentle backdrop to their joyful escapade.

"Who knew a singing river could lead to such a delightful mess?" Lila said, wiping a droplet of water from her cheek.

"I wouldn't have it any other way," Alarion replied, his heart fluttering as he glanced at her. "This has been the best day ever, all thanks to you."

Lila smiled back; her cheeks flushed with joy. "Well, let's make it a tradition then! Every week, we'll come back here for more singing and splashing!"

"I'd love that," Alarion said, his smile wide. "But next time, I promise to keep my feet dry!"

Lila laughed; her eyes sparkling. "No promises! I might just drag you back in!"

With their plans set, Alarion and Lila made their way back along the riverbank, leaving behind a symphony of laughter and a memory that would linger like a sweet melody in their hearts. As the sun dipped low in the sky, painting the world in hues of pink and gold, Alarion knew that this was just the beginning of many adventures to come, filled with song, laughter, and perhaps a little romance—just as enchanting as the Singing Riverbank itself.

Chapter 33: The Shy Fairy

Alarion meets a fairy who is too shy to show her magic. He convinces her to perform a small trick, leading to an unexpected shower of sparkles and laughter!

One breezy afternoon, Alarion found himself wandering through a tranquil glen nestled between the mountains of Tiderune. The sun filtered through the leaves of towering trees, casting a mosaic of light and shadows on the soft, mossy ground. He was in high spirits after his adventures at the Singing Riverbank and was eager to discover more magical surprises in this enchanting land.

As he ambled along, he spotted something unusual—a cluster of flowers shimmering with an ethereal glow. Intrigued, he approached them and was suddenly greeted by the soft flutter of wings. Alarion glanced up and saw a tiny fairy hovering nervously above the blossoms. She had delicate, iridescent wings that sparkled in the sunlight, but her face was turned away, as if she were trying to hide.

"Hello there!" Alarion called, waving enthusiastically. "You're beautiful! What's your name?"

The fairy spun around, her wings catching the light and sending little sparkles into the air. "Um... hi," she stammered, her voice barely above a whisper. "I'm Faye."

"Faye! What a lovely name," he replied, grinning. "You're a fairy! You must have some amazing magic. Why are you hiding away?"

Faye fidgeted, glancing down at her feet. "I'm just... shy. I don't really show my magic much. It's... embarrassing."

Alarion felt a pang of sympathy for the shy little creature. "But your magic must be wonderful! Everyone loves a good show. Why don't you show me a little trick? Just a small one?"

She hesitated, biting her lip. "I don't know..."

"Come on! I promise I won't tell anyone," he encouraged, trying to sound as charming as possible. "How about just one tiny sparkle? It'll be our little secret!"

Faye considered his words, her wings twitching nervously. After a moment, she took a deep breath. "Okay. Just a tiny trick..."

With a determined nod, Faye floated closer, her hands shimmering with a faint light. Alarion's heart raced with excitement as he watched her concentrate. After a few moments, she flicked her wrist, and a small burst of sparkling light shot from her fingertips, cascading down like a gentle shower of stars.

"Wow!" Alarion exclaimed, his eyes wide with delight. "That's beautiful!"

Encouraged by his reaction, Faye felt a flicker of confidence. "Really? You like it?"

"It's more than just like; it's amazing!" he replied. "Can you do it again? Maybe a bit bigger this time?"

Faye hesitated but nodded slowly, her cheeks flushing with a rosy hue. "Okay, just a little bigger..."

She concentrated again, her wings flapping faster as she gathered her magic. This time, when she waved her hands, an even larger explosion of sparkles erupted into the air, swirling around them like a galaxy of twinkling stars.

Alarion laughed in pure delight as the sparkles fell like confetti, landing softly on his hair, skin, and clothes. "You're a natural! This is fantastic!"

Seeing his genuine joy made Faye's heart flutter. Maybe showing her magic wasn't so bad after all. With a newfound sense of bravery, she decided to give it one more try. "Alright! This time, I'll do something extra special!"

With a determined look in her eyes, Faye closed her eyes and began to chant a tiny incantation, her hands weaving intricate patterns in the air. Alarion watched, spellbound, as she summoned a burst of colorful sparkles that exploded like fireworks, filling the glen with light and laughter.

But just as she finished, Faye miscalculated the strength of her magic. Instead of a gentle sprinkle, the sparkles shot out in all directions, showering the glen in a kaleidoscope of colors! Alarion laughed uncontrollably as the sparkles rained down, landing on his nose and making him sneeze.

"Ah-choo!" he laughed, sending more sparkles flying into the air. "You turned me into a glitter bomb!"

Faye giggled at the sight of him covered in sparkling dust. "I'm so sorry! I didn't mean to!"

"No need to apologize! This is the most fun I've had all week!" Alarion chuckled, brushing sparkles off his shoulders. He looked around at the enchanting scene. The flowers shimmered with the light of the fairies' magic, and the entire glen felt alive with joy. "You see, Faye? Your magic brings happiness. You have to let it shine!"

Her cheeks flushed with warmth, and for the first time, Faye felt a spark of confidence. "Maybe I should try to show my magic more often. It is kind of fun!"

"I think it's incredible! How about we create a performance together? We could invite the other fairies! Imagine how much fun that would be!" Alarion suggested, excitement dancing in his eyes.

Faye's wings fluttered with glee at the thought. "Really? You think they'd like it?"

"Of course! And I can help! We'll make it a grand show, the best Tiderune has ever seen!" Alarion said, clapping his hands together with enthusiasm.

Inspired by his encouragement, Faye felt her heart soar. "Okay! Let's do it! I can show them all my magic!"

As they began brainstorming ideas for their performance, Faye found herself laughing and sharing stories with Alarion. With each passing moment, she felt her shyness melting away, replaced by a growing sense of joy and camaraderie.

"Tell me, what's your favorite type of magic?" Alarion asked, his eyes sparkling with curiosity.

"I really like the magic of light and colors. I want to make people smile with my sparkles," Faye replied, her voice filled with hope.

"That's the best kind of magic," Alarion said sincerely. "And with your talent, I'm sure we'll have everyone in Tiderune smiling and laughing!"

The sun began to set, casting a golden glow over the glen, and the laughter of two newfound friends echoed in the air. With a sparkle in her heart and a twinkle in her eyes, Faye felt ready to embrace her magic and share it with the world.

"Okay, let's get started on our show!" Faye exclaimed, her wings shimmering brightly as she flew around Alarion, leaving a trail of sparkles behind her.

Alarion smiled, filled with admiration for his new friend. Together, they created a performance that would be talked about for years, and as they practiced, the shy fairy transformed into a vibrant spark of joy—just like the magic she wielded.

And as the stars twinkled above, Faye realized that maybe, just maybe, being shy wasn't a flaw but a part of her magic waiting to shine. With Alarion by her side, she felt ready to share her gifts with the world, one sparkle at a time.

Chapter 34: The Bubble Trouble

A bubble-blowing competition gets out of hand when Alarion accidentally creates a bubble so big it floats away with him inside!

It was a sunny morning in Tiderune, and Alarion could feel the excitement buzzing in the air like a swarm of fireflies. Today was the annual Bubble-Blowing Festival, an event famous throughout the land for its whimsical competitions and delightful entertainment. Everywhere he looked, colorful banners fluttered in the breeze, and laughter echoed through the lush meadows.

Alarion had spent the entire week practicing his bubble-blowing skills. He had even enlisted the help of his friends, Faye the shy fairy and Benny the mischievous squirrel, who promised to cheer him on. As he made his way to the festival grounds, he couldn't help but smile at the thought of the enormous bubble he was determined to create.

When he arrived, the sight was spectacular. There were booths selling bubble wands of all shapes and sizes, bubble gum galore, and even bubble-themed snacks like bubbleberry pies and fizzy drinks. Alarion's eyes sparkled with anticipation. He spotted Faye and Benny at the edge of the main stage, both wearing matching hats that looked suspiciously like bubbles.

"Hey, Alarion!" Faye called out, waving enthusiastically. "Are you ready to become the bubble champion?"

"Absolutely!" he replied, puffing out his chest with confidence. "Just watch me!"

As the festival began, the townsfolk gathered around the stage for the bubble-blowing competition. The host, a jovial gnome named Wobble, announced the rules. "The contestant who blows the biggest bubble will win a year's supply of bubble gum and the coveted Golden Bubble Trophy!"

Alarion felt a thrill of excitement course through him as he stepped up to the giant bubble wand. It was enormous, and he could already see some of the other contestants struggling to lift it. With a deep breath, he positioned himself, gave a big puff, and watched as a lovely, shimmering bubble began to take shape.

The crowd cheered, and Benny shouted, "Go, Alarion! Blow that bubble like it's a giant balloon!"

Faye fluttered her wings in excitement. "You can do it! Just believe in your magic!"

Feeling encouraged, Alarion took another deep breath and blew harder this time. The bubble grew larger and larger, stretching into the air like a shiny, iridescent balloon. But as it grew, it began to wobble dangerously.

"Oh no!" Alarion exclaimed, realizing he might have gone a bit overboard. "I think I'm going to—"

Before he could finish his thought, the bubble reached an enormous size, far beyond what anyone had ever seen. With one final puff, it expanded so quickly that it lifted him off the ground!

"Whoa!" Alarion shouted, flailing his arms as he floated upward, still trapped inside the bubble.

The crowd gasped in amazement and then burst into laughter. Wobble, trying to regain his composure, exclaimed, "Well, that's certainly one way to win the competition!"

Faye and Benny couldn't believe their eyes. "Alarion! Are you okay?" Faye shouted, trying not to giggle.

"Not really! I'm floating away!" Alarion replied, his voice rising with a mix of panic and amusement.

As he bobbed higher into the sky, he could see the entire village below, a colorful patchwork of fields and cottages. The view was breathtaking, but he quickly realized that he had no idea how to get down. "Someone help!" he called out, but his voice was lost in the wind.

Just then, Benny had an idea. "I'll climb up that tree and see if I can pop the bubble!" he yelled, pointing to a towering oak nearby.

"No! Wait! That might make things worse!" Alarion hollered, but Benny was already scampering up the tree with surprising agility.

Meanwhile, Faye fluttered nervously. "What if I try to sprinkle some fairy dust on the bubble? It might deflate gently!" she suggested, her wings buzzing with determination.

"That's worth a shot!" Alarion encouraged, now spinning slowly in midair.

Benny reached the top of the tree and positioned himself just right. "Okay, here goes nothing!" He leapt from the branch, aiming to land on the bubble.

Alarion's eyes widened as Benny landed with a soft thud, causing the bubble to sway perilously. With a little bounce, Benny stood up and began to stomp, causing ripples in the bubble surface. "C'mon, bubble! You can do it!" he cheered.

Faye sprinkled her fairy dust, which sparkled in the sunlight and drifted toward the bubble. "Be gentle, bubble!" she sang, as if the bubble could hear her.

With each stomp, the bubble began to wobble more violently, and Alarion felt the pressure shift. "This is getting a bit bouncy!" he laughed, as the bubble bounced him higher.

Then, all at once, Benny's stomps created a ripple that reached the surface of the bubble, causing it to pop with a loud bang! Alarion tumbled through the air, laughing as he fell softly onto a patch of flowers, the remnants of the bubble popping around him like confetti.

"Woohoo! I'm free!" Alarion cheered, rolling onto his back to catch his breath, laughter bubbling out of him.

Faye and Benny joined him, collapsing into giggles. "That was incredible!" Faye said between fits of laughter. "You just floated away like a balloon!"

"You should've seen the look on your face!" Benny chimed in, still chuckling. "I thought you were going to get a free ride to the moon!"

Alarion wiped tears of joy from his eyes. "That was the most ridiculous thing I've ever done! I can't believe I floated away!"

Just then, Wobble approached them, a big grin on his face. "Congratulations, Alarion! You may not have won the competition, but you've certainly won our hearts—and a special prize for the most entertaining bubble experience!"

He handed Alarion a sparkling bubble trophy, shaped like a giant bubble, adorned with glitter and ribbons. "May it remind you to never underestimate the power of a bubble!"

As the sun began to set, the trio celebrated amidst the laughter and festivities of the festival, sharing stories of the day's hilarity. Alarion felt grateful for his friends, knowing that even in the most unexpected situations, their camaraderie turned every bubble of trouble into a burst of joy.

And with the Golden Bubble Trophy shining brightly in his hands, Alarion realized that the best adventures weren't always about winning; sometimes, they were just about the laughter shared along the way.

BOOK # 2 ALARION AND THE SECRETS OF TIDERUNE 167

Chapter 35: The Grumpy Gnome

Alarion encounters a gnome who is always grumpy. Through a series of silly attempts, he discovers that laughter is the best way to cheer him up!

In the heart of Tiderune, where flowers danced in the wind and the sun shone brightly on the magical landscape, Alarion was feeling particularly adventurous. He had heard whispers from the villagers about a grumpy gnome named Greeble, who lived at the edge of the Whispering Woods. The locals claimed that Greeble hadn't smiled in years, and Alarion, ever the optimist, took it upon himself to bring a grin to the gnome's face.

One sunny afternoon, Alarion set out on his mission, armed with a satchel full of goodies and a heart full of hope. "How hard can it be to make a gnome smile?" he mused aloud; a confident grin plastered across his face. "I've got jokes, snacks, and some great dance moves!"

As he approached Greeble's tiny mushroom house, Alarion could hear the unmistakable sound of grumbling. "Rumble, grumble, and fuss!" Greeble muttered, clearly in the middle of a rant about the state of the garden, which was overrun with flowers and vines.

Alarion knocked on the brightly painted door, which creaked open to reveal the grumpy gnome. Greeble was short, with a beard so bushy it looked like a mop had taken up residence on his chin. He squinted suspiciously at Alarion; his arms crossed tightly over his chest.

"What do you want?" Greeble grumbled, tapping his foot impatiently.

"Hi there! I'm Alarion, and I'm here to make you smile!" Alarion announced cheerfully, trying to project an air of optimism.

"Don't need no smiling. Don't want no smiling!" Greeble replied, scowling. "Go bother someone else."

But Alarion was undeterred. "Oh, come on! Everyone needs a little joy in their life! How about a joke?" He leaned in closer, eager to share his humor. "Why did the gnome bring a ladder to the bar?"

Greeble raised an eyebrow, the faintest hint of curiosity flickering in his eyes. "Why?"

"Because he heard the drinks were on the house!" Alarion burst into laughter, but Greeble remained as grumpy as ever, crossing his arms tighter.

"Ha, ha," Greeble replied dryly, rolling his eyes. "Very funny."

Alarion decided to try a different approach. He reached into his satchel and pulled out a platter of cookies. "How about some delicious bubbleberry cookies? They're the best in Tiderune!"

Greeble's eyes darted to the cookies, but he quickly returned to his grumpy demeanor. "I'm not interested in treats. They'll just make me grumpier!" he huffed.

"Really? You're going to refuse a cookie?" Alarion said, raising an eyebrow. "What if I sing a song while I eat them? It'll be a duet!"

Greeble rolled his eyes again but seemed to be fighting a smile. "You really think you can sing better than a crow?"

"Challenge accepted!" Alarion declared, launching into a surprisingly catchy tune that he made up on the spot about the joys of cookie-eating. He danced a little jig as he sang, making exaggerated movements with his arms and legs. "Oh, cookie, cookie, so sweet and round! You make me happy when you're around!"

Alarion's performance was so silly that Greeble couldn't help but chuckle, despite himself. "What are you doing? Are you trying to dance or fly?" he said, trying to maintain his grumpy façade.

"Both! Who knows what I'm capable of?" Alarion replied with a wink, performing an exaggerated pirouette and nearly tripping over his own feet. "The more you laugh, the less grumpy you'll be! I promise!"

Greeble shook his head, fighting the laughter bubbling up inside him. "You'll never make me laugh!" he declared, but Alarion could see the corners of the gnome's mouth twitching.

Not ready to give up, Alarion rummaged through his satchel once more. This time, he pulled out a rubber chicken he had borrowed from Benny, who always seemed to have an odd assortment of things. "I've got a special guest!" Alarion exclaimed, waving the chicken around. "Meet Clucky! He's got some very important advice to share!"

With exaggerated seriousness, Alarion held the chicken to his ear. "What's that, Clucky? You say Greeble needs a good laugh?" He then launched into a series of ridiculous impressions of the chicken, flapping his arms and making clucking sounds that echoed through the woods.

Greeble could no longer contain himself. He burst into laughter; a deep, hearty sound that surprised even him. "Stop it! You're ridiculous!" he gasped between breaths.

"That's the point!" Alarion grinned, pleased to see that his antics were finally breaking through the gnome's grumpy exterior. "It's okay to be silly sometimes!"

The gnome wiped a tear of laughter from his eye, shaking his head in disbelief. "You're more trouble than you're worth, you know that?"

"Trouble? No way! I'm just a beacon of joy and silliness!" Alarion replied, doing a little victory dance.

Seeing Greeble's mood lifting, Alarion decided it was time to put the final touch on their newfound friendship. "How about we have a mini party right here? I'll bring the snacks, and you can join in the fun!"

Greeble looked taken aback. "You mean, you want to share cookies and dance with a grumpy old gnome?" His brows knitted together in confusion.

"Absolutely!" Alarion said with a grin. "Every gnome deserves a break from grumpiness. Who knows? You might just like it!"

After a moment's hesitation, Greeble let out a sigh and nodded. "Fine. But don't expect me to be a jolly giant or anything."

Alarion beamed, and together they set up a makeshift party with cookies, laughter, and spontaneous dance moves. Greeble, at first reluctant, slowly began to join in the fun, letting loose a few more chuckles as the afternoon went on.

As the sun dipped low in the sky, casting a golden hue over the woods, Greeble found himself laughing more freely than he had in years. Alarion's silly antics had melted away the gnome's grumpiness, replaced with a lightness in his heart.

"Maybe it's not so bad being cheerful after all," Greeble admitted, a genuine smile spreading across his face. "Thanks, Alarion. You really know how to turn a grumpy day into a delightful one."

"Anytime, my friend! Just remember: laughter is the best magic!" Alarion said, giving Greeble a playful nudge.

From that day on, Greeble was known as the "Jolly Gnome" around Tiderune, always ready with a laugh and a smile, thanks to Alarion's silliness and determination. Together, they continued to share laughter and joy, proving that sometimes, the simplest things—like a joke or a rubber chicken—could make the world a brighter place.

Chapter 36: The Fuzzy Phobia

Alarion meets a creature with a phobia of fuzz. Their journey to help it overcome its fears leads to hilarious encounters with the fluffiest things in Tiderune!

One sunny afternoon in Tiderune, Alarion was taking a leisurely stroll through the meadow when something peculiar caught his eye. Amid the colorful wildflowers and fluttering butterflies, he spotted a creature huddled beneath a tree, trembling as if it had just seen a ghost. It was small and round, with big, glossy eyes and tiny feet that seemed barely able to support its rotund body.

Alarion approached cautiously, crouching down to meet the creature at eye level. "Hello there!" he greeted it warmly. "What seems to be the problem?"

The creature jumped, startled, and looked up at him with wide, frightened eyes. It was covered in smooth, sleek skin, which seemed unusual for an animal in Tiderune. Most creatures here had at least a tuft of fur somewhere. This little one, however, looked as though it would have shrieked if it even saw a single hair.

"I... I... I have a problem," it stammered. "The name's Fibbles. And... and... I have a phobia of fuzz."

Alarion blinked, trying not to laugh. A phobia of fuzz? In a place like Tiderune, where fuzzy creatures roamed everywhere, that was quite an unfortunate condition. "A phobia of fuzz, you say?" he repeated, hoping to clarify the situation.

Fibbles nodded, still shaking. "Yes, fuzz! Fur! Anything soft, fluffy, or furry! It gives me the shivers just thinking about it!"

Alarion scratched his head, pondering how he could possibly help the creature overcome such a fear. "Well, Tiderune is full of fuzzy things, Fibbles. It must be hard for you to get around without bumping into a bunny or a bear."

"You have no idea!" Fibbles exclaimed. "Everywhere I turn, there's fluff! And just this morning, I nearly fainted when a cottonseed floated past me. I've tried everything to avoid it—running, hiding, even trying to live in a cactus patch—but it's no use! The fuzz is everywhere!"

Alarion's lips twitched, holding back a smile at the thought of Fibbles hiding in a cactus patch to avoid fluff. But he felt for the little guy. Having a fear of fuzz in such a fluffy world was no laughing matter—well, almost.

"Fear not, my fuzz-fearing friend!" Alarion declared, suddenly standing tall. "I'll help you conquer this fear! We'll face the fluff together!"

Fibbles looked at him with hope, but also with considerable doubt. "You really think you can help me?"

"Absolutely," Alarion said, giving a confident nod. "I've dealt with dragons, mischievous mermaids, and even ticklish toads. How hard could fuzz be?"

The first step in Alarion's plan was simple: introduce Fibbles to some of the fluffiest creatures in Tiderune but in a controlled and gentle manner. Their first stop was the meadow, where a herd of cotton sheep lazily grazed. These sheep were notorious for their cloud-like wool that made anyone want to lie down and take a nap on them.

"All right, Fibbles, just take a step closer to the cotton sheep. They won't hurt you, I promise," Alarion encouraged, leading the way.

Fibbles stood rigid, staring at the sheep with wide eyes. "N-no way! Look at them! They're like walking clouds of terror!"

Alarion chuckled. "They're harmless. See?" He reached out and gave one of the sheep a gentle pat, its wool bouncing under his hand like a soft pillow. "Nothing scary here."

Fibbles inched closer, his tiny feet dragging in the grass as if they were made of lead. When he finally got close enough to touch the wool, his whole body stiffened. He reached out a trembling hand and gave the sheep the lightest tap possible. Instantly, he jumped back as though he'd been shocked.

"See? Not so bad, right?" Alarion said, trying to suppress his laughter.

Fibbles shook his head, still trembling. "It's... too soft. Too fluffy. I can't... I can't do it!"

"Okay, no worries!" Alarion reassured him, sensing that the cotton sheep might have been too ambitious for the first encounter. "We'll start with something less intimidating."

Next on their journey was Pibble, a small hedgehog who lived in a cozy burrow not far from the meadow. Pibble wasn't as fluffy as the cotton sheep, but he did have soft quills and a rather cuddly demeanor.

"Pibble's a great start!" Alarion said, holding the hedgehog in his hands. "Look at him—he's not even that fuzzy!"

Fibbles peered at Pibble, who yawned lazily in Alarion's hands. "I... I don't know..." Fibbles murmured, his voice shaking. "He's still kind of soft-looking."

"Just give him a little pet," Alarion urged. "I promise he won't bite!"

Fibbles took a deep breath, his eyes locked onto the hedgehog-like he was facing his greatest foe. Slowly, he stretched out his hand again, giving Pibble a quick touch before pulling back, holding his breath as though he was waiting for something terrible to happen.

But nothing did. Pibble simply nuzzled into Alarion's hands and yawned again.

"Hey, that wasn't so bad!" Fibbles said, his voice filled with surprise.

"See? You're doing great!" Alarion grinned. "One step at a time, and soon you'll be hugging bunnies like a pro!"

Fibbles still looked unsure, but Alarion's encouragement had given him a spark of courage. For the next few hours, they travelled around

Tiderune, introducing Fibbles to all sorts of fuzzy creatures: from the soft-winged butterflies in the Enchanted Forest to the furry squirrels in the Evergreen Woods.

The most hilarious encounter, however, came when they stumbled upon a pile of giggle grass—a type of grass known for making anyone who walked on it burst into uncontrollable laughter. Alarion had intended to show Fibbles a simple patch of fuzzy moss, but they accidentally wandered into the Gigglegrass patch.

As soon as Fibbles' tiny feet touched the grass, he let out a high-pitched giggle. His legs wobbled, and he tried to step out of the grass, but the more he moved, the more he giggled. Soon, both he and Alarion were on the ground, rolling with laughter, unable to stop as the giggle grass worked its magic.

"I... can't... breathe!" Fibbles gasped between giggles, clutching his sides.

Alarion, laughing just as hard, finally managed to crawl out of the patch and pull Fibbles along with him. They lay on the ground, panting and wiping tears of laughter from their eyes.

"Well... I think we've found the cure to your fear of fuzz," Alarion said, grinning. "You just need to laugh about it!"

Fibbles, still catching his breath, looked at Alarion with wide eyes. "You know... I think you're right. Maybe fuzz isn't so bad after all... especially when it comes to laughter."

With that, Fibbles' fear of fuzz wasn't entirely gone, but it had lessened considerably. And whenever he felt the urge to run from a fluffy creature, he would remember the giggle grass and laugh instead. As for Alarion, he couldn't help but feel proud of his fuzzy, fear-fighting friend.

Together, they returned to Tiderune village, their journey full of laughter, fuzz, and unexpected friendship.

Chapter 37: The Magical Maze

*A*larion gets trapped in a maze that constantly changes its layout. With the help of a clever mouse, they turn the maze into a game of tag!

Alarion stood at the entrance of the maze, its towering hedges looming over him, their leaves whispering mysteriously in the wind. The sky above was clear, and the sun shone brightly, casting dappled light across the path. He had heard legends about this particular maze, known for constantly shifting and changing, confusing any who dared to enter. But Alarion, ever the adventurer, couldn't resist the challenge.

"This will be easy," he muttered confidently to himself, adjusting his cloak. "How hard could a maze really be? Just follow the walls, right?"

He took a step forward, the gate closing behind him with a soft, ominous creak. As soon as he crossed the threshold, the hedges seemed to come alive, twisting and curling as if they were made of liquid, not plants. The paths ahead seemed to stretch and bend in ways that made no logical sense. One moment, a path stretched straight into the distance; the next, it was coiled like a snake.

Alarion frowned. "Well, this is definitely... different." He scratched his head, glancing around. "Not exactly what I was expecting."

Taking a deep breath, he decided to start walking. The maze, though intimidating, didn't seem too terrible at first. But every time he thought he was making progress, the path would shift, and he'd find himself back where he started.

"Okay... This is a little harder than I thought."

After what felt like hours of wandering, Alarion came to a halt in front of a particularly tricky corner. The path ahead split into two, each direction looking identical. He tapped his chin, unsure which way to go, when he heard a faint, almost imperceptible squeak.

Turning around, he spotted a small mouse peeking out from beneath the hedge, its tiny nose twitching curiously. It looked up at him with beady eyes, as if to say, "What are you doing, standing there like that?"

"Ah, a mouse!" Alarion exclaimed with a grin, crouching down. "You wouldn't happen to know the way through this maze, would you?"

The mouse blinked, then dashed off into the maze, disappearing around a corner. Alarion laughed softly to himself. "Well, if the mouse can navigate this, surely I can, too!"

But just as he took a step forward, the ground beneath him shifted again, and the walls of the maze began to twist and contort. Now completely disoriented, Alarion sighed. "I'm never getting out of here at this rate."

Suddenly, the mouse reappeared, this time with something sparkling around its tiny neck—a small, glowing charm. The mouse ran up to Alarion, squeaking excitedly, as if beckoning him to follow.

Alarion raised an eyebrow. "A magical mouse? This day just keeps getting stranger."

With no better option, he decided to follow the clever little creature. The mouse darted through the shifting walls of the maze, weaving in and out of corners as if it knew every twist and turn by heart. Alarion did his best to keep up, though every time he thought he'd lost the mouse, it would appear again, just ahead of him, always urging him onward.

But then, just as things seemed to be going smoothly, the maze decided to get tricky again. The walls shifted suddenly, trapping Alarion in a dead-end. The mouse scurried back, looking frustrated.

"Oh, don't give me that look," Alarion chuckled. "I'm not the one who's controlling this maze."

The mouse squeaked again and, to Alarion's surprise, darted up the side of the hedge wall as if it was running on flat ground. It perched atop the hedge, waiting for him to figure out what to do next.

"That's cheating!" Alarion called up to the mouse with a grin. "I can't climb like you!"

The mouse squeaked once more, its little whiskers twitching with amusement. Suddenly, the idea hit him. If the mouse could treat the maze like a game, why couldn't he?

"Fine, you want to play tag? Let's play tag!" Alarion declared, his playful spirit returning.

He took off down a different path, knowing full well the mouse would follow. And it did! The little creature zipped along the tops of the hedges, jumping from wall to wall, while Alarion darted down paths that opened and closed in front of him. Sometimes, the maze seemed to work in his favor, other times it didn't, but he was having too much fun to care.

"Catch me if you can!" he shouted, laughing as he dodged yet another twist in the path.

The mouse, now fully invested in the game, chased after him with renewed energy. Every time it came close, the walls of the maze shifted, giving Alarion just enough space to dash ahead. It was like the maze itself had joined in on the fun, turning their race into a chaotic game of cat and mouse—or, in this case, wizard and mouse.

After what felt like an endless game of tag, the maze suddenly stopped shifting. Alarion found himself at the centre, a beautiful garden filled with colorful flowers and a sparkling fountain. He skidded to a stop, catching his breath, and looked around in awe.

"Well, would you look at that," he said, grinning. "We made it to the centre!"

The mouse, triumphant, scurried up to him and hopped onto a stone bench, squeaking proudly.

Alarion chuckled, sitting down beside his new furry friend. "You did it, little guy. You helped me win."

As if understanding the praise, the mouse squeaked happily and began grooming its whiskers, the charm around its neck glowing softly.

Alarion reached into his pocket and pulled out a small piece of cheese he had been saving from his lunch earlier. "Here, a reward for the champion." He placed the cheese on the bench, and the mouse eagerly accepted it, nibbling away contentedly.

For a while, they both sat in peaceful silence, watching the fountain's water shimmer in the sunlight. Alarion smiled, feeling a sense of accomplishment. What had started as a frustrating, ever-changing maze had turned into one of the most enjoyable adventures he'd had in a long time.

"Thanks for the help, little buddy," Alarion said, giving the mouse a gentle pat on the head. "I don't think I could've made it without you."

The mouse squeaked softly in response, its eyes twinkling with mischief. Alarion had a feeling this wouldn't be the last time their paths crossed.

As the sun began to set, the maze's entrance reappeared, and Alarion knew it was time to head back to the village. He stood up, stretched, and gave the maze one last look. "Until next time," he called out, waving to the hedges.

With the clever mouse by his side, Alarion left the magical maze, a wide grin on his face, knowing that sometimes, even the trickiest puzzles could be solved with a little bit of fun—and a whole lot of laughter.

Chapter 38: The Wizard's Challenge

Alarion faces a wizard who challenges him to a magical duel. Their battle quickly turns into a slapstick comedy of misfires and funny spells!

The day began like any other in the magical realm of Tiderune. The sun was high, birds chirped merrily, and Alarion was simply minding his own business, enjoying a rare quiet afternoon in the village square. He'd been planning to visit the local bakery for a loaf of fresh bread when, out of nowhere, a loud voice boomed through the air.

"Alarion! I challenge you to a duel!"

Startled, Alarion looked up to see a figure floating several feet above the ground, dressed in the grandest wizard robes he'd ever seen. The robes were a shimmering emerald, covered in intricate silver runes that twinkled like stars. The wizard's long beard was tied in a braid, which gave him an oddly serious, yet comical look. His staff, topped with a gleaming crystal, pulsed with magical energy.

Villagers around Alarion stopped what they were doing and gasped. Alarion, however, raised an eyebrow and muttered under his breath, "Who is this now?"

The wizard descended with dramatic flair, landing softly on the cobbled street. "I am Gadwen the Grand! And I have heard tales of your so-called 'magical prowess.' But I, the greatest wizard in all the lands, challenge you to a duel!" Gadwen struck a heroic pose, the wind dramatically catching his robes.

Alarion sighed, rubbing the back of his neck. He had faced all sorts of magical opponents, but something about this wizard seemed... off.

"Look, Gadwen, was it? I don't really duel other wizards unless it's absolutely necessary. Plus, I was just about to get some bread. Maybe we can do this another time?"

But Gadwen wouldn't have it. "You cannot back down from a challenge, Alarion!" He twirled his staff in a rather exaggerated fashion. "A wizard's honor is at stake!"

Alarion blinked, then glanced around at the growing crowd. There was no escaping this now. "Fine, fine," he said, raising his hands in defeat. "But let's keep this civil, alright? No turning anyone into a toad."

Gadwen grinned, clearly satisfied. He took several steps back, creating space between them. "Prepare yourself, for I shall not go easy on you!" He lifted his staff, and sparks flew from its crystal tip.

Alarion rolled his eyes. "Sure thing."

The duel began with a bang—or, rather, a sneeze. Gadwen pointed his staff at Alarion, chanting a complex spell under his breath, but just as the final word left his lips, he sneezed violently. A puff of smoke appeared from the end of his staff, and suddenly, a flock of pink pigeons burst out, circling around him.

"What the—" Gadwen sputtered as one of the pigeons perched on his head.

The crowd burst into laughter, and Alarion had to bite his lip to keep from joining in. "Good start," Alarion teased, casually flicking his own wand. He decided to return the favor with a simple, harmless trick. With a swirl of his wand, he summoned a gust of wind that ruffled Gadwen's robes and lifted his hat straight off his head.

The hat landed upside down on the ground, revealing an embarrassing stash of candy hidden inside. The crowd roared even louder, and Gadwen's face flushed bright red.

"That—that was just a warm-up!" Gadwen stammered, hurriedly grabbing his hat and stuffing the candy back inside.

Alarion, now thoroughly entertained, waved his wand again, conjuring a small, playful firework. It popped harmlessly over Gadwen's head, showering him in harmless sparks.

Gadwen, flustered, tried again. This time, he waved his staff with determination, and out shot a stream of bright light. Alarion braced himself, but instead of a powerful spell, a giant bubble floated out of the end of Gadwen's staff. The bubble shimmered in the sunlight, wobbling back and forth before gently floating toward Alarion.

Alarion blinked in disbelief. "A bubble? Seriously?"

The crowd, meanwhile, was losing it. Villagers were doubled over, some wiping tears from their eyes as they watched the "epic duel" unfold.

But Gadwen, ever the determined wizard, refused to back down. "It's a distraction!" he shouted, trying to save face. "And now, prepare for the real attack!"

Alarion chuckled. He wasn't about to let Gadwen have all the fun, so he conjured a bucket of confetti, which rained down on Gadwen from above. The poor wizard sputtered and waved his arms wildly as the colorful paper showered down, getting stuck in his beard.

Desperately trying to regain control of the duel, Gadwen aimed his staff at Alarion one more time. This time, his spell actually hit its mark—sort of. A spark of magic shot toward Alarion, who dodged, but the spell hit the bakery sign behind him instead.

The sign transformed into a massive loaf of bread, which immediately fell off its hinges and landed with a soft "thud" on the street in front of them. It was perfectly baked, and it smelled divine.

"Nice," Alarion said, clapping slowly. "Now I don't even have to go to the bakery."

Gadwen was now red-faced, covered in confetti, and slightly sang from his own misfired spells. In a final, desperate attempt to win back some dignity, he raised his staff one last time and shouted, "Behold! The grandest spell of all!"

But before he could finish the incantation, a gust of wind—perhaps summoned by the universe itself—swept through the village square, ripping Gadwen's hat off once more. This time, the hat flew high into the air, spun a few times, and landed squarely on a passing goat's head.

The goat, seemingly unfazed, trotted away with Gadwen's hat still perched on its head, while the crowd erupted into uncontrollable laughter. Even Alarion couldn't keep a straight face anymore. He doubled over, laughing until his sides hurt.

Gadwen, clearly defeated, slumped his shoulders and muttered under his breath, "I'll, uh, be going now."

But Alarion, still chuckling, approached the flustered wizard. "Come on, Gadwen, that was all in good fun. Why don't we call it a draw and grab some bread? I've got plenty now, thanks to you."

Gadwen, looking sheepish, glanced at the enormous loaf of bread on the ground. After a moment, he let out a reluctant chuckle. "Alright, alright. Maybe we both got a little carried away."

With the duel officially declared a draw, the two wizards sat down on the edge of the fountain, tearing off pieces of the oversized bread and sharing it with the amused villagers. The crowd slowly dispersed, and soon it was just the two of them, laughing about the absurdity of the whole situation.

"You know," Alarion said between bites, "you're not a bad wizard, Gadwen. You've got potential."

Gadwen sighed, brushing confetti out of his beard. "I just wanted to prove I could be as great as the legends say."

Alarion clapped him on the back. "Being a great wizard isn't just about big, fancy spells. Sometimes, it's about knowing when to laugh at yourself."

Gadwen smiled, finally relaxing. "I suppose you're right."

As the sun set over the village, the two wizards sat there, enjoying their bread and newfound camaraderie. And though the duel had been far from serious, Alarion couldn't help but feel like he'd gained something far more valuable than a victory—he'd made a friend.

"Well, Gadwen," Alarion said, grinning, "next time we duel, let's try to keep it under control. Maybe without the bubbles?"

Gadwen laughed, a sound far more genuine this time. "Agreed. No bubbles."

And with that, the two wizards walked off into the evening, their robes trailing behind them, leaving behind a village full of laughter, a goat wearing a wizard's hat, and the memory of a duel that would be talked about for years to come.

Chapter 39: The Rainbow Chaser

Chasing a rainbow leads Alarion to a field where colors come alive. Each color tries to convince him it's the best, resulting in a colorful debate!

It was a brilliant, sun-drenched morning in the land of Tiderune, the kind of morning that made Alarion's heart feel light as air. He had been wandering through the countryside, marvelling at the sights of nature in full bloom—birds flitting between the trees, bees humming busily around wildflowers, and the breeze carrying the scent of fresh rain. All seemed peaceful. Little did he know that today, a simple chase would lead to one of the most peculiar adventures yet.

As Alarion crested a hill, he spotted something magical in the distance—a shimmering rainbow stretching across the sky, its vibrant colors glowing brighter than any he'd ever seen. It arched gracefully over the hills, disappearing behind a distant grove. But this was no ordinary rainbow. Something about it seemed alive, as if the colors themselves were calling to him, daring him to follow.

"Why not?" Alarion muttered to himself, already feeling the excitement bubbling up. Rainbows always led to something special—at least in the stories. And in a land as magical as Tiderune, who could resist the possibility of finding out what lay at the end of one?

With that, Alarion took off, his feet light as the breeze that blew through the grassy fields. He ran toward the rainbow, laughing to himself as the colors seemed to dance ahead, always just out of reach. Every time he thought he was getting close, it shimmered and shifted, pulling him further along. But Alarion loved a good challenge, and this rainbow was certainly proving to be one.

Finally, after what felt like hours, Alarion found himself in a vast, open field that seemed to hum with magic. He slowed to a stop, panting slightly, and looked around. The rainbow arched overhead, but instead of disappearing into the distance, its colors descended right before him, as if anchoring themselves into the ground. And then, something truly extraordinary happened—the colors began to move.

At first, they wavered like ripples on a pond, but then each band of color—red, orange, yellow, green, blue, indigo, and violet—seemed to break free from the rainbow and float toward him. Alarion blinked in disbelief. The colors hovered in the air like living beings, swirling around each other in a playful dance. They shimmered and sparkled; their hues so bright that it almost hurt to look at them directly.

"Uh... hello?" Alarion ventured, not entirely sure how to address a group of floating colors.

To his surprise, the red color, the boldest of the bunch, zoomed toward him and spoke in a deep, booming voice. "Ah, Alarion! You've finally caught up! Well, done, well done! But now that you're here, let's settle something once and for all. Which of us is the best color?"

Alarion raised an eyebrow, completely caught off guard. "Wait... what?"

Before he could get another word out, the yellow color—bright and sunny—chimed in with a cheerful, sing-song voice. "Oh please, Red! Everyone knows I'm the best! I'm the color of sunshine, happiness, and laughter! Who could possibly resist me?"

Green, swaying lazily in the breeze like a gentle leaf, rolled forward next. "Don't be ridiculous, Yellow," Green said in a calm, soothing voice. "I'm the color of nature, of life itself. The world would be dull and barren without me."

"Pfft, nature," scoffed Blue, swirling up with a cool, breezy energy. "I'm the color of the sky and the sea. Without me, the world would be endless land, no beauty, no serenity."

Alarion watched in utter bemusement as the colors began to bicker, each one trying to outdo the others. Orange, not to be outdone, jumped into the fray, insisting it was the color of warmth, creativity, and adventure. Indigo, a little mysterious and brooding, claimed to be the color of twilight and magic. And Violet, regal and elegant, simply stated that it was the color of royalty and wisdom, so clearly it was the best.

"Well, I didn't expect this," Alarion muttered under his breath as the debate continued to escalate.

The colors circled around him, each vying for his attention, each trying to convince him that they were the one he should choose. It was like being caught in the middle of a very bizarre argument at a family reunion.

"Alright, alright!" Alarion finally shouted, raising his hands. "You're all great! But there's no need to argue about who's the best."

The colors paused, floating silently for a moment as they stared at him.

"But there must be a best!" Red insisted, puffing up. "There's always a best."

Alarion thought for a moment, rubbing his chin. "You know, maybe that's where you're wrong. Each of you brings something unique and special to the world. Red, you're bold and full of energy. Yellow, you bring warmth and joy. Green, you're calming and peaceful. And Blue, well, you're... cool and serene."

He glanced at each color as he spoke, trying to smooth things over. "Indigo, you're the mysterious one, full of depth. Violet, you're elegant and wise. And Orange, you're full of creativity and adventure. Without any one of you, the rainbow wouldn't be complete. It's all of you together that makes the world so beautiful."

The colors floated quietly, considering his words. For a moment, Alarion feared he might have offended them, but then Red gave a small huff. "Well... when you put it that way..."

Yellow giggled and swirled around playfully. "He's right, you know. We do look fabulous together."

Green nodded thoughtfully, and Blue seemed to relax a little, its shimmering edges softening. "I suppose a sky without the sunset wouldn't be as lovely," Blue admitted.

Indigo and Violet exchanged glances, and then Violet, always the regal one, said, "Perhaps there is wisdom in harmony."

Alarion breathed a sigh of relief. He hadn't meant to get caught up in a color debate today, but somehow, he had managed to calm things down.

"Well then," Alarion said with a grin, "how about we celebrate by doing what you do best? Let's make the most beautiful rainbow Tiderune has ever seen!"

The colors brightened at the suggestion, and without another word, they zipped back into place, forming the most vibrant, breathtaking rainbow Alarion had ever seen. It stretched across the sky in a glorious arch, its hues blending together perfectly, each color adding its own magic to the display.

As Alarion stood there, admiring the sight, he couldn't help but chuckle. Who would have thought that chasing a rainbow would lead to a lesson in unity—and a rather lively debate among the colors themselves?

He smiled to himself, watching as the rainbow shimmered and sparkled in the afternoon sun. "Just another day in Tiderune," he mused, turning to head back toward the village.

But as he walked away, a soft voice—Violet's—whispered after him, "For the record, Alarion... I'm still the best."

Alarion laughed and waved over his shoulder. "Sure, Violet. Whatever you say."

And with that, he continued on his way, leaving the rainbow to shine brilliantly behind him, knowing that sometimes the best things in life are the ones that work together in harmony—even when they're a little competitive.

Chapter 40: The Sleepy Sandman

Alarion meets a sandman who can't stop yawning. His sleepy antics make it hard for Alarion to stay awake, leading to a humorous struggle!

Alarion had been wandering the twilight fields of Tiderune for what felt like hours, lulled by the soft whispers of the evening breeze. The sky had just begun to turn from pink to deep indigo, and a sprinkling of stars had appeared, shimmering like distant jewels. His journey today had been a long one, and though his feet were tired, he couldn't shake the odd feeling that something was drawing him forward, beckoning him to explore the unknown edges of this magical realm.

As he made his way through a gentle valley, he noticed a peculiar figure sitting on a large, crescent-shaped mound of sand. The figure was tall and lanky, draped in a cloak made entirely of glittering stardust, which shimmered with every movement. His head, though hard to see clearly, was covered in a cloud of sleep-inducing dust that floated lazily around him, as if caught in a perpetual yawn.

Curiosity piqued, Alarion stepped closer. "Hello there!" he called out cheerfully. "What brings you out here all alone?"

The figure slowly turned his head, though it was clear he wasn't in any hurry. As he did, a massive yawn escaped him, so wide and drawn-out that it made Alarion's own jaw stretch in sympathy. He tried to resist, but the yawn was simply too contagious.

"Ahhh... you'll have to forgive me..." said the figure, his voice thick with drowsiness. "I'm... ahhh... the Sandman... and it seems I'm... a bit... sleepy."

Alarion chuckled softly. "A bit? You look like you're about to fall over any second!"

The Sandman gave a slow nod, his eyes—if he even had eyes under all that sand—drooping heavily. "I'm supposed to... bring sleep... to everyone else," he explained between yawns, "but lately, I can't seem to stay awake... long enough to do my job."

Alarion could feel the tug of sleep growing stronger the longer he stood there, the air around the Sandman thick with the promise of sweet dreams. His legs felt heavier, and his eyelids were starting to droop. He shook his head, trying to stay alert. "Well, you certainly have a powerful effect on people. I feel like I could nap for a week just standing near you."

The Sandman yawned again, this time so wide that Alarion nearly collapsed on the spot, fighting desperately to stay awake. "That's... the problem," the Sandman mumbled, his voice trailing off. "I can't seem to stop... spreading sleepiness... wherever I go. It's... ahhh... causing... ahh... problems."

Alarion rubbed his eyes, blinking furiously to stay alert. "There must be a way to fix this! You can't just go around putting everyone to sleep—especially yourself."

But the Sandman, his head bobbing up and down like a nodding sunflower, seemed completely oblivious to Alarion's struggle. "Maybe... if I... just... took... a short... nap..."

Before Alarion could protest, the Sandman had slumped forward, resting on his mound of sand, snoring softly. The soft sound of his breathing created a rhythm so soothing, so hypnotic, that Alarion felt his knees buckle. He sat down, trying to shake the sleep from his mind, but it was impossible to fight. The air around him felt warm and inviting, like a soft blanket wrapping itself around him.

"No… I… I can't…" Alarion muttered, trying to keep his thoughts straight. "I have to… wake him… up…"

But as the soft snoring filled the air, Alarion found himself leaning back into the sand, his body sinking into its warmth. His eyes fluttered closed, just for a moment, just long enough to rest them…

Suddenly, a sharp burst of laughter echoed in the distance. Alarion jolted awake, his heart pounding. His eyes snapped open, and the sleepiness lifted just enough for him to sit up. He blinked, trying to figure out where the sound had come from.

"Ha! I knew it!" a voice called from behind him.

Alarion turned to see a young fairy flitting about, her wings shimmering in the moonlight. She was small and quick, darting in and out of view like a mischievous sprite. "You almost fell asleep, didn't you?" she teased, twirling in the air. "You were about to join Mr. Sleepyhead here!"

"Who are you?" Alarion asked, standing up and shaking off the last bits of drowsiness.

The fairy giggled and landed on his shoulder, her wings brushing against his cheek like a tickle of moonlight. "I'm Elysia," she said with a wink. "And I know all about the Sandman's little problem. He's been like this for days now, spreading sleepiness all over Tiderune. It's becoming quite the issue."

"Well, that's an understatement," Alarion said, rubbing his temples. "I can barely keep my eyes open just being near him."

"Exactly!" Elysia said, flitting off his shoulder and landing near the Sandman's sleeping form. "But I have a plan. We just need to wake him up—properly, this time—and remind him that his power works best when he's well-rested."

Alarion raised an eyebrow. "Wake him up? How? He's practically a professional napper!"

Elysia grinned. "Leave that to me."

With a flick of her tiny wrist, Elysia summoned a flurry of sparkling dust, swirling it into a small, glowing ball. "Now, watch this," she whispered with a mischievous glint in her eyes.

The fairy danced in the air, dropping the ball of dust right on the Sandman's head. The effect was instantaneous. The Sandman's snoring stopped, and his body jolted awake as if struck by lightning.

"Wha—? What's happening?" he stammered, blinking rapidly. "I was... dreaming of something..."

"Exactly!" Elysia said, fluttering around his head. "You've been so busy putting everyone else to sleep that you've forgotten to take care of yourself. You need a proper nap, Sandman—a good, long rest so you can wake up feeling refreshed. Then, and only then, will you be able to do your job without putting the whole world to sleep."

The Sandman scratched his sandy head, yawning yet again, though this time it wasn't as contagious. "But... I'm supposed to bring sleep to others, not myself."

"And how do you think you can do that if you're falling asleep every five seconds?" Alarion chimed in, folding his arms. "You've got to rest if you want to help others rest."

The Sandman thought about this for a moment, then nodded slowly. "I suppose you're right," he admitted. "I've been so focused on everyone else's sleep that I forgot... I need it too."

Elysia landed on the Sandman's shoulder, giving him a tiny pat. "That's the spirit! Now, why don't you take a proper nap—one where you're not worrying about anyone else—and we'll keep an eye on things for you."

Alarion smiled. "We'll make sure no one falls into a deep sleep while you're resting."

The Sandman gave a slow, grateful nod. "Thank you," he said softly. "I think I will... take that nap now..."

With that, the Sandman stretched out on his sandy mound, closed his eyes, and within moments, he was sound asleep. But this time, his snoring wasn't spreading drowsiness—it was peaceful, calm, and almost musical.

Elysia grinned at Alarion, her wings shimmering in the moonlight. "Looks like he'll be out for a while. Come on, let's get out of here before we catch his yawns again."

Alarion chuckled, feeling lighter now that the sleepiness had lifted. "Good idea. I could use some fresh air after all that."

As they walked away from the valley, the stars twinkled above them, and Alarion couldn't help but smile. Sometimes, even the bringers of sleep needed a little rest of their own. And with the Sandman finally taking his well-deserved nap, Alarion was sure that the dreams of Tiderune would be a little sweeter tonight.

"Who knew?" Alarion mused, glancing up at the sky. "Even Sandmen need a nap."

Elysia giggled beside him. "And we all need a good laugh to keep us awake."

And so, they walked on, the night filled with the gentle sound of the Sandman's peaceful sleep and the promise of more magical adventures to come.

Chapter 41: The Jumpy Jelly

A jelly creature bounces around, inviting Alarion to join the fun. Their jumping competition turns into a wacky race with lots of laughter!

The day in Tiderune began like any other. Birds chirped in the treetops, the sun shone brightly, and the breeze carried the scent of flowers blooming in every direction. Alarion found himself wandering down a winding path lined with colorful wildflowers, enjoying the serene atmosphere of the morning. His latest adventures had been a whirlwind, and he was grateful for a moment of calm.

But, as was typical in the magical realm of Tiderune, calm never lasted long.

As Alarion approached the edge of a forest clearing, he noticed something unusual in the distance. At first, it looked like a large, wobbling mass. He squinted, trying to make out the shape. It was... bouncing? Yes, definitely bouncing. A jiggling, shimmering blob of... jelly?

Curiosity got the better of him, as it often did, and Alarion cautiously stepped closer. The bouncing jelly creature was unlike anything he'd ever seen before. It was translucent, with a rainbow sheen that changed colors as it moved, and it wobbled excitedly with every bounce. The closer Alarion got, the more he could see that this jelly was not just bouncing—it was having the time of its life, hopping from one patch of grass to another like it was the happiest creature in the world.

"Well, what do we have here?" Alarion muttered to himself, his eyes wide with amusement. "A jelly creature with a serious case of the giggles, it seems."

As if it could hear him, the jelly stopped mid-bounce and turned to face him—though how it could see him was a mystery, as it didn't seem to have any eyes. Without warning, it gave an excited jiggle and sprang toward him, landing right at his feet.

"Whoa!" Alarion stumbled back, nearly falling over. The jelly wobbled in place, its whole body vibrating with excitement.

"Uh, hello there?" Alarion said, unsure of how one addressed a creature made entirely of jelly.

The jelly gave another enthusiastic bounce in response as if inviting him to join in. Alarion raised an eyebrow. "Are you trying to get me to... bounce?"

The jelly quivered happily, seemingly thrilled at the idea.

Alarion chuckled. "Alright, I'll play along. How hard could it be?"

Taking a deep breath, he bent his knees and gave a little hop. The jelly wobbled excitedly, bouncing higher and higher with each jump. Alarion, not wanting to be outdone by a blob of gelatin, bounced higher as well. Before long, the two of them were in a full-fledged jumping competition, with the jelly leading the charge and Alarion following close behind.

The more they jumped, the higher the jelly seemed to bounce, and soon Alarion found himself soaring into the air with each leap. It was oddly exhilarating, and Alarion couldn't help but laugh as they bounded across the clearing.

"This is ridiculous!" he shouted mid-bounce, though he was grinning from ear to ear.

The jelly bounced in agreement, quivering with delight as they raced from one side of the field to the other. Alarion tried to keep up, but the jelly had an unfair advantage—being made entirely of bounce, after all. Each time it landed, it would ricochet higher than before, leaving Alarion scrambling to match its height.

As they reached the centre of the clearing, the jelly suddenly veered to the left, bouncing toward a cluster of rocks. Alarion followed, laughing at the creature's unpredictable movements. But just as he was about to leap after it, the jelly bounced onto the largest rock, and—without warning—shot straight into the air with a speed Alarion hadn't anticipated.

"Oh no," Alarion muttered, watching the jelly soar high above him. He barely had time to react before the jelly came hurtling back down—right at him.

With a squelching sound, the jelly landed on top of Alarion's head, enveloping him in its soft, wobbly embrace. For a moment, all Alarion could see was a blur of rainbow-colored gelatine as the jelly bounced in place, jiggling uncontrollably.

"Hey!" Alarion sputtered, trying to peel the jelly off his head. "That's not fair!"

The jelly, apparently enjoying itself far too much, quivered with laughter—or at least, that's what Alarion assumed it was doing. It seemed to find the entire situation hilarious.

Finally managing to pry the jelly off, Alarion held the creature in his hands, still laughing despite himself. "You've got quite the sense of humor, don't you?"

The jelly bounced happily in response, its entire body shimmering in the sunlight.

Alarion, his hair now sticking up in all directions from the encounter, couldn't help but grin. "Alright, alright. You win this round. But I bet you can't beat me in a proper race!"

The jelly wobbled with excitement, clearly eager to accept the challenge.

Alarion set the jelly down on the ground, and the two of them lined up at the edge of the clearing, ready to race. Alarion crouched low, preparing for the starting leap. "On your mark, get set... go!"

They both took off, bouncing across the field with abandon. The jelly, unsurprisingly, surged ahead, its bounces growing higher and more erratic with each leap. But Alarion wasn't far behind, pushing himself to keep up with the energetic creature.

The race was chaotic, with Alarion dodging trees and rocks while the jelly effortlessly sailed over them. The field became a blur of colors and laughter as they bounced through the landscape, neither one willing to back down.

As they neared the finish line—a large oak tree at the far end of the clearing—Alarion put on a burst of speed, determined to at least tie with the jelly. But just as he was about to leap past it, the jelly pulled a sneaky move. It bounced sideways, right in front of Alarion, causing him to stumble.

With a yelp, Alarion tumbled to the ground, landing in a heap of grass and laughter. The jelly, having already reached the oak tree, bounced victoriously in place, quivering with excitement.

Alarion sat up, brushing bits of grass from his tunic, and looked at the jelly, who was still wobbling happily by the tree. "Alright, alright. You win again," he said with a chuckle. "But I'll get you next time."

The jelly bounced back toward him, landing softly at his feet. It wobbled once more as if to say, good game!

Alarion smiled and patted the jelly on what he assumed was its head. "You're a tricky one, but that was the most fun I've had in a while."

As the sun began to dip lower in the sky, casting a warm golden glow over the clearing, Alarion and the jelly sat side by side, watching the horizon. The jelly, still bouncing occasionally, seemed content, and Alarion felt a sense of peaceful joy settle over him.

"Well, Jelly," Alarion said with a sigh, "I suppose we'll have to call it a day. But I have a feeling our paths will cross again. And when they do, you'd better be ready for another race."

The jelly gave a small quiver as if accepting the challenge.

With a final bounce, the jelly sprang off into the distance, its rainbow-colored form disappearing into the trees. Alarion watched it go, shaking his head in amusement.

"Only in Tiderune," he muttered to himself, standing up and stretching. "Only in Tiderune."

As he made his way back down the path, Alarion couldn't help but smile at the day's unexpected adventure. Life in the magical realm was never dull, and with creatures like the Jumpy Jelly around, it was always full of laughter and surprises.

And who knew? Maybe one day, he'd finally win that race.

Chapter 42: The Talking Tree

A tree that loves to gossip shares the latest news about Tiderune. Alarion realizes he's in for some juicy and funny tales!

It was a warm and pleasant afternoon in Tiderune, the kind of day that made even the laziest creatures want to stretch out and bask in the sunshine. Alarion, however, had other plans. His curiosity had led him deep into the Whispering Woods, a place where magic hummed in the air and secrets seemed to linger in every shadow. He wasn't quite sure what he was looking for, but in a land like Tiderune, adventures had a way of finding him.

He wandered along the mossy path, the sun filtering through the trees in dappled patterns. Every now and then, a bird would chirp a friendly greeting, and a few squirrels scurried about, chattering to one another in their squeaky voices. But it wasn't until Alarion reached the centre of the woods that he encountered something truly unusual.

There, standing proud and tall in a clearing, was a massive oak tree—its trunk so wide that it would take at least five people to wrap their arms around it. Its bark was gnarly and twisted, giving it the appearance of having seen many, many years of Tiderune's history.

As Alarion approached, he noticed something odd. The branches of the tree were shaking slightly, though there wasn't any wind. And then he heard it—a voice, low and gruff, muttering under its breath.

"... and did you hear what that foolish pixie did last week? Honestly, some creatures have no sense of decorum..."

Alarion froze, his eyes widening. Was the tree... talking?

He inched closer, trying not to make a sound. But before he could get too near, the tree's branches suddenly whipped around, and a pair of eyes—carved into the bark itself—opened wide, staring right at him.

"Oh! A visitor!" the tree exclaimed, its voice now bright and excited. "How delightful! It's been ages since anyone stopped by for a chat."

Alarion blinked, unsure how to respond. He had encountered many strange things in Tiderune, but a talking tree wasn't exactly on his list of usual suspects.

"Um... hello?" he said cautiously. "I didn't mean to intrude."

"Nonsense!" the tree said, its deep voice rumbling through the clearing. "You're not intruding at all! In fact, I've been rather bored lately. There's only so much gossip you can collect when no one's around to share it with."

Alarion raised an eyebrow. "Gossip?"

The tree's branches rustled with what could only be described as excitement. "Oh, yes! I hear everything that happens in these woods—and beyond! You wouldn't believe the stories I've collected over the years. The things I could tell you about the goings-on in Tiderune would make your head spin."

Alarion chuckled. "Well, I do love a good story."

The tree's bark seemed to creak with pleasure. "Oh, where to begin? Let's see... Ah! Have you heard about the time the Fairy Queen caught the Dragon of the East snooping around her garden? She was not pleased, let me tell you. The poor dragon didn't even know the flowers were enchanted—he just wanted a snack!"

Alarion laughed. The idea of a mighty dragon getting in trouble over a few flowers was too ridiculous not to be funny. "What happened next?"

"Well," the tree said, lowering its voice conspiratorially, "she gave him a stern talking-to, of course. But between you and me, I think the Fairy Queen secretly has a soft spot for the dragon. She pretends to be furious, but I've seen the way she smiles when she talks about him. Could there be a little romance brewing, hmm?"

Alarion's grin widened. A dragon and a fairy queen? That was definitely a tale worth remembering.

"And speaking of romance," the tree continued, its voice dropping to a whisper, "have you met the baker's apprentice in the village? Oh, the poor boy has the biggest crush on the village healer, but he's too shy to tell her! Every day, he bakes her pastries and leaves them on her doorstep, hoping she'll figure it out."

Alarion couldn't help but feel a bit touched. "That's sweet," he said. "Has she noticed?"

The tree's branches swayed as it let out a sigh. "Not yet. She thinks it's the wind spirits leaving her gifts. Can you believe it? Sometimes, love just needs a little push."

Alarion nodded thoughtfully. "Maybe I'll give the baker a hand. He could use some courage."

The tree chuckled, its deep voice shaking the leaves around them. "You're a good lad, Alarion. Always helping where you can."

Alarion smiled but then realized something. "Wait a minute... How do you know my name?"

The tree's eyes sparkled with amusement. "Oh, I know a lot more than that, my dear boy.

You've had quite the adventures since you arrived in Tiderune. And let me tell you, word travels fast around here."

Alarion rubbed the back of his neck, feeling a little sheepish. "I suppose I've had my fair share of... misadventures."

"Misadventures?" the tree said with a hearty laugh. "Oh, don't be modest! You've made quite the name for yourself. Why, just the other day, the Pixie Council was talking about that time you accidentally turned their entire village into candy. That was legendary!"

Alarion winced at the memory. "Yeah... that wasn't my finest moment."

"Oh, nonsense! They loved it! Well, after they figured out how to change everything back, of course. But you should have seen them—little pixies with candy wings, flying around with chocolate houses. It was delightful!"

Alarion couldn't help but laugh. "I guess it was a bit of fun."

The tree's eyes twinkled. "Exactly! And that's what makes you so beloved here. You bring a bit of chaos, sure, but you also bring joy. And Tiderune thrives on joy."

Alarion felt a warmth spread through him. It was nice to know that his presence was appreciated, even if things didn't always go as planned.

"So," Alarion said, leaning against the tree's trunk, "what other juicy gossip do you have?"

The tree's branches shook with glee. "Oh, you're going to love this one! Have you ever heard of the Sneaky Wind?"

Alarion's eyes lit up. "Oh, I've met the Sneaky Wind, alright."

The tree let out a booming laugh. "Of course you have! Well, the Sneaky Wind recently got into a bit of trouble with the Cloud Council. Apparently, it's been swiping the clouds' fluff for its own games, and now the skies have been looking a little... patchy."

Alarion grinned. "I can't say I'm surprised."

"And here's the best part," the tree continued, lowering its voice to a dramatic whisper. "The Cloud Council is planning a prank to get back at the Sneaky Wind. They're going to fill the skies with pink clouds made of cotton candy, just to confuse it!"

Alarion burst out laughing. The image of the Sneaky Wind getting tangled up in sticky pink clouds was too good to resist. "That's going to be a sight to see."

"Oh, it'll be spectacular!" the tree said with a mischievous glint in its eyes. "You'd better be there when it happens. It's bound to be one of the greatest pranks in Tiderune history."

Alarion shook his head, still chuckling. "I wouldn't miss it for the world."

As the sun began to set, casting a golden glow over the clearing, Alarion realized that he had spent hours talking with the tree. The stories and gossip had been too entertaining to walk away from.

"Well," Alarion said, standing up and stretching, "I should probably be on my way. But thanks for the stories. I haven't laughed like that in ages."

The tree gave a soft rustle, its leaves shimmering in the fading light. "You're welcome anytime, Alarion. And don't worry—I'll always have more gossip to share."

With a final wave, Alarion turned and made his way back through the woods, the tree's voice fading behind him.

"Don't forget to check on the baker!" the tree called out. "That boy needs all the help he can get!"

Alarion grinned, making a mental note to visit the village soon. Life in Tiderune was never dull, and with a talking tree as his new source of information, he knew there were plenty more adventures—and stories—waiting just around the corner.

Chapter 43: The Dragonfly Dilemma

Alarion encounters a dragonfly that can't remember where it left its favorite toy. Their search leads to some funny misunderstandings along the way.

The sun beamed brightly over Tiderune, casting playful shadows across the lush meadows where Alarion wandered. It was a perfect day for exploration, with fluffy clouds lazily drifting overhead and the air filled with the sweet scent of wildflowers. As Alarion meandered along a winding path, humming a cheerful tune, he heard a faint buzzing sound that caught his attention.

Curious, he followed the noise and soon stumbled upon a dazzling dragonfly, its wings glimmering in shades of emerald and sapphire. The little creature zoomed back and forth; its movements frantic yet graceful.

"Hey there! What's got you buzzing like a bumblebee on a sugar high?" Alarion called out, waving a hand in greeting.

The dragonfly halted mid-air, hovering in front of Alarion with a puzzled expression. "Oh, hi! I'm Dazzle! I've lost something very important and I'm in a bit of a pickle!"

Alarion chuckled at the name. "Dazzle, huh? Quite fitting for such a sparkly creature! What have you lost?"

With a dramatic flourish, Dazzle replied, "My favorite toy! It's a shimmering little pebble that sparkles like the stars! I can't remember where I left it, and without it, I can't do my favorite dance!"

ALARION TILTED HIS head, intrigued. "A pebble? A dancing dragonfly needs a pebble?"

"Not just any pebble! This one is special! It has magical properties that make me sparkle even more when I dance! I must find it!" Dazzle insisted, her wings fluttering with urgency.

"Well, I'm always up for an adventure!" Alarion declared. "Let's retrace your steps. Where did you last see your sparkling treasure?"

Dazzle thought for a moment, her tiny head tilting to the side. "Hmm, I was flitting around the pond when I first found it. Then I showed it to my friend, the ladybug, and after that... I can't remember!"

Alarion grinned. "The pond it is! Lead the way!"

As they made their way to the pond, Dazzle zipped ahead, chattering excitedly about her dance moves. "You should see me! When I dance with my pebble, it's like the stars have come down to join me! I twirl and spin, and everyone stops to watch!"

Alarion laughed. "I'd love to see that! But first, let's find that pebble."

Upon arriving at the pond, they found it as picturesque as ever. The water sparkled under the sun, and the lily pads floated serenely on its surface. Alarion crouched down, scanning the area. "Okay, where do we start?"

"Right here!" Dazzle exclaimed, pointing with a tiny leg at a cluster of reeds. "I was here, dancing with the ladybug when I must have dropped it!"

Alarion began searching through the reeds, pushing aside the tall grass and bending down to examine every nook and cranny. "Do you remember exactly what it looked like?"

"It was small, round, and sparkled like the sun! Oh! And it had a little heart carved into it!" Dazzle added, fluttering nervously.

"Got it!" Alarion exclaimed, pulling out a perfectly ordinary rock from behind a clump of grass. "Is this it?"

Dazzle squinted at the rock. "Um... not quite. That one looks a bit... ordinary. But keep looking!"

With a shrug, Alarion tossed the rock back into the water, sending ripples across the pond. "Alright! Let's try over there!" He pointed towards a patch of wildflowers blooming nearby.

As they sifted through the flowers, Alarion couldn't help but notice how Dazzle kept flitting from flower to flower, occasionally getting distracted by a particularly colorful bloom. "Focus, Dazzle! The pebble!" he reminded her.

"I can't help it! They're so pretty!" Dazzle giggled, her wings sparkling with delight. "But you're right; I need to concentrate!"

They continued their search, and as Alarion bent down to check under a blossom, Dazzle suddenly cried out. "Wait! I remember something else! I might have dropped it while flying over the old oak tree!"

Alarion's eyes widened with realization. "The old oak tree? That's quite a distance from here!"

"Yeah, but it's the last place I remember before I got all confused!" Dazzle insisted.

"Alright, then! Let's go!" Alarion said, and they took off towards the tree, Dazzle buzzing excitedly around him.

As they reached the old oak, Dazzle zipped around the branches, calling out, "Pebble! Where are you?" But after an extensive search of the area, the pebble remained elusive.

"I can't believe I lost it again! What if it's gone forever?" Dazzle lamented, her wings drooping slightly.

"Don't worry! We'll find it," Alarion assured her. "Let's think. You said you were dancing, right? Maybe we should try recreating the dance you did when you lost it!"

Dazzle's eyes brightened. "That might just work! Okay, I remember a little bit. Just a little spin, a little twirl, and a buzz!"

Alarion watched as Dazzle began to flit about, spinning and twirling in the air, her little legs moving in an oddly infectious rhythm. "Come on, Alarion! Dance with me!" she called.

Alarion, feeling silly but willing to give it a go, began to twirl along with Dazzle. He spun and flailed his arms, trying to keep up with the dragonfly's intricate movements. Dazzle burst into laughter, and soon, Alarion couldn't help but laugh, too. They danced around the base of the oak tree, creating a comical spectacle of jumping, twirling, and spinning.

Suddenly, Dazzle paused mid-spin. "Wait! I just remembered! I did a big flip right here!"

And as she did a dramatic flip, Alarion stumbled backward, tripping over his own feet. He flailed his arms, trying to regain his balance, but ended up crashing into a pile of leaves.

Dazzle hovered above, laughing uncontrollably. "That was so funny! You should have seen yourself!"

"Very funny!" Alarion laughed, brushing off the leaves. "But did it help you remember?"

Dazzle tilted her head, deep in thought. "Hmm, I remember a flash of sparkles when I flipped! And then... I think I saw it roll towards the bushes!"

"Then let's check there!" Alarion exclaimed, scrambling to his feet and heading toward the bush.

As they searched through the foliage, Alarion spotted a glimmering object nestled among the leaves. "Could it be...?"

"Is it my pebble?" Dazzle buzzed with excitement.

With a triumphant grin, Alarion reached in and pulled out the pebble. It sparkled brilliantly in the sunlight, and just as Dazzle had described, a little heart was indeed carved into its surface.

"I found it!" Alarion cheered, holding it up for Dazzle to see.

"Oh, my goodness! Yes! Yes! Yes!" Dazzle danced in mid-air, her joy bubbling over. "You did it! You found my pebble!"

Alarion felt a rush of satisfaction as he handed the pebble to the ecstatic dragonfly. "Now you can dance again!"

With the pebble secured, Dazzle zipped around in circles, her wings shimmering as she executed an extravagant series of spins and twirls. "Look at me! Look at me! I'm dancing!" she cried, her laughter echoing in the air.

Alarion watched, his heart warming at the sight. Dazzle's delight was infectious, and he couldn't help but smile as she danced with all her might, glittering like a star in the sky.

Suddenly, Dazzle landed beside Alarion, her eyes sparkling with gratitude. "Thank you so much! You've saved my dance and my day! I couldn't have done it without you!"

"Anytime, Dazzle! I had a blast," Alarion replied, chuckling at the memory of their silly dance. "And next time, try to keep a better eye on your favorite toy!"

Dazzle giggled, her wings flickering with joy. "You bet! And hey, if you ever want to join me for a dance, just let me know! We could use some more laughter in Tiderune!"

"I'll take you up on that," Alarion said, grinning. "But let's just skip the flipping part next time, alright?"

As they shared a laugh, Alarion felt a surge of warmth for the lively little dragonfly. Their adventure had turned into something unexpected and wonderful, and he realized that sometimes, the best moments in life came from the most delightful dilemmas.

With their hearts light and laughter lingering in the air, Alarion and Dazzle set off together, ready to tackle whatever new adventures awaited them in the enchanting world of Tiderune.

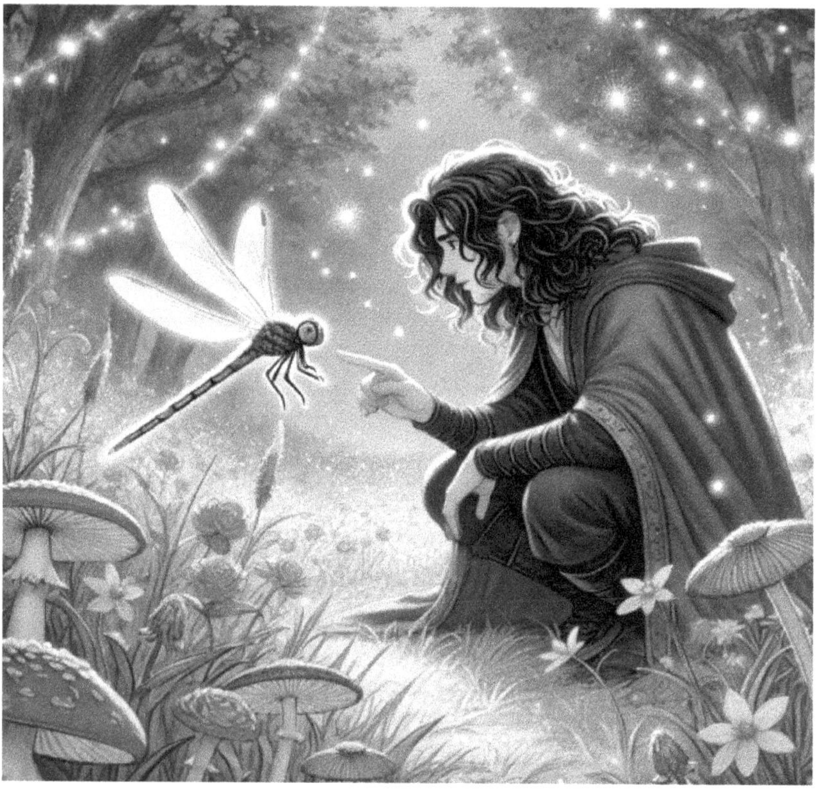

Chapter 44: The Bubblegum Potion

In a quest for knowledge, Alarion tries a potion that makes everything taste like Bubblegum. His serious discussions quickly turn into sweet chaos!

In the magical realm of Tiderune, where the air was always fragrant with blooming flowers and the sun painted the sky in vibrant hues, Alarion found himself standing before the grand, mystical library of Eldoria. With towering shelves filled with ancient tomes and bubbling potions, it was a haven for anyone seeking knowledge—or trouble, as was often the case for Alarion.

Today, he was on a quest for a special potion that promised to enhance one's intellect and sharpen one's wit. The potion was said to be hidden deep within the library, guarded by an eccentric old wizard named Professor Whimsy. The stories about him were legendary; he had a knack for turning the mundane into the bizarre.

"Just one little potion and I'll be the smartest mage in Tiderune!" Alarion muttered to himself, puffing out his chest in determination. He adjusted his satchel, feeling the weight of his ambitions, and stepped into the library.

The inside was as magical as the tales suggested. The walls shimmered with enchanted dust, and every book seemed to whisper secrets. As Alarion wandered through the aisles, he spotted Professor Whimsy, a tall figure with wild white hair that looked like it had been styled by a particularly mischievous wind.

"Ah, young Alarion!" the professor exclaimed, peering at him through thick spectacles that magnified his eyes comically. "What brings you to my sanctuary of wisdom today?"

"I'm here for the potion of enhanced intellect, Professor!" Alarion announced, hoping to sound more confident than he felt.

"Ah, yes! The potion of enhanced intellect!" Professor Whimsy echoed, rubbing his chin thoughtfully. "However, I must warn you—this potion comes with a catch. Are you ready for a surprise?"

Alarion's curiosity piqued. "What kind of surprise?"

"Just a little side effect," the professor grinned. "Once consumed, everything you taste will turn into Bubblegum flavour! It's quite delightful but can lead to, shall we say, unexpected outcomes!"

Alarion's eyes widened. "Bubblegum flavour? Like, everything I taste?"

"Indeed! Now, are you interested?" Professor Whimsy asked, his eyes twinkling with mischief.

With a mix of excitement and hesitation, Alarion nodded. "Sure, why not? I'll take the risk!"

The professor clapped his hands, and a bubbling cauldron appeared before them, filled with a swirling, luminescent liquid. After adding a few strange ingredients—like a pinch of fairy dust and a sprig of mint—he ladled some potion into a crystal vial. "Drink this, and may your intellect soar like an eagle!"

Alarion took the vial and gulped it down. The taste was surprisingly pleasant—a burst of sweetness exploded in his mouth, reminiscent of summer days and carefree laughter. "Wow, this is amazing!" he exclaimed.

Just then, Professor Whimsy clapped his hands again, and a small bell chimed. "Now, let's discuss the latest theories on magical energy!"

Alarion nodded, eager to engage in serious discussions. But as he opened his mouth to respond, a strange sensation took hold. "Umm, well…" he began, only to burst into laughter as his words transformed into sugary sounds. "Everything tastes like Bubblegum!"

The professor's expression shifted from scholarly to bewildered as Alarion struggled to articulate his thoughts through fits of giggles. "Exactly!" the professor said, chuckling. "Bubblegum thoughts, I see!"

Alarion tried to regain his composure, but every serious point he attempted to make was met with a pop and a fizz. "This potion might be too… sweet!" he laughed, clutching his stomach. "I was ready to dive into the intricacies of magic, but all I can think about now is cotton candy clouds and Bubblegum rain!"

As Alarion continued to flounder in his attempts to discuss magical energy, the room around them began to change. The more he spoke, the more whimsical and colorful it became. The shelves transformed into candy cane pillars, and the air filled with the sweet scent of spun sugar. Books flapped their covers like wings, and Alarion found himself in the middle of a candy wonderland.

"Oh, this is getting out of hand!" he exclaimed, his laughter mingling with the sweetness. "I didn't sign up for a candy party!"

"Indeed, but it seems your intellect has taken a backseat to your taste buds!" the professor replied, laughing heartily. "Let's see if we can turn this chaos into a learning experience!"

Suddenly, a group of animated candies—gummy bears, lollipops, and chocolate bars—began to dance around them, performing a hilarious routine. Alarion couldn't help but join in, twirling and hopping as he tried to keep up with their sugary steps. The dance was utterly ridiculous, with Alarion flailing about, and he felt lighter and more carefree than ever.

Amid the colorful mayhem, Dazzle the dragonfly buzzed in through an open window. "What on earth is happening here?" she laughed, seeing Alarion caught during a candy-inspired frenzy. "Are you throwing a Bubblegum party without me?"

Alarion waved his arms. "Dazzle! You have to try this potion! Everything is Bubblegum flavored, and I can't stop laughing!"

"Sounds like you're having a blast!" Dazzle giggled, zipping around him. "But I hope you don't forget about your studies!"

"Studies? What studies?" Alarion shouted, still caught in the whirl of candy chaos. "I'm just trying to figure out how to stop this giggle fest!"

Professor Whimsy, thoroughly entertained, waved his wand, and with a sprinkle of sparkling dust, the library began to return to normal. The shelves straightened up, the animated candies retreated, and the swirling colors faded. Alarion stood in the center, panting and breathless, a goofy grin plastered on his face.

"Looks like the potion has worn off," the professor said, still chuckling. "Though it seems you've learned an important lesson today."

"What's that?" Alarion asked, wiping away a tear of laughter.

"That knowledge doesn't always come from seriousness. Sometimes, it's found in laughter and lightness!" Professor Whimsy replied, his eyes twinkling. "And in your case, perhaps a little too much Bubblegum."

Dazzle landed on Alarion's shoulder, her wings still sparkling. "You know, Alarion, I think you might have stumbled onto something wonderful. A serious discussion mixed with laughter could bring the best ideas to light!"

Alarion nodded, realizing that while he had come in search of knowledge, he had left with a valuable lesson on the importance of joy. "You're right! Maybe I don't always need to be so serious. Learning can be fun!"

With a newfound perspective, Alarion looked at Professor Whimsy, who smiled knowingly. "Would you like to try another potion, perhaps one that enhances your creativity instead of your intellect?"

Alarion grinned, this time with a hint of mischief. "Only if it doesn't turn everything into Bubblegum!"

As laughter echoed through the library, Alarion realized that sometimes, the sweetest moments were the ones filled with laughter, and perhaps a little Bubblegum chaos was just what he needed to remind him of that joy. With that thought in mind, he was ready for whatever magical adventures awaited him next in Tiderune.

Chapter 45: The Funny Shadows

Alarion finds that his shadow has a mind of its own, mimicking all his movements in a hilariously exaggerated way, leading to a shadowy showdown!

In the whimsical land of Tiderune, where the extraordinary was commonplace, Alarion had become quite the adventurer. He had faced dragons, danced with fairies, and even managed to charm a rather grumpy gnome. But nothing could prepare him for the day his own shadow decided to take centre stage.

It all began on a bright morning when Alarion was preparing for a stroll through the enchanted woods. The sun filtered through the leaves, creating dappled patterns on the forest floor. As he stepped outside, he felt a familiar flutter of excitement. "Another day of adventure awaits!" he declared, puffing out his chest in triumph.

However, as Alarion took his first step, he noticed something peculiar: his shadow seemed to be lagging behind, looking a little... lazy. "Come on, Shadow! We have places to go!" he called out, laughing. To his surprise, his shadow responded by stretching out like a cat, yawning exaggeratedly before it finally followed suit.

"Are you always this dramatic?" Alarion chuckled, shaking his head as he continued on his path. Little did he know, today was about to get much more entertaining.

As Alarion strolled deeper into the woods, he began to notice his shadow behaving in the most peculiar ways. Each time he lifted his arm, his shadow would send it sky-high, as if trying to take flight. "What are you doing, Shadow? You're not a bird!" he laughed, but his shadow only responded with a cheeky twist, as if to say, "Watch me!"

Soon, the antics escalated. Whenever Alarion bent down to pick a flower, his shadow would perform an elaborate somersault. Alarion burst into laughter, clapping his hands. "Now that's impressive! But can you do this?" He tried to imitate his shadow's dramatic movements, only to end up tumbling into a bush of flowers, sending petals flying everywhere.

Just as he was emerging from his floral mishap, Alarion heard a giggle nearby. Turning around, he spotted Dazzle the dragonfly, perched on a shimmering leaf, her wings fluttering with amusement. "You and your shadow make quite the comedy duo!" she exclaimed, trying to stifle her laughter.

"Right?" Alarion replied, brushing petals off his clothes. "I think it's trying to steal my spotlight!" He paused, narrowing his eyes playfully at his shadow. "Are you trying to upstage me, little guy?"

To Alarion's shock, his shadow seemed to nod enthusiastically. It then mimicked his exaggerated pout, causing Alarion to laugh uncontrollably. "Alright, alright! You're in charge for today!" he said, holding his hands up in surrender.

As they continued their walk, Alarion noticed that his shadow was becoming more and more animated. It began to mimic not just his movements but also his facial expressions, going as far as to pull silly faces. Alarion could hardly contain his laughter, especially when it scrunched up its "face" in a ridiculously exaggerated pout, mirroring his attempts at seriousness.

"Let's have a little contest, shall we?" Dazzle suggested, her eyes sparkling with mischief. "How about a shadow showdown? Who can perform the best moves?"

Alarion, always up for a challenge, grinned widely. "You're on!" he declared. "I'll go first!"

With that, Alarion started off with a series of dramatic dance moves. He spun around, twirled, and even attempted a little jig. His shadow, however, took it a step further, executing each move with exaggerated flair. It spun like a whirling dervish, its "arms" flailing about in ways that defied the laws of physics.

As Alarion leaped into a graceful pirouette, his shadow responded by puffing up and then crashing down in a hilariously ungraceful tumble. The contrast was so absurd that Dazzle burst into laughter, her tiny wings sparkling in the sunlight. "Your shadow has some serious style!"

"Alright, Shadow! You win that round!" Alarion chuckled, giving it a playful salute. "But let's see how well you can mimic this!" He decided to switch it up and launched into a series of exaggerated karate chops, channelling his inner martial artist.

To his astonishment, his shadow began to mimic him perfectly—only it exaggerated every move even more. It performed an entire routine of karate moves that included wildly flailing limbs, twisting and turning in every possible direction. Alarion couldn't help but double over in laughter. "This is the best shadow ever!"

Dazzle clapped her tiny hands together. "You should really take your shadow on stage! It could be a star!"

\But just as Alarion was about to respond, something unexpected happened. His shadow, emboldened by the applause, suddenly took off running down the path ahead, causing Alarion to gasp in surprise. "Hey! Where do you think you're going?" he called out, chasing after it.

The chase was on! Alarion darted through the trees, his shadow zipping ahead, hopping over logs and skirting around bushes as if it were a living entity. Dazzle zipped along beside them, cheering Alarion on. "Go, go, go! Don't let it escape!"

Alarion's laughter filled the air as he tried to catch up, but his shadow seemed to have its own agenda, veering off in every direction.

It pretended to slip on imaginary banana peels, doing a little dance whenever it fell, which made Alarion laugh even harder.

Just when Alarion thought he had his shadow cornered, it dashed behind a tree. He skidded to a stop, peering around the trunk, and saw that his shadow was now doing the chicken dance! "You've got to be kidding me!" he exclaimed, clutching his sides in mirth.

"Looks like it's found its groove!" Dazzle laughed, her wings shimmering in delight.

Determined to outsmart his mischievous shadow, Alarion devised a plan. "Alright, Shadow, you want a showdown? Let's see who can do the funniest move!" He quickly started flapping his arms like a bird, waddling in place, and doing a ridiculous little jig.

To his surprise, his shadow not only copied him but took it to a whole new level. It wobbled, fluttered, and made funny little jumps that made Dazzle roar with laughter. "That's not a dance; that's a shadow spectacle!"

Realizing that this was more fun than any serious contest could ever be, Alarion decided to lean into the silliness. He danced and pranced, letting his shadow take the lead. The forest echoed with laughter as they became a chaotic duo, their movements spiralling into a whirlwind of comedic antics.

Eventually, they both collapsed in a fit of giggles, lying on the grass as the sun began to dip below the horizon, painting the sky in shades of orange and pink. "You know," Alarion said, breathless from laughter, "I think I've learned something important today."

"What's that?" Dazzle asked, her voice still tinged with glee.

"Sometimes, you just have to let loose and be a little silly," Alarion replied, looking at his shadow, which was now lying next to him, mimicking his relaxed pose. "Life's too short to take everything so seriously."

As the last rays of sunlight faded, casting long shadows across the forest floor, Alarion felt a warm sense of camaraderie with his playful shadow. It had turned a simple day into an unforgettable adventure filled with laughter, friendship, and a dash of magic.

With a satisfied sigh, Alarion stood up, brushing off the grass from his clothes. "Alright, Shadow, what do you say we head back home and plan our next adventure?"

His shadow sprang to life, leaping to its feet with a playful bounce, clearly eager for whatever hilarious escapade lay ahead. With Dazzle fluttering above them, Alarion and his silly shadow ventured back through the woods, their hearts light and laughter echoing in the air—a reminder that sometimes, the funniest moments come from the unexpected.

Chapter 46: The Flying Fish

During a trip to the ocean, Alarion meets fish that can fly! Their aerial antics create a splash, leading to a flurry of fishy fun!

The salty breeze whipped through Alarion's hair as he strolled along the sun-kissed shore of Tiderune's coastline. It was a day meant for adventure, the kind where the sky melted into the ocean, and the horizon promised mysteries beyond imagination. The waves danced playfully, inviting him closer. Little did he know, today's escapade would be like none other.

As Alarion wandered, he spotted a cluster of vibrant colors flickering beneath the water's surface. Intrigued, he squatted down, peering into the crystalline depths. Just then, a peculiar fish leaped out of the water, flipping gracefully into the air before splashing back down, sending droplets glimmering like jewels all around.

"Whoa!" Alarion gasped, leaning forward. "Did that fish just... fly?"

A chorus of laughter erupted behind him, and Alarion turned to find Dazzle the dragonfly hovering nearby, her eyes sparkling with mischief. "Oh, Alarion! You haven't seen anything yet!"

With a playful twinkle in her eye, she darted toward the water, beckoning him to follow. Eager to see more, Alarion chased after her, the sand squishing between his toes. He soon reached the water's edge, where the fish were putting on a show like no other.

They jumped and soared, performing acrobatic flips in midair, their scales shimmering in the sunlight. Each leap sent a cascade of water droplets flying, creating a sparkling rainbow in the sky. "Look at them go!" Alarion shouted, clapping his hands in delight.

Dazzle giggled, her wings fluttering with excitement. "They're called Flying Fish! They can glide through the air to escape predators. Isn't it magnificent?"

Alarion could hardly believe his eyes. "This is incredible! Can I join them?" he asked, his curiosity piqued.

"Why not?" Dazzle replied, winking. "Just don't forget your swimming skills!" With that, she zipped down to the water's edge, ready to dive in.

Alarion hesitated for a moment, then took a deep breath, stripping off his shirt and rolling up his pants. He waded into the ocean, feeling the cool water envelop him. The fish, sensing his presence, began to gather around him, their playful spirits infectious.

"Hey there, friends!" he called out, splashing playfully. "I hear you can fly! Show me your tricks!"

One particularly bold fish, adorned in bright hues of blue and gold, swam up to him. "Care to join our aerial dance?" it chirped, its voice bubbling with excitement.

"Absolutely!" Alarion exclaimed, his heart racing. He was ready for an adventure that would take him beyond the waves.

With a playful flip, the fish launched itself into the air, gliding effortlessly above the water. "Follow me!" it called, zipping back and forth. Alarion watched, captivated, as the fish soared higher and higher, diving and twisting through the air with such elegance that it looked as if it were choreographing a grand ballet.

Alarion took a leap of faith, pushing off the water's surface. To his astonishment, he found himself gliding after the fish, riding a small wave. He couldn't believe his luck! "This is amazing!" he shouted, laughing as he attempted to mimic their moves.

As he soared, the other fish joined in, creating a colorful formation. They flipped and spun around him, creating a flurry of movement that made Alarion feel like a part of their aquatic world. "Let's do a loop-de-loop!" the blue and goldfish suggested, darting around in a circular motion.

"Alright! On three!" Alarion replied, excitement bubbling within him. "One... two... three!" They twirled in the air, laughter echoing across the ocean as they created a whirlpool of splashes and sparkling droplets.

However, just as Alarion was about to complete his loop, he miscalculated his leap. Instead of gliding gracefully, he belly-flopped back into the water, creating a massive splash. The fish erupted into giggles, their bubbly laughter ringing in his ears.

"Nice dive, Alarion!" Dazzle teased, hovering above him. "But I think you need to work on your aerial skills a bit!"

Flushing with embarrassment but unable to hide his grin, Alarion swam back to the surface. "Alright, alright! I'll stick to the ground for a while." He took a moment to catch his breath, wiping droplets from his face before he noticed something shimmering beneath the waves.

"Hey, what's that?" he pointed curiously.

The blue and goldfish swam closer. "That's our treasure! Follow me!" It led Alarion toward a patch of vibrant coral, where something glimmered enticingly among the seaweed.

As Alarion approached, he discovered a small chest partially buried in the sand. "A treasure chest? Here?" he exclaimed; eyes wide with excitement.

"Absolutely! We've kept it hidden for ages!" the fish exclaimed, its fins flapping eagerly. "Let's open it!"

With the help of the other fish, they dug out the chest and hoisted it up to the surface. Alarion couldn't believe his eyes as they cracked it open, revealing a collection of sparkling seashells, shiny coins, and a note that read: "To those who embrace adventure, may your days be filled with laughter and joy!"

Alarion beamed at the treasure, but more than that, he felt a deep sense of camaraderie with his newfound friends. "This is incredible! Let's share this with everyone!"

The fish chirped excitedly in agreement. "Yes! Let's throw a party on the beach!"

As they splashed back to shore, Alarion helped gather shells and other treasures to share with the villagers. By the time they reached the beach, a festive atmosphere was already brewing. Children laughed and played, and the sun began its descent, painting the sky in hues of pink and orange.

With the help of Dazzle and the flying fish, Alarion organized an impromptu beach party. They set up decorations with colorful seashells, while the fish entertained the villagers with their incredible aerial performances. Alarion couldn't stop laughing as they leaped into the air, performing dazzling tricks and splashes, each jump accompanied by cheerful squeals.

As night fell, the atmosphere transformed into a magical celebration. Lanterns lit up the beach, casting a warm glow on everyone gathered. Alarion watched as the villagers enjoyed the fish's antics, dancing and cheering, their laughter blending with the sounds of the ocean waves.

"Alarion!" Dazzle called, flitting toward him, her wings sparkling in the soft light. "You should join in on the fun! Dance with me!"

Feeling bold, Alarion took Dazzle's tiny hands and twirled her around, leading her into a playful dance. The music from the village mingled with the sounds of the ocean, creating a joyful melody that echoed into the night. "I never imagined today would be so magical!" he exclaimed, laughing as Dazzle twirled, her tiny form illuminated by the lanterns.

As they danced under the stars, Alarion couldn't help but feel a connection to the world around him—an appreciation for friendship, adventure, and the beauty of unexpected moments. He looked around at the happy faces, the shimmering sea, and the joy in his heart.

Just then, the flying fish soared overhead, leaving trails of shimmering water in their wake. One particularly cheeky fish landed on Alarion's shoulder, wiggling its fins playfully. "Thanks for the fun, Alarion!" it bubbled, nuzzling against him.

"You're welcome! You all made this day unforgettable!" Alarion replied, reaching up to give the fish a gentle pat.

As the party continued, he realized that Tiderune was not just a land of wonders but also of connections—whether with flying fish or playful dragonflies, adventures were made richer when shared. Underneath the starry sky, he knew he'd carry these memories in his heart forever, ready for whatever whimsical adventure awaited him next.

Chapter 47: The Dancing Shadows

Alarion discovers that shadows can dance when no one is looking. He accidentally becomes the star of a shadow dance party!

The sun had just dipped below the horizon, painting the sky in hues of purple and gold, casting a warm glow over the enchanted land of Tiderune. Alarion found himself wandering through the Whispering Woods, a place known for its shimmering leaves and curious creatures. He had always loved exploring here, especially when the sunset, as it seemed to breathe a different kind of magic into the air.

As he ventured deeper into the woods, he noticed the gentle rustle of leaves and the soft sounds of creatures settling down for the night. "Tonight feels special," he mused, feeling a flutter of excitement in his chest. But little did he know, that magic was already brewing around him.

While walking, Alarion stumbled upon a clearing bathed in the fading light. It was then that he spotted something peculiar—a series of shadows dancing across the ground, swirling and twirling as if they were alive. He rubbed his eyes, convinced he was imagining things. "Am I losing it?" he chuckled to himself.

Intrigued, he stepped closer, and suddenly, the shadows froze, as if they were caught in a moment of surprise. "Okay, this is just weird," he said aloud, tilting his head in confusion. But then, the moment he turned away, the shadows sprang back to life, kicking and twirling in a joyful frenzy.

Alarion couldn't help but laugh. "Alright, shadows, you want to dance? Let's see what you've got!" he declared, and to his astonishment, the shadows responded, forming a semi-circle around him. It seemed they were eager for a dance partner.

Taking a deep breath, he twirled around, his arms outstretched. The moment his shadow hit the ground, it erupted into a flurry of movement, mimicking him with exaggerated grace. The shadows began to copy his every move but with a twist—each step was adorned with silly flourishes that made him laugh uncontrollably.

"Oh, so you think you can dance better than me?" he teased, doing a little jig. The shadows swirled faster, moving in sync with his playful antics. Soon, Alarion found himself lost in the moment, forgetting all about the world outside the clearing.

With every turn, jump, and spin, the shadows grew bolder. They leaped and lunged, creating a mesmerizing performance that had Alarion giggling like a child. "This is amazing!" he exclaimed, clapping his hands as they danced around him, their movements a delightful mix of humor and grace.

But as he danced, he noticed something peculiar—the shadows were starting to take on personalities of their own. One shadow, a rather cheeky fellow, began to twirl and flip, trying to impress Alarion. "Is that all you've got?" Alarion called out playfully. The shadow puffed up its chest, clearly accepting the challenge.

As the shadows competed for his attention, a competitive spirit ignited in Alarion. "Alright, let's make this a dance-off!" he proclaimed, striking a dramatic pose. The shadows cheered silently, as their forms twisted and stretched in excitement.

Alarion began a series of ridiculous dance moves—silly slides, the moonwalk, and even the chicken dance. The shadows, always eager to keep up, mirrored him flawlessly but added their own hilarious interpretations. Alarion laughed until his stomach hurt as he watched his shadow kick its legs out wildly, looking as if it were caught in a fit of giggles.

"Okay, okay! Let's see who can do the best spin!" he challenged, spinning in place with all his might. The shadows responded in unison, their forms spinning faster and faster, creating a whirlwind of darkness and light. The air was filled with joyous energy as if the very forest was alive with laughter.

In the fun, Alarion couldn't help but feel a warm connection with these dancing shadows. It was as if they understood him in a way that no one else could, responding to his laughter and joy. As he took a break, panting from the exuberance, the shadows gathered closer, their shapes shifting as if they were forming a circle around him.

"Alright, you shadow dancers," he said, still catching his breath. "What's next? A grand finale?"

At that moment, one shadow moved forward, its form elongating dramatically. It twirled in a graceful arc before leaping into the air, soaring higher and higher until it seemed to float just above Alarion's head. Then, with a flourish, it came crashing down, creating a soft landing that sent a ripple of giggles through the other shadows.

Alarion clapped, utterly amazed. "That was incredible! You're all amazing!"

Feeling inspired, he joined the shadows for one last dance. They moved in unison, a swirling mass of limbs and laughter, creating a beautiful tapestry of movement against the backdrop of the darkening sky. The world around them faded away as the shadows took centre stage, twirling and leaping under the soft glow of the moonlight.

Just when he thought the night couldn't get any better, a soft voice floated through the air. "You're quite the dancer, Alarion!"

Startled, Alarion turned to see Lira, the graceful fairy he had met during one of his previous adventures. She floated above him, her wings sparkling like stardust. "I've been watching from the trees. You've made the shadows come alive!"

Alarion's heart skipped a beat, not just from surprise but from joy. "Lira! You should join us!" he urged, his eyes sparkling with mischief.

"Oh, I don't know," she giggled, her cheeks flushing slightly. "I might not be as good as your shadows."

"Come on! It's all in good fun!" Alarion replied, gesturing for her to join. "We're just here to dance and enjoy the night!"

With a twinkle in her eye, Lira descended, landing gracefully beside him. "Alright, but only if you promise to teach me some of those silly moves!"

Alarion laughed, feeling a surge of excitement. "Deal!" And with that, the three of them—Alarion, Lira, and the dancing shadows—formed a delightful trio, twirling and spinning beneath the stars.

As they danced, the shadows became more animated, adding whimsical touches to their movements. Lira laughed as she tried to imitate the shadows, her own graceful dance style intertwining with their silly antics. Alarion couldn't help but admire how beautiful she looked under the moonlight, her laughter blending with the soft sounds of the night.

Hours seemed to pass in what felt like mere moments, and soon the night grew late. Breathing heavily, Alarion and Lira collapsed onto the grass, laughter bubbling between them like a joyful melody. The shadows, too, seemed to tire, gathering in a gentle heap around them, settling down as the night wore on.

"Thank you for tonight, Alarion," Lira said softly, her voice a soothing whisper against the night. "It's not every day you find dancing shadows and a fun partner."

"Thank you for joining in! I couldn't have imagined this night without you," Alarion replied, smiling warmly. They exchanged a glance, the kind that held a promise of more adventures to come.

As they lay there, gazing up at the stars twinkling overhead, Alarion felt an unexpected warmth spread in his chest. It was a feeling of connection, of joy, and perhaps something a little more—something magical.

With the sounds of the Whispering Woods cradling them, Alarion made a silent promise to cherish moments like this, where laughter, shadows, and newfound friendships intertwined in the most unexpected of ways. As he closed his eyes, he couldn't help but smile, knowing that tomorrow would bring another adventure, another dance, and perhaps more delightful surprises in the enchanting world of Tiderune.

Chapter 48: The Topsy-Turvy Treehouse

Alarion finds a treehouse that's built upside down. As he navigates the crazy structure, he learns that sometimes things can be funnier when they're topsy-turvy!

In the whimsical world of Tiderune, where magic danced in the air and adventure lurked around every corner, Alarion woke up one sunny morning with a sense of excitement bubbling inside him. Today, he had decided to explore a part of the Whispering Woods he had never ventured into before. Whispers of a strange and enchanting treehouse had reached his ears, and he was eager to see it for himself.

As Alarion journeyed deeper into the woods, he stumbled upon a clearing where an enormous tree stood majestically. But this wasn't just any tree—it was an extraordinary sight, with its roots twisted high in the air and its branches stretched downwards, forming a most peculiar treehouse that appeared to be completely upside down!

"Now that's something you don't see every day," Alarion chuckled to himself, scratching his head in disbelief. He approached the treehouse, his curiosity piqued. How on Tiderune could anyone even get up there?

Just then, a cheerful squirrel scampered down the trunk. "Hey there, Alarion! You here to check out the Topsy-Turvy Treehouse?" it chattered excitedly, its bushy tail twitching with enthusiasm.

"Uh, yeah! How do you get up there?" Alarion asked, looking up at the strange structure that hung precariously from the tree.

"Easy peasy!" the squirrel said, gesturing to a nearby set of colorful ropes. "Just climb the ropes and enjoy the fun! But be careful—things can get a little kooky inside!" With that, the squirrel zipped back up the tree, leaving Alarion chuckling at its antics.

Feeling adventurous, Alarion grabbed hold of the ropes and began to climb. Each step felt thrilling, and soon he found himself reaching the entrance of the treehouse. He hesitated for a moment, glancing back down at the ground, but the excitement of exploring this topsy-turvy wonder outweighed any hesitation.

With a deep breath, he swung open the door and stepped inside. The moment he crossed the threshold, a delightful confusion greeted him. The floor was on the ceiling, and furniture was stuck to the walls, swaying slightly as if anticipating his every move. Alarion's eyes widened in amazement as he took in the sight of upside-down chairs, dangling light fixtures, and a rather confused-looking cat hanging lazily from a bookshelf.

"Welcome!" the cat said, yawning widely as if this was the most ordinary thing in the world. "I'm Whiskers. Care for a cup of tea?"

"Um, sure!" Alarion replied, suppressing a laugh at the sight of the cat balancing a teapot on its head. It poured tea into an upside-down cup resting on the ceiling, sending a stream of liquid tumbling towards the floor. Alarion couldn't help but burst into laughter as he watched the teapot do a little jig, bouncing off the ceiling in an attempt to keep up with the cup.

"Careful! That one's a bit rambunctious," Whiskers said, grinning as the cup rolled away. "But it's all part of the charm in here."

Alarion took a seat on an upside-down chair, which felt surprisingly comfortable. "This place is incredible! I've never seen anything like it!"

"Oh, it gets better," Whiskers winked. "Just wait until you see the sliding board."

"Sliding board?" Alarion echoed, his curiosity growing. "How does that work in a treehouse that's upside down?"

Whiskers gestured to a colorful slide that seemed to emerge from the ceiling and curl around the walls. "Why don't you give it a try? It's the highlight of the treehouse!"

With a mischievous grin, Alarion decided to embrace the whimsy of the treehouse. He climbed up to the start of the slide, which felt like a ride through a funhouse. With a slight push, he launched himself down the slide, the world blurring into a whirlwind of colors and laughter as he spiralled through the air.

When he finally landed with a soft thud on the "floor" (which was really the ceiling from the outside perspective), he found himself laughing uncontrollably. "That was amazing!" he shouted, eyes wide with delight.

Just then, the entrance door swung open, and a young girl appeared, her eyes sparkling with mischief. "Hey! Did I hear someone having fun without me?" she exclaimed, her voice bright and cheerful.

"Who are you?" Alarion asked, getting to his feet and brushing off imaginary dust from his shoulders.

"I'm Bella!" she said, bouncing on her toes. "I live nearby, and I've heard all about this place. Mind if I join the fun?"

"Not at all! The more, the merrier!" Alarion said, gesturing for her to come in.

Bella stepped inside and looked around in awe. "Wow! It's even crazier than I imagined!" She immediately darted over to the wall where a collection of plush cushions hung like a tapestry. "Can we jump into the cushions? They look so soft!"

"Let's do it!" Alarion replied, racing over to join her. They both leaped onto the cushions, which bounced them back up into the air. Laughter filled the treehouse as they played, rolling and tumbling through the fuzzy, floating cushions.

"This place is the best!" Bella exclaimed between fits of giggles. "I love how everything is upside down! It makes everything feel so… magical!"

Just then, a burst of colorful confetti rained down from above, seemingly from nowhere, causing them both to erupt into fits of laughter. "Okay, now that's just silly!" Alarion said, wiping tears of laughter from his eyes.

After a while, they settled down, lying back on the cushions and looking up at the ceiling, which, from their perspective, was the floor. "You know," Bella said, her voice softening, "this topsy-turvy place makes me think about how sometimes, life can be really unpredictable. But that's what makes it fun, right?"

Alarion nodded thoughtfully. "Yeah! It's like this treehouse. Things don't always have to be straight and perfect. Sometimes, the wackiest experiences turn out to be the most memorable." He glanced over at her, feeling a warmth in his heart as he realized how much he enjoyed her company.

Just then, Whiskers the cat sauntered over, licking its paws. "You two are quite the pair! Maybe you should come back and visit more often. We could have tea parties and cushion races every day!"

"Tea parties sound wonderful!" Bella said enthusiastically, her eyes lighting up. "I'd love to come back and have more adventures here!"

Feeling a sense of camaraderie forming, Alarion turned to Bella with a bright smile. "How about we make a pact? We'll return to this treehouse whenever we need a little adventure or just want to escape from the ordinary!"

"Deal!" she replied, holding out her Pinky finger for him to seal the agreement. They both giggled as they intertwined their pinkies, feeling as if they had just created their own little secret world.

The sun began to set outside, casting an enchanting golden light that streamed through the upside-down windows, filling the treehouse with a warm glow. Alarion couldn't help but feel grateful for this unexpected friendship and the topsy-turvy adventures they had shared.

As the evening wore on, Alarion and Bella enjoyed a delightful tea party with Whiskers, sipping tea from their upside-down cups and laughing at the antics of the bouncing cushions. They shared stories, dreams, and giggles that echoed through the enchanting Topsy-Turvy Treehouse, creating memories that would surely last a lifetime.

As the stars began to twinkle in the night sky, Alarion and Bella knew that this was only the beginning of their adventures in Tiderune. With each visit to the treehouse, they would uncover more delightful surprises, laughter, and perhaps a touch of magic that made life feel wonderfully topsy-turvy.

And as they eventually bid farewell to the treehouse, Alarion felt a sense of joy swell in his heart. Sometimes, it took a little upside-down adventure to find the right path, and he was excited to see where their newfound friendship would lead them next.

Chapter 49: The Great Giggle Hunt

A treasure map leads Alarion on a quest to find the greatest giggle in Tiderune. His journey turns into a hilarious adventure filled with laughter!

In the vibrant land of Tiderune, where the skies shimmered with hues of lavender and the fields danced with wildflowers, Alarion awoke to the sound of laughter wafting through his window. Today was a special day; a treasure map had mysteriously appeared at his doorstep the night before, and the whispers of adventure tickled his imagination.

Grabbing a piece of toast and stuffing it in his mouth, Alarion rushed outside to examine the map. It was decorated with colorful doodles and whimsical arrows that pointed toward "The Greatest Giggle in Tiderune." He chuckled to himself, wondering what exactly that could mean. Was it a hidden treasure? A legendary joke? Or perhaps a giggling creature? Whatever it was, Alarion was determined to find it.

With the map tucked safely in his pocket, he set off on his quest, his heart racing with excitement. The first stop on the map led him to the Fluttering Fields, a place known for its enchanting butterflies that flitted about, carrying stories of joy. As Alarion walked through the fields, he noticed a group of butterflies dancing around a large dais.

"What's happening here?" Alarion asked, approaching them with curiosity.

"Welcome, traveller!" said a particularly large butterfly, flapping its wings dramatically. "We're practicing our dance for the annual Flutter Festival! But it's missing something—laughter! Would you help us?"

"Of course!" Alarion replied, a smile spreading across his face. "What do you need?"

The butterflies explained that they wanted to incorporate giggles into their dance, but they weren't sure how to make it happen. "We need someone with a funny story! Can you share one?"

Alarion thought for a moment and remembered a tale of a wobbly dog he once encountered. "Alright, here goes! There was once a dog named Wiggly who had a peculiar habit of slipping on banana peels! One day, he slipped and landed right in a tub of pudding—plop! When he got up, he looked like a walking dessert!"

The butterflies erupted into giggles, their wings fluttering in delight. The sound of their laughter filled the air, and Alarion found himself laughing along with them. They danced together, twirling and spinning, and Alarion felt the joy radiating from the butterflies.

As the dance concluded, the butterflies showered him with flower petals. "Thank you, Alarion! You've helped us find our laughter!" one of them said, as they settled down.

"Just wait until you see what else I discover today!" he said, waving goodbye as he continued on his adventure.

Next on the map was the Silly Stream, known for its babbling waters that sounded remarkably like giggles. Alarion hurried to the stream, eager to see if the rumors were true. When he arrived, he was greeted by a sight that made him burst out laughing—a family of frogs wearing tiny hats and glasses were sitting on the bank, croaking in harmony.

"Hello there!" Alarion called, amused by the scene. "What are you up to?"

"Preparing for the Great Frog Symphony!" croaked one frog, adjusting its glasses. "But we need a maestro! Would you conduct us?"

"Absolutely!" Alarion said, feeling a surge of enthusiasm.

He took a deep breath and began waving his arms dramatically, leading the frogs through their performance. They hopped and croaked in sync, creating a bizarre yet delightful melody that echoed through the woods.

As the frogs reached their crescendo, Alarion couldn't help but add his own sound effects, imitating the frogs' croaks in exaggerated tones. The entire scene turned into a cacophony of laughter as the frogs tried to keep up with him, each misstep resulting in hilarious hops and slips into the water.

"Bravo! Bravo!" the frogs cheered, their tiny hats bobbing in excitement.

After finishing the symphony, Alarion thanked the frogs and continued on his quest, the giggles of the stream still ringing in his ears. He consulted the map again, which now pointed toward the Wacky Woods, home to some of the most mischievous creatures in Tiderune.

As Alarion entered the woods, he noticed a cluster of giggling squirrels leaping from branch to branch, each one trying to outdo the other with their silly antics. "Hey! What's going on here?" he asked, watching them with amusement.

"We're on a mission!" shouted one squirrel, clutching a small acorn. "We're trying to collect the best giggles in Tiderune, but we need help! Can you join our game?"

"Count me in!" Alarion grinned, feeling the infectious energy of the squirrels.

They explained their plan: each squirrel would perform a silly trick, and if Alarion could keep a straight face, he'd win. If he laughed, they would get to keep the giggle!

One by one, the squirrels took turns showing off their ridiculous stunts—one tried to juggle acorns while balancing on a tightrope made of twigs, another performed an interpretive dance while wearing a tiny hat, and a third squirrel simply rolled down a hill, and ended up tumbling into a bush.

Alarion found himself laughing uncontrollably as he watched their antics. "Alright, alright! You win!" he said, clutching his stomach.

"You're a great sport!" the lead squirrel said, beaming with pride. "Let's celebrate our victory with a giggle feast!"

The squirrels led Alarion to a clearing where they had gathered various snacks—nuts, berries, and a huge cake that seemed to be made entirely of frosting. As they indulged in the feast, the air was filled with laughter and stories, making it the perfect end to a delightful day.

As the sun began to set, Alarion consulted the map one last time. It directed him to the final destination: The Giggle Grove, where he hoped to uncover the "Greatest Giggle" of them all.

When he arrived, he found a large tree with a door carved into its trunk. He knocked gently, and to his surprise, the door swung open to reveal a tiny creature with twinkling eyes and a contagious smile.

"Welcome to the Giggle Grove!" it chimed, bouncing up and down. "I'm Snicker, the Giggle Keeper! What brings you here?"

"I'm on a quest to find the greatest giggle in Tiderune!" Alarion announced, feeling both excited and a bit nervous.

Snicker clapped its tiny hands, giggling softly. "You've already found so many giggles today!

But let's see if you can find the greatest one. You must tell the funniest joke you know!"

Alarion thought for a moment, recalling all the laughter he'd shared that day. "Okay, here goes! Why did the scarecrow win an award?"

"I don't know! Why?" Snicker asked, eyes wide with anticipation.

"Because he was outstanding in his field!" Alarion exclaimed, bursting into laughter at his own joke.

At that moment, the ground beneath them began to tremble, and a symphony of giggles erupted from the trees, cascading down like sparkling confetti. Alarion couldn't help but join in, his laughter mingling with the joyous sound all around him.

"That's it! You've done it!" Snicker squeaked, clapping excitedly. "You've discovered the Greatest Giggle in Tiderune! And it's yours to share!"

As the giggles continued to echo through the grove, Alarion felt a warmth in his heart. It was a reminder that laughter was indeed the best treasure of all. He thanked Snicker for the experience and headed back home, the magical sounds of Tiderune still resonating in his ears.

On his way back, he reflected on his day filled with laughter, fun, and unexpected friendships. He knew he would cherish this adventure and share the joy he'd found with everyone in Tiderune.

As Alarion approached his home, he looked up at the twinkling stars and made a promise to always seek out laughter and spread it wherever he went. After all, the world was full of delightful surprises waiting to be uncovered, and he couldn't wait for the next giggle hunt to begin!

Chapter 50: The Celebration of Secrets

In the grand finale, Alarion and his friends gather to celebrate all the secrets they've uncovered. With laughter and magic in the air, it's a party to remember!

The sun rose over the enchanted land of Tiderune, casting a golden glow across the meadows and shimmering lakes. Today was a day like no other; it was the grand finale of Alarion's adventure—a Celebration of Secrets! The entire realm buzzed with excitement, and Alarion could hardly contain his joy as he prepared for the festivities.

Word had spread throughout Tiderune about the secrets Alarion and his friends had uncovered on their journeys. From the giggling waters of Silly Stream to the topsy-turvy antics of the Wacky Woods, every corner of the land held stories that had sparked laughter, friendship, and a little magic. Today, everyone would gather at the Great Meadow to share those secrets and celebrate the joy they had brought into their lives.

Alarion stepped out of his cozy cottage, the smell of freshly baked treats wafting through the air. He spotted his best friend, Lira, a sprightly fairy with shimmering wings, fluttering about as she hung sparkling decorations from the branches of the nearby trees.

"Lira!" Alarion called, waving excitedly. "Everything looks amazing!"

"Thanks, Alarion! But I can't take all the credit. The squirrels helped with the decorations!" Lira giggled, pointing to a group of squirrels who were bouncing around, draping colorful streamers made of leaves and flowers.

Just then, Alarion's other friends arrived—Brom, the silly dragon, and Snicker, the giggle keeper. Brom soared down from the sky, landing with a flourish and a puff of smoke that sent the squirrels tumbling backward.

"Ta-da!" Brom announced with a dramatic bow, his scales glimmering in the sunlight. "I've brought the most fabulous fruit from the Mystic Orchard! It's rumored to make anyone who eats it burst into song!"

"Let's save that for the party!" Alarion laughed, clapping his hands in delight. "We'll need something special to keep the energy up!"

As the day progressed, creatures from all over Tiderune gathered, each bringing their own secrets to share. The wise old owl, Professor Hoots, arrived with tales of the stars, while the mischievous pixies floated around, playfully sprinkling glitter on everyone.

The meadow transformed into a vibrant tapestry of laughter, music, and magic. Alarion took a moment to step back and soak it all in, his heart swelling with happiness. He had never felt more connected to his friends and the world around him.

When the sun began to dip low in the sky, casting long shadows across the meadow, Lira called everyone's attention. "It's time for the first round of secret sharing! Who wants to go first?"

A hush fell over the crowd, and a small creature—a timid hedgehog named Higgly—stepped forward. "Um, I have a secret!" he squeaked, adjusting his tiny glasses. "I'm actually really good at singing!"

The crowd erupted into cheers, encouraging Highly. With a deep breath, he cleared his throat and began to sing a surprisingly beautiful melody that filled the meadow. The audience listened, enchanted, as his voice wove tales of bravery and adventure. When he finished, everyone clapped wildly, and Higgly beamed with pride.

"Wow, Higgly! That was incredible!" Alarion exclaimed. "Who's next?"

The next to share was a trio of cheerful bunnies, each trying to outdo the other with their own secret talents. One bunny could balance carrots on its nose, while another could hop backward faster than anyone. The third, however, could pull off the best impression of Professor Hoots, complete with glasses and a wise demeanor, causing everyone to laugh until their sides hurt.

As the sun began to set, casting a warm orange glow over the meadow, it was Alarion's turn to share. He stood up, heart racing a bit. "Alright, everyone, I have a secret of my own! You see, I've been on quite an adventure this year, uncovering not just secrets but friendships and laughter. I've learned that the best secrets aren't just about what we discover; they're about the connections we make along the way!"

With a flourish, Alarion pulled out the sparkling fruit that Brom had brought earlier. "And I think it's time to try this special fruit! Let's sing and dance the night away!"

With that, he took a bite of the fruit, and to everyone's surprise, a melodious tune erupted from his mouth, a sweet and catchy rhythm that had everyone tapping their feet. Alarion began to dance, and soon everyone joined in, their laughter ringing through the air like music.

The meadow transformed into a lively dance floor, with Brom blowing smoke rings that formed into colorful shapes, and Lira sprinkling her magical fairy dust that made everyone twirl and spin effortlessly. Even the shyest creatures found themselves swept up in the celebration, giggling and dancing under the starry sky.

As the night deepened, Alarion and Lira found a moment to catch their breath, sitting on a large mushroom that served as the perfect vantage point. The meadow was a sea of twinkling lights and vibrant laughter, and Alarion felt a warmth in his heart that he could hardly describe.

"Can you believe how wonderful this all turned out?" Lira said, her wings shimmering as she leaned in closer.

"I know! I never imagined so many secrets would lead to something so magical," Alarion replied, a soft smile spreading across his face.

Their eyes met, and for a moment, the world around them faded. The laughter, the music, the magical glow of Tiderune—they were all just background to the connection they shared. Alarion felt a flutter in his chest, a warmth that was more than just friendship. But before he could say anything, Brom swooped down, interrupting their moment.

"Hey! You two lovebirds!" he teased, a cheeky grin on his face. "Come join the fun! I just taught the squirrels how to fly!"

"Alright, alright!" Alarion laughed, shaking off his thoughts as he and Lira jumped down to rejoin the party.

As the night wore on, Alarion realized that the Celebration of Secrets was more than just a party; it was a celebration of everything that made life in Tiderune extraordinary. Laughter echoed through the trees, magical moments were created, and the bonds of friendship were strengthened.

As the final song played and the stars twinkled overhead, Alarion looked around at his friends, feeling an overwhelming sense of gratitude. At that moment, he knew that no matter what adventures lay ahead, they would face them together—filled with laughter, secrets, and a little bit of magic.

With hearts full and spirits high, they celebrated not just the secrets they had uncovered, but the promise of new adventures waiting just beyond the horizon. The magic of Tiderune was alive, and so were the dreams of all who dared to chase them.

BOOK # 2 ALARION AND THE SECRETS OF TIDERUNE 245

A Note of Thanks to Our Wonderful Readers

Dear Readers,

As we close the chapter on "Alarion and the Secrets of Tiderune," I want to take a moment to express my heartfelt gratitude to each and every one of you. Your support, enthusiasm, and curiosity have been the driving forces behind this journey, and it fills me with joy to know that you have joined Alarion on his whimsical adventures through the magical realm.

Thank you for diving into the enchanting world of Tiderune and for embracing the laughter, friendship, and lessons that Alarion has encountered along the way. Your willingness to explore this fantastical realm and connect with its characters means the world to me. Writing this book has been a labour of love, and your engagement has truly brought it to life.

As we bid farewell to Tiderune, I am excited to invite you to continue this journey with me in the next instalment, "Alarion and the Oracle of Atheron." An ancient oracle foretells Alarion's destiny, setting him on a path toward a dangerous prophecy. As he seeks answers in Atheron, he will discover that fate and fortune are forever entwined, leading him to even more thrilling adventures and unexpected twists.

I look forward to sharing this next chapter with you, filled with new challenges, deeper mysteries, and the enduring magic that makes Alarion's journey so special. Until we meet again in Atheron, keep the spirit of adventure alive, and may your own paths be filled with wonder and joy.

BOOK # 2 ALARION AND THE SECRETS OF TIDERUNE 247

With immense gratitude,
Anant Ram Boss

Acknowledgment

As I pen these words in the acknowledgment section of "Alarion and the Secrets of Tiderune," my heart is filled with gratitude for all those who have been part of this enchanting journey. Writing this book has been a magical experience, and I am truly thankful to everyone who has contributed to its creation.

First and foremost, I would like to express my deepest appreciation to my family and friends, whose unwavering support and encouragement have been my guiding light. Your belief in my dreams has inspired me to chase after stories that spark joy and imagination. Thank you for listening to my countless ideas, sharing your thoughts, and cheering me on through every twist and turn of the writing process.

I am also incredibly grateful to my readers, both new and returning. Your enthusiasm for Alarion's adventures fuels my passion for storytelling. I hope that this tale brings a smile to your face and ignites your imagination, just as your support ignites mine. The joy of knowing that my words can inspire laughter and wonder keeps me motivated to create even more.

A special thank you goes to my wonderful editor and beta readers, who provided invaluable feedback and insights. Your keen eyes and thoughtful suggestions have helped shape this story into something I am proud to share. Thank you for your patience and for pushing me to refine my craft—this journey would not have been the same without you!

I must also acknowledge the countless writers, artists, and creators who have come before me, lighting the path for those of us who dare to dream in ink and paper. Your works have inspired me in ways words cannot fully express, and I hope to carry that legacy forward through my own storytelling.

Finally, to the magical realm of Tiderune itself—thank you for your endless inspiration! As I delved into your vibrant landscapes and whimsical characters, I found joy, laughter, and adventure at every turn. May this journey continue to captivate the hearts of those who dare to explore your secrets.

As you step into Alarion's world, I hope you find a piece of magic that resonates within you. May your own adventures be filled with laughter, friendship, and the courage to seek out the unknown. Thank you for joining me on this journey, and here's to many more magical tales to come!

With heartfelt gratitude,
Anant Ram Boss

Disclaimer

"Alarion and the Secrets of Tiderune" is a work of fiction, crafted from the boundless realms of imagination and creativity. While the characters, events, and places portrayed within this book are entirely fictional, any resemblance to actual persons, living or dead, or real events is purely coincidental.

This story is intended for entertainment purposes only. It aims to inspire joy, laughter, and a sense of wonder in readers of all ages. However, it should not be interpreted as a factual representation of any magical practices, creatures, or realms. Magic, as depicted in this tale, is a whimsical and fantastical element that serves to ignite the imagination and transport readers to a world where anything is possible.

As you dive into Alarion's adventures, please remember that the journey through Tiderune is not meant to be taken literally. The magic found within these pages is a reflection of the limitless possibilities of storytelling, where creativity knows no bounds.

While I encourage readers to explore their own imaginations and embrace the wonders of fantasy, I must stress that the practices, spells, and lore mentioned in this book are purely fictional. They are designed to entertain and delight, not to provide guidance or instruction in any real-life context.

By engaging with this book, you agree to embrace the spirit of adventure and fun that lies within these pages. I hope you enjoy the journey as much as I enjoyed creating it!

I am also thankful to all great personalities whose thoughts have been considered in this Book.

With endless gratitude,

[ANANT RAM BOSS]

Please contact us for any quarry/suggestions if any at : anantramboss@gmail.com

About the Author Anant Ram Boss

Anant Ram Boss is an accomplished author with a passion for creating immersive worlds and captivating stories. His journey into the realm of writing began at an early age when he discovered the magic of words and the power of storytelling. Anant's dedication to his craft and his relentless pursuit of literary excellence have made him a notable figure in the world of fantasy literature.

With an imaginative mind that knows no bounds, Anant can transport readers to enchanting and mysterious realms. His writing is known for its vivid descriptions, well-drawn characters, and intricate plots that keep readers eagerly turning pages. He has an innate talent for weaving intricate tales filled with magic, adventure, and profound themes.

Throughout his career, Anant has received acclaim for his ability to craft epic sagas and captivating series that resonate with readers of all ages. The Series, in particular, has garnered a devoted following, and it showcases Anant's mastery of the fantasy genre.

When he's not lost in the worlds he creates, Anant enjoys exploring the great outdoors, indulging in his love for photography, and seeking inspiration from the beauty of the natural world. His appreciation for nature often finds its way into his storytelling, enriching his narratives with a deep connection to the environment and the magic that exists within it.

Anant Ram Boss is not only a storyteller but also a world-builder, a dreamer, and an explorer of the human experience through the lens of fantasy literature. With each new book he writes, he invites readers to

BOOK # 2 ALARION AND THE SECRETS OF TIDERUNE 253

embark on journeys of the imagination, fostering a love for the magical and the wondrous that resides within us all.

Don't miss out!

Visit the website below and you can sign up to receive emails whenever ANANT RAM BOSS publishes a new book. There's no charge and no obligation.

https://books2read.com/r/B-A-GGLBB-NCRDF

BOOKS 2 READ

Connecting independent readers to independent writers.

Did you love *Book # 2 Alarion and the Secrets of Tiderune*? Then you should read *Book # 1: Alarion and the Cryptic Key*[1] by ANANT RAM BOSS!

Step into "The Chronicles of Alarion," a captivating series filled with humor, adventure, and magical wonder! This enchanting journey follows the life of Alarion, an ordinary boy who stumbles upon an extraordinary artifact—an ancient key that unlocks not just doors, but a portal to an entirely new world. Each book in the series offers readers a fresh and exciting tale of magic, mystery, and hilarious mishaps as Alarion faces ever-evolving challenges in a realm where nothing is as it seems.

In the first book, "Alarion and the Cryptic Key," readers are introduced to Alarion's quirky, fun-loving personality as he embarks

---

1. https://books2read.com/u/bxGDQd

2. https://books2read.com/u/bxGDQd

on a quest to discover the secrets of the magical world he accidentally stumbles into. Alongside his loyal but forgetful giant friend Grog, Alarion encounters talking keys, mischievous goblins, and sassy sorcerers—all while trying to figure out the deeper purpose of the mysterious key that appears to have its very own psyche. From goblin negotiations to enchanted forest adventures, this book sets the tone for a laugh-out-loud yet heartwarming journey.

Key Points of the Series:

Humor and Heart: The series is packed with light-hearted humor, fun twists, and relatable moments that will make readers laugh out loud. Yet, beneath the jokes, there's a story about friendship, bravery, and self-discovery.

An Unforgettable Cast of Characters: Alarion is joined by a colorful array of characters—like the lovable Grog, the giant with a knack for snacks, and a sarcastic, talking key who loves riddles. Each character adds charm and excitement to the series.

Unique Magical World: The books immerse readers in a magical universe where logic bends, trees talk, and even mountains have personalities. The world-building is vivid and imaginative, ensuring every page is a discovery.

Action-Packed Adventure: From escaping goblin traps to bargaining with dragons, the series never lacks action. Alarion's journey is full of suspenseful moments, clever puzzles, and epic showdowns.

Themes of Growth and Courage: Despite its fun tone, the series subtly explores important themes like finding courage, embracing one's uniqueness, and the power of friendship. Alarion's growth throughout the series is one that readers will relate to and cheer for.

Engaging for All Ages: While designed with young readers in mind, The Chronicles of Alarion appeals to anyone who enjoys a well-crafted adventure story with heart, humor, and a touch of magic.

As the series progresses, each book unravels new layers of Alarion's quest, with more surprises and magical mysteries waiting around every corner. From deciphering cryptic clues to facing shadowy forces, Alarion's journey is a delightful blend of laughter, danger, and unexpected twists. Readers will be hooked as they root for Alarion to unlock the ultimate secrets of the key and fulfill his destiny.

If you're a fan of humorous, action-packed fantasy adventures, "The Chronicles of Alarion" will take you on a journey you won't want to end. Whether you're 12 or 112, Alarion's world has something magical waiting for you!

Also by ANANT RAM BOSS

1
The Chronicles of Alarion -Part-6 "Alarion and the Nexus of Netheron"
"The Chronicles of Alarion -Part-7-"Alarion and the Legacy of Luminarya"

2
Mystic Alliances

Alarion Chronicles Series
The Dawn of Magic
Shadows Embrace
Book#3: "Phoenix's Flight"
Book 4: "Warriors of Light"
Echoes of Wisdom
Captivated Woodland
Kingdom of Crystals
Book 8: "Lost Legacies"
Book 9: "Siege of Hope"
Book 10: "Veil of Light"

The Astral Chronicles
Awakening Shadows
Awakening Shadows
Celestial Convergence
Whispers of the Himalayas
Riddles of Rishikesh
Portals of the Past
Echoes from Vijayanagara
Veil of Varanasi
The Astral Nexus
Eclipse of Eternity
Beyond the Veil

The Chronicles of Alarion
Book # 1: Alarion and the Cryptic Key
Book # 2 Alarion and the Secrets of Tiderune

Standalone
Love's Delectable Harmony
Adventures in Candy land
Adventures in Candy land
Canvas to Catalyst: Parenting Mastery
Guardians of Greatness: Our Children Are Our Property in Cultivating Tomorrow's Leaders
Guardians of Greatness: Cultivating Tomorrow's Leaders
Space Explorers Club
The Enchanted Forest Chronicles
Mystery at Monster Mansion

Robot Friends Forever
Underwater Kingdom
Underwater Kingdom
Time Travel Twins
Time Travel Twins
The Giggle Factory
Dreamland Chronicles
The Case of the Vanishing Cookies
Dragon Knight Chronicles
The Wishing Well
Trade Tactics Unveiled: Mastering Profit Secrets
Whispers in the Graveyard
Love after Dawn: A Second Chance Romance
Exodus: A Hopeful Dystopia
Death at Blackwood Manor
Orient Express: Murder Redefined
Poirot & the Raven: Digital Legacy
The Brave Little Elephant
The Little Robot That Could
The Adventures of Little Star
Dream World
Unique Friendship
The Courage of the Lion
The Art of Building Wealth: A Strategic Guide

About the Author

Anant Ram Boss is an accomplished author with a passion for creating immersive worlds and captivating stories. His journey into the realm of writing began at an early age when he discovered the magic of words and the power of storytelling. Anant's dedication to his craft and his relentless pursuit of literary excellence have made him a notable figure in the world of fantasy literature.

With an imaginative mind that knows no bounds, Anant has the ability to transport readers to enchanting and mysterious realms. His writing is known for its vivid descriptions, well-drawn characters, and intricate plots that keep readers eagerly turning pages. He has an innate talent for weaving intricate tales filled with magic, adventure, and profound themes.

Throughout his career, Anant has received acclaim for his ability to craft epic sagas and captivating series that resonate with readers of all ages. The Sries, in particular, has garnered a devoted following, and it showcases Anant's mastery of the fantasy genre.

When he's not lost in the worlds he creates, Anant enjoys exploring the great outdoors, indulging in his love for photography, and seeking inspiration from the beauty of the natural world. His appreciation for nature often finds its way into his storytelling, enriching his narratives with a deep connection to the environment and the magic that exists within it.

Anant Ram Boss is not only a storyteller but also a world-builder, a dreamer, and an explorer of the human experience through the lens of fantasy literature. With each new book he writes, he invites readers to embark on journeys of the imagination, fostering a love for the magical and the wondrous that resides within us all.